BLOOD MONEY

A gripping crime thriller full of twists

CHARLIE GALLAGHER

JOFFE BOOKS

Published 2017 by Joffe Books, London.

www.joffebooks.com

© Charlie Gallagher

ISBN-13: 978-1-912106-54-7

For my wife, who suffers this obsession every day.

Author's Note

I am inspired by what I do and see in my day job as a front-line police detective, though my books are entirely fictional. I am aware that the police officers in my novels are not always shown positively. They are human and they make mistakes. This is sometimes the case in real life too, but the vast majority of officers are honest and do a good job in trying circumstances. From what I see on a daily basis, the men and women who wear the uniform are among the very finest, and I am proud to be part of one of the best police forces in the world.

Charlie Gallagher

CHAPTER 1

Something was wrong. Tony Robson had been here more times than he could remember and the routine had always been the same. They saw the same people, did the same things. Daniel received his treatment. And Tony and his son never left each other's side the whole time.

And now Tony was all on his own, sitting on a black leather chair with polished metal frame. The consultant sat opposite. Doctor Ngaye was sitting on an identical chair and he was fidgeting. Eventually he seemed to settle on leaning forward, just like Tony. He looked concerned.

'Is there a problem, Doc?' Stupid question.

He was in the specialist wing of the hospital, a place for people with rare genetic disorders. His seven-year-old son had developed one of the least known forms of muscular dystrophy. In fact, it was so rare that no one in the UK had ever seen a case like it. It had been terrifying for Tony, taking his little boy to the hospital, only to be met with shrugs and bemusement. After all, that's what you did when your kid got sick, you took them to the hospital and the doctors made them better. But they hadn't made Daniel better. Instead, they had been brutally honest, admitting they'd never seen this disorder manifested in

1

quite this way before, and they didn't really know where to start.

Tony had found the answer in America. He had spent hours online, finding out everything he could about the shadow that was threatening to engulf their lives and, through forums and chatrooms with people just like him, he'd found that doctors in the States were much further ahead with this sort of thing. Hell, some of them had even heard of Daniel's condition. Somehow he got speaking to a pharmaceutical company who thought they might be able to make a difference. They made no promises, but they would eventually be offering a new drug that might just be a breakthrough. America and the UK's NHS then spoke to each other, and Daniel was on the trial.

It *had* been a breakthrough. The expectation for Daniel at the time of his diagnosis was that he would suffer muscle wastage in all the key areas. He'd be confined to a wheelchair within just a couple of years and then the disease would continue its attack on his mobility, his speech, the very process by which he breathed in and out. His quality of life would be gone, maybe even his life altogether. Daniel would reach this stage before his eighteenth birthday. Death would likely rob him of his twenty-first. Tony couldn't let this happen. It was his doing. He and his wife, and their genes, had cursed him with this awful, degenerative disease.

That was four years ago. These days, Daniel looked no different from other seven-year-old West Ham-supporting kids. He was doing well at school, he was in three football teams, he picked on smaller kids occasionally, and then at the end of the day he got a bit more tired than most. The drugs had all but halted the disease, stopped it dead in its tracks. Their son was doing fine.

Now the consultant looked concerned. What was happening? Dr Ngaye took his time, appearing to choose his words carefully. Then he just said it.

'The trial is over.'

Tony swallowed. Initially he was confused, then came hope. 'You mean Daniel's cured?'

'Mr Robson, we know that Daniel may never be cured.'

'But this drug, this breakthrough, you said that if they can halt it, then maybe they can stop it altogether? So how can the trial be over?'

'As you know, the NHS took Daniel on as a trial patient in conjunction with an American pharmaceutical company at considerable expense and with some trepidation, to see if we could further our understanding of these types of conditions—'

'And we know it works,' Tony cut in, and immediately wished he hadn't. Doctor Ngaye was a large part of the reason the NHS had even considered the trial in the first place. Tony knew he was on their side. 'I'm sorry,' he continued. 'I don't mean to be rude, Doc, but we're doing well here — Daniel is, I mean.'

'We are. The trial has been a success for Daniel but, as you know, this was a wider trial and the other patients that were put on this drug have not responded.'

'But Daniel has.'

'Mr Robson, this will not be easy to hear and it is not easy for me to say about an organisation I have dedicated my life to, but Daniel's treatment costs three thousand pounds a month. It has halted the progress of his condition, but he is the only person in the country who has benefited in this way. We knew the challenge right from the start, when we realised just how rare your son's condition was.'

'So Daniel's life on its own isn't worth saving? They're just going to take it away and let him die slowly and with total loss of dignity, when there's a way they can prevent it?'

'The NHS will continue with conventional treatment, Mr Robson, as we would have done had we not been given this opportunity—'

'But we were, we were given an opportunity and we know it works. Conventional treatment? You people might as well stand over him banging a wok — it would have the same effect as your conventional damned treatment. It's painful and it's a waste of time and we both know it.'

'I hear you, I do. But the NHS has been cut to within an inch of its life, Tony. This government really isn't on our side, and the people who control our budget have looked at what they can do with three thousand pounds a month. It could make a massive difference to many, many more people if put to a different use.'

'But Daniel will die.' Tony couldn't even begin to comprehend what he was being told. Surely, if you got ill, you went to the hospital and they did what they could to make you feel better? Now he was being told that they wouldn't do what they could. They were about to stop lifesaving treatment for a seven-year-old boy, *his* seven-year-old boy, because of money.

'I'm very fond of Daniel, you know that. I can assure you I didn't take the news well either, and we will do what we can with the resources we have.' The doctor shook his head. 'I wanted to be the one to tell you.'

Tony's mouth was dry. He pursed his lips tightly to stop them quivering, and looked down. He took in a rushed breath. This couldn't be it, couldn't be the end. 'Now you've told me,' he said, and his eyes lifted to meet with Doctor Ngaye's, 'Who's going to tell Danny? And his mum?'

'I'll talk to them if you want me to.'

Tony shook his head. 'How? How are you going to tell Danny? What can you say to him? We're sorry but we're going to have to let you die? This is crazy.'

The doctor leant back into his chair, and the leather creaked a little. 'You have the contact at the pharmaceutical company. I spoke to them briefly before speaking to you, so they are aware of the situation. The drugs were already heavily discounted for the NHS.' The doctor expelled air in a sigh. 'They said to me that they will continue to discount the treatment directly to you, and they will contact you to tell you how to make that possible. If you can secure the drugs for Daniel we can continue to manage him here.'

'Three thousand pounds a month?'

'Yes.'

'Or my son wastes away to nothing.'

'There are websites. You can set up these JustGiving pages, spread the word on social media. People are very generous with—'

'You want me to beg month on month for my son's life?' Tony lifted his hands, clenched in fists, and brought them back down onto the table. He found his feet and the leather chair slid backwards. He was a big man. Previously he'd trained his body hard, using the regimen of a powerlifter, but he'd used it to wrestle, and at a good level. Then Daniel had come along, with his health problems, and there hadn't been so much time, but he was still muscular, with broad shoulders.

'It's not like begging,' offered the doctor, his voice soft.

Tony's anger started to ebb, replaced by an emotion he rarely experienced — fear. 'People will help, I'm sure, but for how long? He's seven now. A few years maybe, but then he's a teenager and then a man. He'll not be a poor little boy anymore, and people won't want to know. There'll be an earthquake or a tsunami somewhere and he'll be forgotten, left to just waste away.'

'I'm sorry. Really I am.'

'I know that.' Tony started pacing, talking fast, thinking out loud. 'Three thousand a month. I can earn that if I get back to being busy, back like it was when things were good. I can make it up with Lorraine. We'll have to sit down and have a talk, but if we get back together, under the same roof, split the bills, maybe we can do it. I'll eat jam on toast for the rest of my life if I have to. I like jam.'

'There you are, Tony. This is bad news, I know, but with a bit of time maybe you can come up with a plan.'

Tony put his hands to his head. Realism hit back. 'I'm a carpenter, Doc, self-employed. I was doing three grand a month once when Lorraine was pregnant — worked every hour God sent and it damn near killed me. I took it easier when my little man was diagnosed, you know, to spend time with him. I didn't want to miss a thing. Not when I thought I mightn't have him long.' Tony paused to compose himself but it was too late. He did nothing to wipe his tears away. Tears were a new thing to him.

'What do I do now, Doc? What do I do now?'

* * *

Daniel had been outside the office playing football with a ball of scrunched-up paper. He'd roped in one of the nurses who was playfully kicking it back at him. He'd been a slow starter but his confidence was increasing all the time. Daniel was just starting to become the person he was supposed to be.

They walked to Tony's car in silence. It was an electric blue Skoda Octavia Estate, the sporty vRS model with 'vRS' stitched in an angry red on the front seats. Daniel was turned towards his dad, feeling the raised lettering with his finger, like he always did. He loved this car. It was getting old now, but Tony could never get rid of it, not while Daniel was so obviously in love with the turbo whistle and the power, the suspension so hard that a pothole would have them yelping, then giggling out loud. They'd bought this car together. He had driven the car home with Daniel in the booster seat in the front, his mother making do in the back. She didn't mind a bit. They had smiled all the way home. The car was a celebration. It was a time when everything looked like it might just be all right. They had been so desperate at the start. The doctors hadn't held back with their worst-case scenarios and Tony had taken a few weeks to accept what he had been told. But eventually, with the new treatment, they had been able to control it, even almost *forget* about it at times. Four years later they were back to square one, but even worse. This time he knew the answer: three thousand pounds a month. That was what his son's life would cost.

Tony sat up straight. There was a general election next April, just half a year away, and the politicians were starting to show their faces. An episode of *Question Time* was being filmed today at Canterbury University, five miles away, tops. He'd heard it on local radio this morning. He thought he'd heard that it was a big deal, senior politicians, people who could reverse the decision maybe. If he could just get to talk to them.

'Are you okay, Dad?' Daniel looked concerned but his face softened with a smile as his dad turned to face him.

'Yeah, fine, son.'

'Can we go to McDonald's before you drop me back at Mum's? I think she's cooking shepherd's pie tonight,' Daniel said, checking around him before continuing in a whisper, 'And she doesn't make the best shepherd's pie.'

On any other day, Tony would have laughed with his son. Today, he managed a tense half smile.

'We need to go and see someone quickly, then we'll think about food,' he said. He reached down and switched the radio on, turning the volume up loud enough so Daniel wouldn't try to make any conversation.

They drove to Canterbury University in silence. The car park was full, Tony couldn't see any actual spaces. He opted to bump the Skoda up onto a small grassy verge close to the front of the building. He was watched by two stocky men standing on the steps up to the entrance.

Tony hadn't been thinking straight. He hadn't reckoned on security staff. The first man wore an expression that told Tony he wasn't getting past.

'Sir?'

The other man stepped in closer too. They were cut from the same block. They wore the same uniform and the same defiant, if slightly bored, expression.

'I need to get in. I need to speak to the politicians about my son. He's seven and without their help he's going to die.'

Tony flicked a glance back at Daniel. He had left him in the car and he had already moved to the driver's seat and was pretending to steer. Tony screwed his face a little and rubbed at his forehead with frustration. It was such a long story. He wanted the men to understand, then they might help. But that wasn't going to be possible. He saw the two men exchange glances.

'Sir, the minister is currently committed to a debate. Following that, he will be leaving and is on a tight schedule. There are proper channels if you want to make contact with him and we can—'

'The minister in there might be my only hope. Please, he can save my son's life. And he might . . . you just need to let me talk to him!'

'Sir, I'm sorry but—'

The steps to the glass doors of the entrance were so close Tony could almost reach them with his foot. He made a rush for the gap between the two men, but they closed it quickly. The man who had been doing the talking took hold of Tony by his left forearm and bent it up behind his back in a neat move that took Tony off balance and bent him forward, so he was staring wide-eyed at the ground. Tony was beyond pain. The frustration, the injustice, the desperation reared up inside him. He planted his feet and snapped his head upwards. The doorman was caught a little by surprise and was forced to take a step away, releasing his hold, and Tony saw another opportunity.

The other man, who had been waiting, silent, at the back, shifted his weight and, as the first guard tried to get a hold back on Tony, he stalled him enough for his colleague to bring his fist up in a solid uppercut that met with Tony's onrushing body, catching him hard in the abdomen. The oxygen left Tony's body and he folded onto the pavement.

Tony was gasping for breath but he was still trying to fight, his arms flailing helplessly towards the two men who now stood over him.

The front man looked at his colleague. 'Jesus, man,' he said, 'Was that really necessary?'

'He came at me. Fuck him.'

'He weren't coming for us.'

'Fuck him,' he repeated.

'But here? All the world's press are here for fuck's sake!'

The man bent down to where Tony's fight had been reduced to a helpless, whimpering wheeze.

'Hey, big man. Let's get you away from here and get some air back into you.' He reached under Tony's shoulders and pulled him to his feet in a single movement. 'There's a mobile round the corner here. I'll get you a water, or I can do a shit tea.'

'My son,' Tony managed to say, and pointed to the car.

The security man followed Tony's finger. 'Does he like tea?'

Tony nodded. The man gestured at the car and after a few moments the door opened. Daniel ran to his dad and hugged him.

'You okay, Dad?'

* * *

'What's this all about then? I'm John, by the way. My mate out there is Alan and he ain't normally such a twat. I'm kinda responsible for him which means I can apologise for him too.'

Tony had been led to a Portakabin that had been set up for the event. Tony perched on the edge of a plastic stool that was slightly too high. The space was largely empty, a few trails of wire and some specialist-looking lighting stacked untidily in the opposite corner. He sat next to a steaming urn.

'My name is Tony,' he said, bringing a cup of tea to his lips and narrowing his eyes to the steam. He waved his other hand. 'Forget it. I was being an idiot and he was doing his job. It's just been a hard day.'

'You was telling me about your son out there, that's why you wanted to speak to the top man?'

Tony suddenly looked panicked, and his eyes flitted to where Daniel was sitting, swilling a plastic cup of cold water, watching it intently.

John turned to him too. 'Hey,' he said to the little boy, 'Do you like football?'

Daniel nodded and smiled enthusiastically. 'There's a football we kick around over there. If your dad don't mind there's a grassy patch just outside the door — you can practise your kick-ups.'

Daniel looked at his dad and Tony nodded. 'Just a few minutes,' he said, but Daniel was already on his way out.

Tony started talking. To some doorman whose mate had just punched him in the stomach. But he felt relieved to be talking to someone. Someone who wasn't emotionally involved.

John listened. He listened intently. Then a silence fell over the interior of the Portakabin. The steaming urn and an occasional loose football bouncing off the flimsy walls were the only sounds.

'You need three grand a month?' John said.

'That's where I am.'

John reached into his pocket and took out a phone. 'What's your number?'

'Why do you need that?'

'I'm going to pass it on to someone. This person needs reliable people to do some work. It might be just the odd night, but he pays well.'

'Three grand a month well?'

John paused and looked up, the light from the screen illuminating his face. 'Prove yourself trustworthy and you'll earn that in a night.'

'Three grand for a night's work? There ain't nothing the right side of the law that pays that much.'

'It's a courier job. You turn up somewhere, drive a car somewhere else, go home. I don't ask why or what for. I can take your number and pass it on, or we can both forget this conversation and get on with our lives. Your choice.'

Tony took a few seconds. The football bounced off the side of the cabin again. 'Pass it on. I'm interested, sure.'

'Good decision.' John smiled. 'What's your full name, date of birth, and your address?'

'I didn't think this was legit. So why would you need all that?'

'You'll get checked out. If you're not right, you won't be called. If they're happy, someone will call you.'

'When?'

John shrugged. 'Maybe never.'

* * *

A few minutes later John watched Tony and his kid walking away. He already had his phone to his ear.

'Yeah.' John knew the voice. Lee Chivers. A horrible waste of skin, even his friends didn't like him. He was the enforcer for cleverer men, but he was also the buffer, the monkey holding the phone for the organ grinder.

'Gee, you still looking for someone to do some delivery work?' Gee was Lee's street name. Normally John would avoid using it just to piss him off, but today he needed him compliant.

'J., you sad old fuck. Yeah, me and the man looking for someone to do a job or two. The filth got tight tabs right now, we can't even fart down here.'

'I met someone. He could be perfect.'

'Could be? *Hey yo! Shut up, bitch!*' John heard the sound of someone being struck and a soft female whimper. 'Could be, John? I don't need no *could-be*s.'

John made himself stop and think, he didn't need to be biting back. 'I'll send his details through but I think he's clean. He's got no ties to no one and he just needs the money. He'll do what you need and the cops won't even look at him.'

'He ain't stupid now, is he, John? Stupid enough to start thinking for himself? You know what happened to the last man you sent my way who started thinking for himself?'

'Stupid enough to do as he's told. Clever enough to do no more than that.'

'Then send him through.'

CHAPTER 2

'You need to give me something!' Helen Webb's voice sounded desperate and angry.

Ed Kavski allowed himself a little time before answering. He used it to lean back into his patio lounger and smile. He was enjoying himself immensely. He always enjoyed his telephone conversations with the detective chief superintendent at Lennokshire Police, the woman who doubled as area commander for the east of the county.

'I don't *need* to do anything,' he said.

'You don't seem to understand the pressures I'm under here — and don't think that you're sitting comfortable either, because if they come after me, they'll come after you too.'

'But you know to make sure that doesn't happen, don't you, Chief Superintendent? They really don't need to hear what I have to say.'

'Oh, fuck right off, it's getting boring now. Every time we speak, you make the same idle threat to tell the world about me. We both go down if you open your mouth and we both know that ain't gonna happen.'

Ed smiled again. Helen was often stressed, always curt, but rarely swore. She must be rattled, and she was right to be. Ed was the main supplier of class A drugs to her county, and she was a big reason for this.

'So, what do you need?' he said.

'You know very well what I need. That job you pulled, the Whitfield robbery with the booze and fags, I need a result on it. Shop someone who was with you, give me a handler, anything to keep the chief off my back.'

'The chief?' Ed sat forward a little. He had closed his eyes and they now opened and fell on the lush green grass of his manicured lawn. He was sitting in the rear garden of a large manor house in a stretch of exclusive residences in the seaside town of Hythe. Lennokshire Police were paying through the nose to cover his rent every month. This little agreement had been made with Helen, who had managed to bury it in some budget or another.

'Yes, the chief. The security guard that you beat to within an inch of his life? Well, that inch appears to be getting smaller and smaller and now it looks like the old man might die. We've taken a bit of a hit in the media down here, as you can well imagine, and the last thing the chief wants is another violent crime. The man was an ex-copper and we've got a lot of unhappy cops who feel like more should be being done. Seems he's become a bit of a symbol for them all after recent events. The chief's under pressure, getting a lot of shit, and that shit is running downhill.'

'You seem to have convinced yourself that I have any idea what you're talking about. A half-dead security guard and a robbery ring no bells with me. That's not really my style now, is it?' Ed was an ex-copper himself. He'd been a damned good one once, but then it became very clear to him what policing in good ol' England was all about: the media. That was all that mattered to these people. It wasn't about keeping the streets safe, arresting the bad guys and protecting the vulnerable. It was about looking like you were keeping the streets clean, looking like you were arresting a load of bad guys, and giving the impression that you were protecting the vulnerable. If he needed any more proof, then this conversation was it. She couldn't care less about the man in the hospital bed, just what the world would make of his demise and her part in it. Nothing is easier to exploit than ambition.

Ed Kavski's had reached his moment of clarity after ten years of unblemished service. From that point, it had taken him two years to use this realisation against his former employers. He was now at the head of an organised criminal network. He was known as 'the Russian' on the street. Kavski was no more Russian than the rest of the white middle-class population that filled the townhouses and bistros of his current hometown of Hythe, but his name sounded Russian, and the moniker had stuck. He was sure his Polish ancestors would forgive him.

His drugs empire had been established with the assistance of some of the most senior police officers in the county, and since then, Ed had started to branch out a little. Into people trafficking, a little movement of weapons and, most recently, the robbery of a P&O storage depot in Whitfield. This last job was almost purely for fun. Ed had used inside knowledge that police resources would be rather stretched on that particular night.

'Don't take me for a fool.' Helen Webb's voice was a little more hushed now. Ed pictured her at work, hunched over the phone in her office with the door shut.

'You knew we were all over the place that night. You were the only person who *could* know. What were the chances of a secure unit with a fast-response silent alarm getting hit at the exact same time as my entire police force was chasing a car heading in the opposite direction?'

'You've had a shit run of luck recently, haven't you?' Ed chuckled.

'The chief is here tomorrow. He'll be speaking to the security guard's family who are at his bedside, then to the forty-odd serving officers holding a vigil in the hospital grounds. Then he is coming to me for an update on the investigation and for a memorial service for the fallen officers that I'm pretty sure he thinks I'm responsible for. I need to be telling him about some pretty monumental breakthrough. I need to find out who put the security guard in hospital, and so far I've got next to nothing. I am on the bones of my arse here, Mr Kavski. The chief has already had a conversation with me regarding my future, and it probably involves demotion and movement to a distant corner of the free world. That will leave both of us in the wilderness, won't it? Now — where is the stuff being held? Who's stashing up the van?'

'Jesus, you really haven't got much, have you?' Ed's enjoyment had diminished a little. Helen was right. Her demotion and posting would remove her influence in the area completely and that left him vulnerable. He didn't need her so much anymore for furthering his business but, pissed off and demoted, she could become very dangerous to him.

Most of the stuff from the robbery had already gone out to street dealers — small-time crooks doing pubs and clubs in London and the surrounding area. None of the distribution was in Lennokshire, it would be too obvious where it was from. The van was stashed up. He was waiting for the heat to die down before moving it to its final resting place, but he couldn't give that up. It was a key location.

Helen was back at him. 'I suggest you start boxing some stuff up then, *Mr* Kavski, because your nice little number by the seaside comes to an end in four days. I won't have any budgets where I can hide two grand a month rent for a scumbag.'

'Now, Helen, there's no need to get personal. I can give you something. It's nothing to do with your robbery but it will give you a few days, and soon I'll get you the van and maybe a name or two.'

Helen was quiet for a second. 'What do you have?'

'Tomorrow morning I have a large movement. I've got a courier picking up a package. He'll be moving it along the coast to a point where it will stay for a while until I can move it on again. I'll give you details of when he'll be on the road. He'll have a couple hundred grand of brown and white on-board. The brown is still in blocks — it'll be seventy per cent pure if it's true to form, not even cut for the street yet.'

'Where's the pick up?'

'You don't need to know anything more than my man's route.'

'Who's he delivering to?'

'Do you want the details or not? You'll get enough information to make the stop. Nothing more. You understand that I know the value of the gear because I've already paid for it, yes? This is going to hit me hard in the pocket. I'm giving you this for nothing.'

Actually, £200,000 wasn't a huge hit for Ed. Besides, he could use it to his advantage. He would blame a leak from within his organisation, pick someone out and make an example of them. Give his people a bit of a kick in the arse, remind them about the price of disloyalty.

'Of course I do. Is our man a major player? Someone we know well?'

'No, actually. The poor sod came to me out of the blue. We had him checked out as best we could, and he's got nothing with you lot. Just got himself in a situation where he needed money quick. He's a fucking carpenter. He'll be using his own car to make the trip. It's a bright blue Skoda Estate vRS, distinctive — even your lot shouldn't miss that. The reg is SD60 HSN.' Ed stopped and waited.

'Go on.'

'He'll be on Dymchurch Road between eight and nine o'clock tomorrow morning. We wanted him to blend in with the rush hour traffic.'

'What's his direction of travel?'

'West to east. Assuming he's on time — and he fucking wants to be — he should be easy to pick out.'

'I need to know where he's going. You know I don't want to hit this car on the run, Ed. There's risk attached to that. We both need this to succeed.'

'No way. This goes later today. I don't have the time to isolate this bloke, so you've got what you've got. I can't make it any easier for you — this life we chose is all about risks, is it not? I'm sure you can get this done.'

'You people use any concealment methods?' Helen asked.

'This bloke's picking up a holdall and delivering. He's not one of my people — what he does with it when it's in his car is down to him. My guess is that he sticks it on the passenger seat and wonders what the fuck he's got himself into all the way home, but he might be stashing it in fake Michelins for all I know. You're gonna have to do *some* work at least. I can't give it to you any more on a plate than it already is.'

'Fine.'

'You're welcome.' Ed chuckled.

'You think this is funny? You think this solves all our problems and you can relax? This is a token gesture at keeping us both out of the shit, and it may not have the desired effect. Rest assured, Ed, I will be back soon. I'll need a break with the Whitfield robbery.'

'I told you I'll see what I can do with that. I need time myself. And a word of warning, Helen.' Ed paused but got no reaction. 'You need to hit this bloke long before he gets anywhere near Hythe. I will be keeping a sharp eye on the job. Any suggestion that you're getting ambitious and trying to follow the drugs to the drop site, I'll cut him loose and you'll get nothing from me. Understand?'

'You're hardly in a position to be giving me warnings, Ed.'

'Whatever my position is, you have been warned. I've given you your job. Hit the car hard and clean and everyone's happy. For now. I'll get you something more by the end of the week.'

'You'd better, or you might find that I won't be able to have any influence on your business. Positive or negative.'

Helen Webb hung up and the smile returned to Ed's face as he conjured another image of the chief superintendent, swearing silently at her phone, and squirming in her chair. His mind switched to the new guy. He'd only contacted Ed's people a few days ago — no criminal record and just needing some easy money, fast.

'No such thing as easy money,' he said out loud, getting to his feet. He stretched, then walked to the kitchen where he turned on the coffee machine.

CHAPTER 3

The spotter, PC Lee Howiss, picked up the electric blue Skoda Octavia vRS estate vehicle with ease. The spotter was disguised as a dog walker, wearing jeans and a long sleeved T-shirt, with a frenetic springer spaniel on a leash. They had found a lookout point from a sandblasted wooden bench on the windswept seafront of the small town of St Mary's Bay. Lee was sitting sideways with a takeaway coffee, intently studying every moving object on the dead straight road behind him. The bench was right next to a pinch point, manufactured by the strike team using parked cars. It was 7.40 a.m. The target was early and had the seated police officer been just a few minutes later he would have missed it.

For a few seconds the vRS came almost to a stop directly in front of him. It was plenty of time for a positive identification, even before he had seen the registration number as the car pulled away. The type of car was not common, the colour was distinctive, but it was the behaviour of the man at the controls that was the real giveaway. The car had accelerated hard up to the parked obstruction and the braking had been late and firm. The driver had his hands tight on the wheel, his eyes forwards.

Everyone else seemed to appreciate the view. Even the locals used the opportunity of slowing their vehicle to gaze sideways and take in the wiry grass waving on the dunes, the smattering of polished pebbles and that deep blue backdrop.

Lee knew the follow cars were four minutes from his location. He let the Skoda get a short distance away and reached into his top pocket where a clipped microphone was concealed.

'Sierra One One, permission.' The spaniel turned to his master at the sound of his voice.

'Go ahead, Sierra One One.'

'Confirm vehicle Skoda Octavia colour blue, Sierra Delta Six Zero Hotel Sierra November passed my location. One male occupant, white male, shaven head, large build. He is wearing a black polo shirt and travels east on Dymchurch Road towards Hythe.'

'Receive that, Sierra One One. Sierra One Two, did you receive the last?'

'Sierra One Two, yes, yes. Confirm target vehicle approaching our location, I will call up when I have the eyeball.'

'Receive that, Sierra One One.'

Lee took a deep breath and turned to face out towards the sea. He met the spaniel's keen eyes. 'Well, you were awesome, Jack.'

Jack accepted a pat on the head. His owner's attention had already returned to his earpiece.

'Sierra One Two, I've got the eyeball.'

* * *

Barry Lance listened intently to his radio. The briefing for this job had come from the chief superintendent herself, and she had made it quite clear that it needed to be quick and clean. Barry had pulled out all the stops to get this done right.

His first call had been to a contact at Highways, where he had been able to call in a favour. He had sourced a set of "stop" and "go" signs, to be held up and spun by undercover police officers in hard hats, high-visibility vests, khaki shorts, and steel-capped boots. For all the world they looked like temporary traffic signs, safely moving traffic around a parked Transit van and a small clear area beyond. The whole façade would create a second pinch point where they could bring the Skoda to a forced stop right next to another Transit van, its interior packed with five uniform officers. It would be cramped and hot, but they would be ready to strike. Barry had been clear on his instructions: Sierra One Two's Ford Mondeo would follow the Skoda through the traffic signs and a Land Rover would then pull out and come the other way. The Skoda would have to come to a stop. By this time, the rear doors of the Transit would have spat out the five-man arrest team, backed up by the undercover officers, and the man would be in custody with the evidence secured by the time Barry had driven the half mile from his holding point. Everyone on the team knew their part.

The Skoda passed Sierra One Two. They pulled out directly behind it as it rolled up towards the signs. The target slowed as it approached a man in sandy-coloured work boots and a hi-vis vest who scratched his hip as he spun a tall, circular sign displaying 'Stop.'

Barry had been forced to transmit a hurried message to a concealed transmitter in the man's right ear telling him that the Land Rover hadn't managed to get into position yet. He was to hold up the target car.

* * *

Barry's frustration was almost tangible. His team had been caught out by the Skoda being earlier than they had expected. He held the radio mouthpiece in his hand, holding his breath for an update, his frustration mounting.

'*Sierra One Two. Target vehicle is left, left onto Burmarsh Road. Confirm Burmarsh Road, speed increasing. Vehicle is now making off.*'

'Shit!' Barry thumped the steering wheel of his grey Range Rover Sport. His car was two up, accompanied by a sturdy Volvo four-by-four vehicle and a brand new BMW 5 Series that had been the subject of a pleading phone call by Transport Services for it not to be "broken."

Barry had a digital map on the centre console and he swiped a finger over it, trying to plot the change of direction. The road they had taken was effectively a long crescent. It had other roads jutting off it that skewed deeper into the marshland, but it also looped round, back onto the A259.

'Sierra One Two the target vehicle continues to increase his speed, we are attempting to make up ground and will keep the zero.'

Barry banged on the steering wheel again. He had raised the mouthpiece of his car radio to his mouth to call the chase car off, to tell them to give it some room. This might have appeased the target and saved the situation, but the Mondeo had accelerated after it. It was now a chase.

Barry Lance selected drive, and the V8 roared out into the traffic. He could take the next right and it would put him on the same road as the target vehicle — but it would be coming straight for him. It was never ideal to strike a vehicle from a head-on position, not when the target was moving at speed, but Barry needed a quick end. The roads were narrow enough for him to force the Skoda to slow at least, then they would have to play it by ear.

Barry checked his rear-view mirror. The BMW had fallen in behind him, followed by the Volvo. 'Sierra One Zero, we have moved onto Burmarsh Road but we are coming in from the other end. We will force the target vehicle to slow. Sierra One Two, you are to put the box on as soon as the opportunity arises.'

'Sierra One Two, receive the last.'

The Range Rover continued down the street. A Ford emerged from a pub forecourt and nearly pulled right out in front of the speeding convoy. The BMW pulled out and round the offending vehicle's protruding bonnet and the

Volvo followed in close formation. After the pub it was a hard left onto Donkey Street, which became Burmarsh Road.

From his lofty position in the Range Rover, Barry could see the front of an electric blue Skoda coming towards him. The road wasn't wide enough for both to pass on the tarmac and he moved out into the middle. In his mirror he saw the BMW drop back. The Skoda kept coming, the Ford Mondeo clinging to the back. The vehicles were almost on each other, then the Skoda jerked left. Barry stomped on his brakes as the target rode up onto the slippery grass that dropped away quickly to a watery dyke. It found sufficient grip to scramble past the Range Rover. Barry flinched as the Mondeo came to within inches of his front bumper. The BMW suddenly made a desperate last play and veered to the right, meeting with the front offside wing of the blue Skoda.

The rear of the Skoda skipped up off the ground. The bonnet of the BMW rippled and bent and the Skoda bounced left. There was nothing now to stop the Skoda's momentum. It hit the water hard. The Skoda dropped, its left side suddenly flipping downwards, the wheels bucking out towards the road. The nearside windows blew in and the car scratched and scraped, digging itself sideways into the bed of the six-foot-deep dyke.

Barry was already out and running towards the stricken Skoda. It was filling with water. The man in the driver's seat was clearly in trouble, with his head almost submerged by the ditch water. Barry's team acted quickly, clambering over the car, and wrenching open the driver's door. They pulled the man to the bank and smoothly moved his head back to open his airway. He was soon breathing normally and reacting to their voices. This was not Barry's idea of clean.

'He's going to be okay.' One of his officers gave him a thumbs-up.

'Well, it's a start,' Barry replied, turning his attention back towards the Skoda. The left side, and most of the front, was completely submerged in dirty ditch water. 'Now we just need to carry out a quick search of the car and we're fucking done.'

One of the lads on his team joined him on the bank, where they looked down at the wreckage.

'We'll get it,' he said. 'It'll just take a little longer.'

CHAPTER 4

'Good morning, Jim, how are we doing today?' Inspector Martin Young said.

'Sir.' The jailer stood up hurriedly, straightened his glasses and visibly took a breath. 'I'm doing good.'

It was 11 a.m. and the back office of Langthorne's custody suite seemed pretty quiet, not unusual for a midweek morning. A quick glance at the wall-mounted whiteboard showed Martin that just four of the cells were occupied.

'And the cell block, Jim? As much as I like to know you're doing okay.'

'Can't moan this morning, sir. The sarge has just booked a shoplifter in, and that takes us to four. Uneventful night it seems, nothing juicy in the bin either.'

'I'm glad of that, Jim. Juicy usually suggests a large amount of paperwork.'

'Good point, but we do have a little paperwork, I'm afraid. The two from overnight are due reviews. You can speak to the female that's just come in if you want to, but she seemed pretty out of it to me.'

'I'll pop my head in on them all.'

'Understood. Well, you've got two lorry drivers in, stopped inbound at the Port of Dover and nicked for human trafficking — load of illegals found in the trailers. Might be that some were in the cabs as well but I can't recall.'

Martin shrugged. 'I'm not interested in the investigation side of it, Jim. I assume our drivers are foreign?'

'Both Polish.'

'Speak English?'

'The usual story. Not when they were nicked but they suddenly remembered the lingo when they got hungry. I don't doubt they'll speak to you if they think it will get them out quicker.'

'They will be sorely disappointed then.'

'You've got a bloke who came in half hour ago or so for concern in the supply of Class A and failing to stop for police. He was stopped by the Tac team, load of heroin on the passenger seat of his car apparently. Bit of fun and games stopping him I think, a couple of our cars are gonna need some new panels. Our man ended up in a ditch full of water down on the marsh. All the evidence is drying off upstairs and he's had a trip to hospital to get checked out before coming here.'

Martin rolled his eyes. 'I swear those Tac team boys go round driving into people just for fun.'

'Good job, though. Fair amount of Class A, a couple of hundred grand they reckon. Just as soon as they wring it out!'

'I take it the man has accepted his arrest and isn't making an issue of his injuries? I'm not dealing with a complaint here, am I?'

'Nah. He got a bang on the head and shoulder but he's been checked over at A&E and they're perfectly happy with him.'

'Who is he?'

Jim swung his eyes back to the whiteboard. 'A fellow called Tony Robson, thirty-eight years old, local.'

Martin scowled a little. 'Local?'

'Yeah, Twelve Wartam Gardens, Langthorne.'

'Wartam Gardens!' Martin smiled. 'I used to live on that road. I don't know the name though.'

'I don't think he's lived there long, sir.'

'I don't mean I might know him as a neighbour, Jim, I mean as a criminal.' Martin was good with names, and this wasn't one he'd heard before.

'No, he's not known to anyone. Not on our system, never nicked. Not even a stop-check on the bloke.'

'And he suddenly appears with two hundred thousand pounds' worth of heroin on his passenger seat?'

Jim nodded. 'Just like that. Maybe he's one of those that are good at it, that go under the radar?'

'Until now.'

'Until now,' Jim agreed.

'Maybe.'

'And then there's the girl we just booked in. She's your standard skaghead, nicking meat from the twenty-four-hour Tesco to sell for her hit later in the day. She'll be on half-hourly checks 'cause she seemed a bit monged out. I'm due to go and see her in a minute. She wanted a coffee and might want a breakfast.'

Martin waved him away. 'Don't worry. I'll include her in my rounds, and I'll ask her if she fancies the breakfast.'

Martin left Jim to fill the office kettle in preparation for his return. As the duty inspector, Martin was in charge of making sure that everyone in custody was being treated fairly, was there for the right reasons and, most importantly, was being kept alive. Generally, these things looked after themselves and a lot of the duty guv'nors would simply put their stamp on prisoners' custody records after peering through the Perspex peephole. Martin liked to visit every cell, open every door, speak to every prisoner. He was too close to retirement for a death in custody to cost him his pension. He still cared anyway.

First Martin popped into the second kitchen where the cheap coffee, along with powdered milk, was kept and was already divvied up in individual cardboard cups stacked under a hissing urn. He filled one for his first prisoner, a convenient way to build rapport from the offset and make his own life easier. He stuffed several sachets of sugar and a plastic stirrer in his trouser pocket then fiddled with the keys to open the first cell. Affectionately known as the "drunk cell," the bed was lower there.

Martin recognised the odour all too well, the familiar smell of urine, vomit and unwashed body. He stood in the doorway looking at the slumped figure of the female shoplifter.

* * *

The woman's face was pressed against the ground. The intense cold from the solid concrete floor bit into her cheek and she was glad of the pain. It almost overrode the agony that racked the rest of her body, beating behind her eyes if she opened them to the light, aching in her fingers and toes. She was exhausted. Her addiction had been her only consistent bedtime companion for three years now, ensuring that sleep was neither deep nor prolonged. A person hooked on heroin was never truly asleep, never truly awake.

She moved her arm up under her head. The oversized, filthy hoodie that she had acquired at some point was pulled tight against her pointed elbows and tiny frame. Her throat stung with vomit and saliva trickled from her closed lips.

She heard a noise at the door and forced open an eye. Her hair had fallen over her face and into her eyes, and she could not see clearly. A blurred figure stood over her with arm outstretched, holding something in its hand. Her focus moved to the hand. The addict wanted to see exactly what her mark was carrying, what she could snatch.

It was a cup of coffee. Her eyes moved beyond the steaming cup to silver, raised pips sewn into epaulettes that marked him out as someone of senior rank. An inspector, in fact. Well, she knew the system. She wasn't going anywhere until she'd been interviewed, and for nicking meat it would be a beat copper, probably some new recruit.

The woman moved. She fixed on the man's face now. It was stern and a little judgmental — as she might expect — but there was softness there too. The lips formed a smile containing genuine warmth.

The man dropped to a squat, the coffee still held towards her.

Her head felt like lead, heavy and out of control, and the base of her neck was stiff and painful. She swept her matted hair away from her eyes and rose to an awkward sit. Her head thumped. Her dry lips formed something approaching a smile and she coughed to clear her throat.

'Hello, Dad.'

CHAPTER 5

George Elms was covered in blood.

Not his.

He held the blade at chest height, his feet firmly planted, his whole body tense. He panted from the sudden exertion. The men had stopped coming at him. Two had backed well away, bleeding from crude slash wounds onto the shower tiles. Three more sized him up but made no move. He'd caught them out. They hadn't expected him to be ready for them, to be carrying a blade made from a piece of broken mirror and a steel ruler from the workshops, that he waved at each one of them in turn. Should they attack again, George wasn't sure how much damage he would be able to do. His weapon was a slasher, it was not going to stop a man permanently.

'A fucking blade, pig! You gonna take us all with that?' the leader spat the words out.

'Come find out.' George thrust the weapon towards him.

'Three of us, George. We're gonna take that off you and then I'll show you just how to use it.'

George motioned at the two men clutching at abdomen and chest respectively. 'Your mates here gave it a good go.'

'It was going to be a beating, pig. But you wanna up the stakes? Well, I see your fucking homemade blade and I raise you.'

The man reached to his waistband and pulled out a solid-looking meat cleaver. He held it up close to his eyes, twisting it like a beautiful object that he was taking in for the first time. His lips puckered, ready to kiss the blade. He looked like he was enjoying himself.

His two accomplices were watching this performance and George saw his opportunity.

He lurched forward. It was two paces between him and his would-be assailant, whose lips were resting against the edge of the blade. George struck the flatter side of the ugly blade with the bottom of his fist, pushing it firmly into the man's face. He yelped, from surprise at first, and then pain. The blade was blunt, but sharp enough to draw blood and solid enough to dislodge a tooth. George used the moment to grab at the cleaver's handle and yank it downwards, but the man wasn't letting go easily. The two men grappled for control of the weapon. The man jerked his head forwards, catching George hard, forcing him backwards onto an ankle held together by a newly inserted pin and an oversized medical boot. The pain from his head and ankle was enough to take his breath away, and he crumpled to the floor. His adapted weapon skittered across the tiles. The man took a second to steady himself, and his smile returned as he looked down on the figure of George Elms, whose hands were clutching his right ankle.

The two men who had been watching now moved in. They took an arm each, pulling them out sideways. One man landed a heavy punch that split George's nose and pushed the back of his head hard into the solid tiles. Another blow struck, harder, and the men leaning over him became a dazed blur. The blows stopped. The lead man stood over him. A large globule of spit hit George on the chin.

George's head rocked from side to side. He was groggy but still determined. His face felt like it was broken all over, but he managed a smile. He looked at the cleaver.

'You could've just taken the beating. We weren't gonna finish the job for a few weeks yet. Maybe even months if I enjoyed it enough.' The man lashed out and the kick connected with the sole of George's right foot. Pain from his shattered ankle shot through him again.

George's body contorted in agony but he steadied himself quickly. He breathed, deep and long, and his mouth opened and closed as he tried to form words. 'There's me, fucking up my future again. Fucking do it then. Get it done'.

The man raised the cleaver, his feet firmly planted either side of George's legs. He was close enough to smash it through his skull.

'What the fuck!' A panicked shout came from somewhere behind them. The man standing over George hesitated.

George just made out the uniform as the voice drew near. 'You said it was a fucking word! A bit of a slap! How do I explain away a man chopped to fucking pieces?'

'This don't concern you!' The uniformed officer grabbed the cleaver man's arm.

'Drop the fucking blade — now! This weren't the deal.'

The ringleader seemed to be running over his options. Suddenly, his arms lost their tension. He lowered the weapon and allowed it to be taken off him.

The guard backed away, and took in the two bleeding men. 'For fuck's sake!' he muttered. 'Get them cleaned up in the showers. I'll get you some dressings and a new tracksuit. If you need sickbay, then give it as long as you can and make it fucking believable.'

No one moved. The scene was frozen like a still from a movie as the credits rolled.

Then the man relinquishing the cleaver gave George one last look. 'This is just the start, *Sarge*. You're gonna wish we'd finished this today.'

'Get the fuck out of here!' shouted the prison guard.

The men moved towards the separate shower area. George watched them leave, then grimaced as he pulled himself up to his elbows, his legs still splayed out in front of him.

'Where are your crutches?'

George gave a harsh laugh. 'What the fuck do you care?'

'You need to be somewhere else. Now.'

'What, so you can save your skin? This didn't quite go to plan, did it? Why the fuck should I help you?'

'You don't need to help me. And I don't need to take you with me. You can follow me out or you can stay and finish your conversation with your mates in there.'

'And live to fight another day. Or at least until you decide to throw me back to the wolves.'

The guard tensed his jaw. 'You coming or not? I need to clean you up.'

'Course you do. Bit difficult explaining the state of me to your bosses.'

'My *bosses* hate you more than the blokes you're in here with. They wouldn't fucking blink, Elms. It's them on the outside that I have to clean you up for. It only takes one to think you're human enough for human rights, and there's all sorts of writing to be done to cover arses. Like we should fucking have to.'

George had pushed himself backwards against a wooden bench. It was bolted to the floor and was low enough for him to pull himself up to a sitting position. His ankle throbbed. He'd taken a good few blows to his head. His vision was still a little blurred and he could taste the blood from his nose. The tinnitus in his ears made a whooshing noise, interrupted by the sound of his own racing heartbeat.

'The outside?'

'That's right. Fifteen minutes. Get yourself looking something like normal. You've got a visitor.'

George gripped his nose and sniffed. He was satisfied it wasn't broken but his hand still came away covered with blood.

'You know I don't see visitors.'

'It's your solicitor.'

'I definitely don't want to see him.'

'You do look a right fucking state. Probably best I tell him you can't make it.'

George finally processed the guard's words.

'Human rights, you say? Nah, fuck it. Maybe I should have a little chat.'

The guard sneered. 'You don't seem to understand what goes on in here, George. My advice to you is to keep your head down and play the game. The people that are keeping you safe in here won't appreciate you rocking the boat.'

George gestured at his battered face. 'This is safe, is it?'

'You ain't dead, are yer?'

'Not yet I'm not.'

'Exactly. You ain't dead till I say you are.'

CHAPTER 6

Martin Young emerged from the drunk cell and closed the door quietly behind him. He leaned against the solid wall of the passage, eyes on the floor.

'You okay, sir?' Jim said.

'Oh yes, Jim, fine.' Martin forced a smile.

'She okay?' Jim the jailer nodded at the closed door. 'The skaghead?'

'Maybe we should show a little more professionalism when we refer to prisoners. We don't know what's caused them to be here, do we?'

'Sorry, sir, you're right. I get a bit loose sometimes, you know, working with these people all day.'

Martin pushed past him to the next cell, where he fiddled with the lock. He swore as the heavy bunch of keys slipped from his hands and clattered to the floor. He was aware of Jim passing behind him.

The prisoner was sat up on his bed when he pushed the door open.

'Good morning,' Martin said. He sounded hesitant, his thoughts were still very much on the next-door cell.

'Good morning.' The prisoner looked at him expectantly.

Martin lifted a blue folder which contained the prisoner's notes. 'You must be Tony Robson?'

'That's right.'

'And this is the first time you've been in custody, I understand?'

'It is, yeah.'

Martin held the man's gaze. 'Never in trouble with the police, and here you are with bricks of heroin on your passenger seat?' Martin was suddenly angry. Shits like this were responsible for flooding the streets with Class A drugs, making sure the addicts stayed addicted. Addicts like his daughter, lying on the cell floor next door.

'I fucked up.' Tony sounded sincere. He seemed genuinely sorry. Probably sorry for being caught, thought Martin. He was a big man, strongly built and thuggish looking.

'You haven't eaten or drunk a thing since your arrest. You should have something.'

'I can't eat.'

'A coffee though?'

'They're shit here, machine crap.'

Martin flickered a smile. 'True.' A shadow passed the cell door. 'Jim!' Martin called out.

The jailer appeared at the door. 'Boss?'

'I'll have my coffee in here if I may, please, and can we make Mr Robson here a real one too? In a mug from the staff stash. I'll sit with him while he finishes it.'

Jim hesitated for a second. The rule was that the prisoners drank the instant rubbish out of small cardboard cups. 'I'll bring them down.'

Martin turned back towards the seated prisoner. 'There — a proper coffee. I'll have to stay with you while you drink it but at least I know you're not going to dehydrate on my watch.'

'Thanks.' There was a pause. 'You think I'm some scumbag drug pusher,' Tony said, looking at the floor.

'I'm not the one to decide what you are. I just get to make sure whoever is down here is being treated right.'

'You got angry though, earlier, when you spoke about heroin. Like you don't like me for what I did. I don't like me either. I only did it for my son. I know you probably hear it all the time, but I got pushed into a desperate place and I thought I saw a way out of it. I'll have made that place a hell of a lot more desperate if I go to prison. Time is not something I have to waste.'

'It was unprofessional of me. It's just a subject that's a little raw. Think of a copper who's had to mop up a terrible road accident caused by someone on their mobile phone. One day you'll be on yours, sitting at some traffic lights, chatting away happily. That same officer will tear your head off for it. We all have things that are sensitive for us. I shouldn't speak to you about the reason you're here, and you shouldn't either until you've spoken to a brief.'

'I'm not having a solicitor.'

'Why not?'

'I know what I did. You know what I did. A solicitor can't change that.'

'It's your choice, but if there are extenuating circumstances? Even if there aren't, you should take some advice.'

'I should take some responsibility for once.' The man raised puffy eyes to Martin. 'Will I go to prison? I can't tell you how important it is for me to be at home.'

'I don't want to jump ahead. You'll get interviewed, they'll tell you what they think they know and you'll tell them your side. Go from there. And if you get charged, you'll have your opportunity to go to court and put your reasons for making your decisions. You'll get to go home whatever happens, I would imagine. They will likely bail you out while they do the tests. We need to know that what you had was definitely drugs before you get charged with anything.'

'It's a stay of execution, then.'

Martin didn't reply.

Jim blustered in and handed them two steaming mugs of coffee. Martin glanced up at the camera in the top corner of the cell. He'd already talked too much. He knew the rules about discussing cases outside the interview rooms. The cameras in the cell didn't record sound, but the ones in the corridors did. The last thing he needed was to be caught offering legal advice to a prisoner. Both men swigged at their drinks in silence.

'What's your issue with drugs? I mean, I know police officers must hate drugs, but you said it was sensitive, like you might have had an experience with them. Was you a druggie once?'

'No,' Martin said too loudly, then more quietly, 'No, I was never a druggie.'

'So . . . what? Just pissed off with them because of your line of work?'

Martin looked up at the camera again. He moved further into the cell. 'I have a family member, a close one, who has an ongoing battle. I've seen what those chemicals do to people. They take everything from them, strip everything away until all that's left is the need for more drugs. When good people get into drugs it takes all the good away.' Martin felt weak all of a sudden. He found a perch on the end of the bed. His voice was low, to avoid being overheard. This was the first time he'd ever spoken out loud about it. He couldn't talk to his wife — he'd tried more times than he could remember, back when Sally started showing the first real signs. The money disappearing from his wife's purse was put down to forgetfulness or misunderstanding. Then jewellery went, including her nan's ring, a precious heirloom. After that, his wife became increasingly angry and bitter. She seemed to think Sally should just pull herself together and snap out of it. Martin knew it wasn't so easy, and that anger was counterproductive, even destructive.

'Your kid?' Tony's question didn't register at first. Martin was thinking about his wife, and whether he would even bother to mention that their daughter was back in custody.

'Your son?' Tony persisted.

Martin shook his head. 'My little girl.' The day was starting to get on top of him and he was afraid he might start crying.

'You'd do anything for your kids, wouldn't you?'

'Anything.'

'Muscular dystrophy,' Tony said.

'Muscular dystrophy?'

'My boy. He's seven. He was diagnosed a few years back and should be pretty severely disabled by now. It's basically a muscle-wasting disease. It hits mobility first but eventually it attacks every part of you. Until there's nothing left.'

Martin looked at Tony. '*Should* be disabled?'

'Yeah. The Americans have got this drug that has pretty much stopped it in its tracks. We were in the most desperate place I've ever known, and then there was hope, you know. It was better than anyone imagined. We have a normal boy with a football at his feet, full of energy and mischief, me telling him off for never leaving me alone and breaking down my fence with his ball.'

'That's great.'

'It was. Our doc spoke to me a few days back. Basically, the NHS won't pay for Daniel's treatment any more. His condition is rare, and saving his life alone isn't worth the three grand a month it costs for the drugs. Just like that, they cut us loose, told us we're on our own. So now it's down to finding three grand a month or watching my son waste away to nothing in front of my eyes. Maybe we're not so different, you and me.'

Martin sighed, and shook his head. 'I feel bad. All my woes are caused by self-inflicted drug abuse, and here you are fighting a terrible disease that your son did nothing to bring on himself.'

'I've seen these crackheads, the way they live. No one would choose to live like that. Your daughter's got a disease too. At least with Daniel, I know what the cure is.'

'Three thousand pounds a month,' Martin said.

'Three thousand pounds a month,' Tony confirmed.

'Hence you suddenly turn up on our radar with three bricks of heroin on your passenger seat.'

Tony rubbed his cheeks hard, distorting his mouth. Both men took a long drink of coffee. 'Is that what it was?' Tony spoke into his cup, his eyes glazed and empty. 'I mean, I guessed, but . . .' He ran out of words.

'If you did have a brief, they'd probably tell you to answer every question with "no comment."' Martin blurted this out before he could stop himself. What was he doing? He shouldn't be advising a prisoner how to answer questions in a police interview.

'But that won't help in the long run. I was caught red-handed.'

'You've not committed any offence until we've proved that what you had was heroin. That takes time, six weeks or so. If you don't reply to their questions there'll be no reason to keep you. You'll get six weeks with your son before you have to come back.' Martin's pulse had quickened, his stomach had tightened up. He was close to having one of his anxiety attacks and needed to get out of there. He stood, swept up the empty coffee cups, and made for the door.

'Six weeks. I suppose I should count myself lucky if that's what I get,' Tony said as Martin reached the door. 'I was thinking they might just cart me off to prison. What am I going to do if they send me to prison?'

Martin stopped, a hand on the cold metal of the door. He stepped out and put down the cups. Closing the door was a two-handed job. He leant back into the cell, his eyes wide open, furtive and intense.

41

'No comment,' he repeated. 'Play for time.'
Martin slammed the cell door shut.

CHAPTER 7

'We need to stop meeting in such circumstances, George.' Solicitor Howard Staples shook George's hand.

'Thanks for ignoring my requests to stay away and coming down anyway. Your timing is impeccable.' George sat down on the wooden bench. It was fixed to the floor at just the right distance to make it impossible to lean comfortably on the table.

'Thanks? Really? You've spent the last few weeks avoiding any contact at all. Here we are with a trial looming, *your* trial, and your solicitor can't even get to speak to you.'

'Is this a bollocking?' George's expression lightened a little.

'Yes.'

'Noted.'

'I'm only here for you, George, you know that. The only reason I need to have a chat is because I need to look after your best interests and I can't do that if you hide behind these brick walls, can I?'

'Like I said, noted.'

'Bollocking over.'

George sat back in his chair, smiled, and immediately flinched in pain. 'Well, that wasn't so bad.'

'I assume I'm here because someone beat some sense into you.'

George gingerly pushed at his cheek, then gripped his aching nose. 'The showers get very slippery in here.'

'You wanna be careful they don't kill you, George. Is that why you finally agreed to speak to me?'

'Well, to be honest, I had no intention of speaking to you this morning. In fact, had you been an hour earlier you still wouldn't have got your meeting, but the option was to continue with the conversation I was having or come and drink a coffee with you.' George shifted, seeking a more comfortable position. The room was used for prisoners to speak to their legal advisors. The only bright colour in the beige room was provided by two red panic buttons on Howard's side of the table. A notice on the wall read, "Anyone causing damage to this room will be charged."

'So you don't want to talk about the case?' Howard prompted.

'You're a good man, Howard, and I really don't like wasting your time.'

'And you didn't even get a coffee.'

'Water's fine.'

'I just want to help you, you know.'

'And you have. Like I said, perfect timing.'

'Change your plea. Go not guilty, talk to the cops about what happened and why, and I can have you out of here in weeks. Maybe less. The CPS have no real case, just circumstantial bits and bobs. I'm sure they wouldn't even take it to court if they didn't have your confession and your continuing insistence on your own guilt.'

'But they do.'

'But they do,' Howard repeated. 'And here we are. You're stuck in here. This is a remand prison, George, you know how this works. If they sentence you for real and to a Cat A prison you are looking at far worse than just never seeing your family again.'

George said nothing.

Howard knew that he had touched a nerve. He waited.

'I'm here for my family.'

'You think they're thanking you for that?' Howard's face was etched with frustration.

'I don't know what they think. How can I?'

'That you're a monster, George. That's what your wife is trying to come to terms with, and that's what your daughter will grow up thinking of her dad. Whatever you think you are achieving by keeping up this façade is meaningless to the people you care about most. You are hurting them, George.'

'There is no other way.'

'Not guilty. You get to say two words in a room of your peers and we're in business.'

George was shaking his head. 'No one but you wants me to change my plea. It's all nice and tidy. Lennokshire Police won't ever let me out of here.'

'Lennokshire Police don't get to decide. And you still have some friends that are asking the same questions as I am about the lack of evidence.'

'What friends?'

'Paul Baern. He was speaking to me almost daily at one point, and it's still regular. Seems he doesn't think it all adds up.'

'Then he's a fool. They'll get him too. He has no idea how deep the issue with me runs.'

'I get the impression he stopped giving a shit about that a long time ago. He wanted to come up here and speak to you himself. I told him—'

'You can't let him do that!'

'Okay, okay! Don't worry. I told him it would be a wasted journey, I said you wouldn't speak to him.'

'He can't come here. I can't be seen speaking to the police.'

'We had that covered. Paul has a contact here, one of the prison officers. His visit would be recorded as a solicitor visit. There would be no mention of the police anywhere.'

'What guard?'

'I don't know, it's Paul's man.'

'I haven't met a guard in here yet that doesn't seem hell-bent on making my stay in here as unpleasant as possible.'

'I can only tell you what he told me. He said he had someone in here that he could tug on to get it done. They could get him sat in front of you with no one else having any idea what was going on.'

'And Paul trusts this man, does he?'

'He said he did.'

'Then he's a bigger fool than I thought.'

'I'll pass that on.'

George sat back and put his hands behind his head. He felt tired all of a sudden. Speaking to deaf ears has that effect. 'Speak to him again,' George said, without looking up.

'To Paul?'

'Yeah.'

'And say what?'

'Firstly I want you to tell him to stop and think. He needs to know that his actions out there can have a massive knock-on effect. I know Paul, he's headstrong and he's like a dog with a bone when he gets hold of something. You need to tell him to reel it in a bit. Get the name of this contact he reckons he has in here and find a way of getting the name to me. And I want you to be satisfied that this guard's not going to be talking about me meeting with a copper. I need you to be sure.'

'Why do *I* need to be sure?'

'Because I trust your judgment.'

'And not Paul's? He's already assured me that—'

'Not in this case, no. He can get sucked in, can Paul, and he doesn't mind taking a punt or two. I can't be taking punts, not with the stakes as they are.'

'So you're saying that if we can meet your criteria, then you'll meet with Paul?'

'I'm not saying that. I can contact Paul if I need to, through you. It's an unnecessary risk to bring him in here. I just want the name, so I know who he's talking about. It might be relevant. Might not.'

'Well, I'm glad we got that set in stone!'

George stood, arching his back and grimacing with sudden pain.

Howard noticed. 'The ankle still?'

'Yeah. It is getting better. Just slowly, and I've not exactly been treating it right.'

'I like the footwear.' Howard towered over George when he stood. He looked down at the supporting boot.

George extended his hand. 'Thanks again. Like I said, I hate wasting a good man's time.'

'And yet you do it so well.'

George gave a sort of laugh. 'I can't promise I won't do it again either.'

CHAPTER 8

Martin Young was confused. He found he was sitting up, the duvet thrown aside. His bedside clock showed 3.12 a.m. Then he heard the noise that must have woken him, a buzzing sound that came from the hallway downstairs. It was his landline, switched to low. At this time of night, it had to be an important call. He padded downstairs. The phone was in the hall, through a set of wooden double doors that always rattled loudly when they were pulled apart. He was lucky his wife was a heavy sleeper. The phone, still ringing, was out of its cradle, still on the shelf. The number on the display beamed bright in the dark.

'Hello?'

'You know Sally?' The voice was female, hushed. It sounded frightened.

'Sally? I have a daughter called Sally.'

'She's crashing at Peto Court. She came home today with some paperwork from the cop shop. She had this phone number written on the back. Are you "Dad?"'

'Yes, yes I am, I mean that's me. Is she okay?' Martin had written his phone number on the back of a leaflet about a drug support group that had been given to his daughter while she was in the cell. He'd contemplated writing a further message, and had stood in the custody area for a full five minutes before someone had entered and he'd settled for drawing a smiley face and scuttling back to his office. He hadn't expected his daughter to look at the piece of paper at all, and he certainly hadn't expected a phone call.

'She had a fight. With some bloke she stays with here — he's been getting pretty nasty recently. She's pretty bad.'

'Bad?' Martin tried to compose himself but his legs gave way. He stood bent forward in a sort of crouch.

'She's taken a beating. He got pissed 'cause she got nicked.'

'Who did? Where is she now?'

Silence. There was a noise as though someone was rubbing the mouthpiece with a piece of cloth. Martin held the phone pressed against his ear and could make out another voice, male. He sounded angry, shouting, then a female voice pleading. The shouting male suddenly became louder, Martin heard swear words. Then the line went dead.

Martin sprinted back up the stairs. He'd left the door to his room ajar and he pushed it hard, so that it hit the wall. His wife sat up immediately.

'Martin! Whatever's the matter?'

'Sally. I need to go out and check on her.'

'Sally? Has she called?' His wife squinted and rubbed her ruffled hair as Martin switched on the main light. He grabbed at trousers and a fleece jumper. 'Is she hurt? I'll come with you.' His wife started to get out of bed.

'No.' Martin's tone was firm. 'You stay here. I'll call you the second I have news. I don't know what's going on yet and I don't know what I might find.'

'I'll make sure my phone's switched on.'

Martin left the house two minutes later. His Volvo burst into life, the lights illuminating his wife's Toyota as he backed out onto the road. The blinds in his bedroom parted, his wife watched him leave.

* * *

Martin knew Peto Court well. As a constable and then as a sergeant, he had been a regular visitor. It was one of those places that just kept dragging you back. It was situated on Langthorne's seafront at the bottom of a steep hill, a solid, featureless block of seventy-eight dwellings, mostly bedsits. The miserable greyish exterior had slashes of faded red under each of the windows and two entrances at opposite sides. Both had security doors with access gained by waving a key fob at the sensors. Martin didn't have a fob, but he'd never had a problem getting in. As his Volvo pulled into the car park, he could see lit windows where he was sure he could get someone's attention. This was a building that never slept.

Martin got out of the Volvo and ran towards the entrance door, trying to get a view into the two nearest flats that had signs of life. The flat to the right of the door had its curtains wide open and the lights from within arrowed out into the car park. He stepped closer to the window and almost kicked the prone figure of a woman lying almost directly under the window. She was on her side, her left hand stretched out to rest against the brick, her back towards him. She was dressed in a vest and white knickers. Even in the poor light, Martin could make out significant bruising on her leg, which spread up towards her buttocks. He put his hand on her arm, gently. She pulled it back, with a grunt.

'Sally.' Martin's lips drew together and his chin quivered.

Sally turned her head towards him. Her face was puffy and red. Her left eye had a fresh swelling that would blacken, and dried blood coated her nostrils. Her hair was caked with blood.

'Dad,' she managed. Her face crumpled, and tears formed in her eyes.

'Are you badly hurt?' Martin knelt down beside his daughter. He wanted to scoop her up, hold her tight, but he didn't know where to touch her. Her whole body looked like it hurt, everywhere raw to the touch. She was so small now, so fragile.

'No.' Sally rose to a sitting position and pulled at her vest top, stretching it over her knees.

'Where are your clothes?'

She shook her head. 'Doesn't matter.'

'Of course it matters.'

'I have some at your house,' she said. Her red eyes were now open, and her tears flowed. 'Take me with you — just for a place to crash?'

'Of course, Sally. Jesus!' Martin helped his daughter scramble to her feet. 'Are you okay? Do you need me to carry you to the car?' His voice broke a little. She pressed her body into his and wrapped her arms round him. He hugged her back, holding her tight. She shook her head against his chest. He let out a sob. Her hair smelled stale, like cigarette smoke and mould, but it hardly registered.

'Sorry, Dad.'

'Don't be silly.'

They drove back to the house in silence. Martin kept a rain jacket in the boot of the car, which he used to cover Sally. The night wasn't cold but she was shivering. Martin held back the flood of questions. He wanted to know who had done that to her, why, and what she was doing about it. What he could do about it. Someone had tossed his daughter out of that block of flats like a piece of rubbish. But he knew Sally was not good with questions. She had always put walls up, and they kept getting higher.

'Oh, good god!' Sally's mother was less restrained when they came in. She was standing in her dressing gown, nursing a cup of black tea. 'What happened to you?'

'Nothing, Ma.' The inevitable response.

'Martin, what are you doing about this?' His wife's reply was equally predictable.

'Denise, I've said that Sally can have a shower and a comfortable bed, something to eat, a cup of tea —

whatever she wants. She knows she can talk to me about anything she wants to. If she wants to.'

Sally looked at the floor.

'We should get her checked out at the hospital,' his wife said.

'She's an adult. If she wants me to take her to hospital, I will.'

'A cup of tea sounds like a good idea.' Sally cracked a smile.

'Love, would you pop the kettle back on?'

'You're not doing anything about this, Martin? This is your daughter.'

'*This* has a name,' Sally spat. She raised her head and met her mother's disgusted look.

'Well, I wonder sometimes. I mean, if you can't have any respect for yourself, how do you expect other people to have respect for you?'

'I don't. I don't expect anything of anyone. I didn't come here for you to *respect* me. I came here because I had nowhere else to go. I should have known I wouldn't be welcome here either.'

'There you go!' Her mother's voice was raised, her neck and chest flushed red. 'Making me out to be the wicked mother again, just because I care when you come back here black and blue with no trousers on. How could you let yourself get into this state?'

Martin stepped between them, facing his wife. 'Something happened to Sally tonight. This isn't her fault. She needs our help to get herself cleaned up and sorted out. That's all.' He stepped to the side, and softened his tone. 'And Sally, your mother is trying to say that we care about you so much that we don't like to see you hurt and vulnerable. That's all. I'll go and start the shower for you and we'll get you some of your old clothes sorted. Okay?'

Sally was staring at the floor again. 'I can start my own shower and sort my own clothes. Maybe I'm not as *vulnerable* as you think I am.'

'I didn't mean it like that . . .' But his daughter was already halfway up the stairs. Martin sighed.

'Aren't you going to talk to her?' Denise insisted.

'Not right now. You and I both know that she won't speak when she doesn't want to, it will only result in us arguing. It's been nine months since I've seen her, and God knows how long since she's been here. The last thing we need now is an argument.'

'Fine. But at least let me go and check on her. She might need a medical assessment — we can get the doctor out. We've got no idea what's happened to her.'

Martin held out his hands, palms down. 'Just leave her to have her shower, get clean clothes and a cup of tea, and we can assess her then. I really think she just needs some sleep and maybe she'll talk to us a bit more in the morning.'

'I'm going up to see her.' Denise started to push past him, but Martin took hold of her shoulder.

'*No!*'

Denise stopped in her tracks. Her husband's expression was as firm as his grip. She shrugged him off and went back into the kitchen. Martin stood still, a little shocked at himself. He heard the kettle start, and then the door closed against him. He turned and went towards the stairs, stopping at the bottom. He could hear the faint sound of the shower running. He wanted to see his daughter again. He saw her so rarely. He knew that he had a better chance than his wife of getting through to her. He went upstairs to check that the bed in her room was made, even though he knew it would be. Sometimes he would go in and just stand there.

He could still hear the shower running and he continued into Sally's room. He immediately spotted that the window was wide open, the net curtain sucked out in the breeze. Martin's stomach knotted. He hurried to the window and leaned out, looking down at the flat roof of the extension. It was damp with dew, and a footprint was clearly visible under the window. He pulled his head back into the room. The wardrobe door was open, a hanger still rocked on the rail. The bathroom was filling with steam — the shower running for no one. His daughter was gone.

'Did she speak to you?' his wife asked.

'No.'

Denise was still standing in the kitchen. She crossed her arms when he came in. Martin hated the pitiless tone his wife used whenever she talked about Sally.

'Well, I'm not taking her tea up. She can come down for it and speak to us like an adult.'

'She's gone, Denise. Out the window.'

Denise turned her eyes to the ceiling. 'Well, that's just brilliant. Running away as usual. Our daughter comes back here all beaten up and half-naked and you seem quite happy to do nothing about it! Well, I won't stand for it! We need to report this to the police, Martin, I hope you realise *that*.' The phone sat in a charging cradle on the kitchen counter. Denise reached for it but Martin was closer.

'We're not calling the police.'

'Why the hell not?'

'I'll go out in the car and look for her. See if I can reason with her. She said herself that she didn't have anywhere to go. She might not have gone far. And then when everyone's calmed down a bit, maybe we can talk about what happened and start making some progress with her. If we send the police after her, she'll never come back to us. She hates the police.'

'Well, maybe if she stopped breaking the law they would stop giving her a reason to dislike them.'

'Maybe you're right,' Martin conceded.

'She had a good upbringing. We did the very best we could by her and this is how she repays us. Twenty-five years old and still giving us dramas in the middle of the night. Lord knows what she's on today and who she's upset.'

'I'll go and look for her, Denise.' Martin had already put on his shoes and had one arm in the sleeve of his coat.

'You know what? I wouldn't bother. There's nothing we can do for that girl. She doesn't want our help — ungrateful little brat. She'll end up dead, we both know it, dead on the street, and it'll be muggins here left picking up the pieces.'

'*Denise!*' Martin shouted, catching them both by surprise. 'Maybe this is her fault, but whatever's happened she's still my little girl. I'd do *anything* for her. That never changes.'

Martin didn't wait for a reply. He walked out of the house and towards his car.

Martin wasn't looking for his daughter. He knew he wouldn't find her. She would be a good distance away by now and could have gone in any direction. He knew nothing about her or her associates, but he did know she would find shelter somewhere. She always did.

His drive was aimless to start with — there were very few places to go at half past four in the morning. Anywhere would do, but home and his wife. After running through his options, he decided on the only one he really had. He was due to start an early shift in just over two hours. He had a spare uniform at work, there was a shower, and on the top floor was a coffee machine that never got turned off.

Ten minutes later, the Volvo drew up in the car park of Langthorne House. The corridors on the fourth floor were silent and dark. The response officers manning the station were on the ground floor and had no reason to venture any higher at this time of night. The inspectors' office was also vacant, a gliding screensaver on one of the two computer monitors the only movement. The inspector on night duty was based at Margate and would only come over if there was a major incident. Tonight had been quiet across the county.

Martin made his way to the metal filing cabinet. Each of the inspectors based here had a personal drawer. He unlocked his and it slid open with a loud, high-pitched squeal. Martin pulled out a litre Evian water bottle and a glass tumbler that lay beside it. He twisted the lid, releasing the scent of vodka. Martin closed his eyes as he breathed it in. It had been weeks. He was a little more regular at home, but at work . . . it could only ever end badly. He was out of hours now though, wasn't he?

Martin sat back in his chair and savoured the reassuring burn of the alcohol as it slid down his throat. He wished he'd brought whiskey with him. Vodka was just a means to an end, it didn't taste of much. He bumped the table as he fidgeted in his seat, shifting the mouse so the screensaver disappeared. The screen now displayed a list of the prisoners currently in custody downstairs. Martin's eyes rested on "*T. Robson, PWITS class A drugs,*" and his mind returned to the conversation of earlier in the day. He'd liked Tony. He'd felt a connection with the man. They weren't so very different really. Both were totally devoted to their children, both desperately caught up in their kids' respective illnesses, both powerless to help.

Except Tony wasn't powerless. He might still be able to do something. He wasn't a criminal. He'd just been desperate to help his son.

Martin read the words again — *T Robson, PWITS class A drugs* — and thought about how unfair the world could be sometimes. Good people could be punished for simple mistakes, for just trying to do the right thing for their families. Martin considered what he could do for Tony. An idea flashed through his mind. No, crazy. He dismissed it with a shake of his head.

But his tumbler was empty and he was already picking up the Evian bottle to pour himself another.

CHAPTER 9

'I came in this morning, opened up, and found it like this.' Alessandra, or Ali as she was usually known, pointed at the smoking mess. Bits of grey foam still oozed from the bottom of the specialist drying machine. When she'd left the previous afternoon, it had been quietly drying what was suspected to be three kilo blocks of heroin and the sports holdall that had contained them. In fact, her explanation wasn't entirely true. She'd opened the door to flames and smoke, and she herself had applied the foam via a fire extinguisher hanging off the wall. The contents of the machine were lost completely. What the fire hadn't consumed had been washed away in the effort to put it out.

'You're going to have to do a whole lot better than that,' snarled Helen Webb. She stood with her feet apart and her hands on her hips. 'The chief himself is coming down here today and he has taken a personal interest in the heroin that was drying in here, under your supervision. What do I tell him when he walks into my office and enquires about the quarter of a million pounds' worth of hard drugs taken off the street?'

Ali shrugged. 'Well, you can tell him the drugs are definitely off the street.'

Helen Webb gave her the coldest of looks. 'You can make your jokes to Professional Standards when they launch their enquiry with my blessing. I suggest you get out of my sight now and start your very detailed statement about just what happened here.'

Ali's smile faded. She bit her bottom lip, considering a reply. She decided against it. She picked up her bag and walked away from the smoking mess and blackened glass that was all that remained of a £6,000 specialist piece of drying equipment. And sole evidence against a man caught moving a quarter of a million pounds' worth of Class A drugs across the county.

* * *

Paul Baern was in the office twenty minutes before an eight o'clock start. He always arrived early, despite the fact that he was pretty sure no one gave a damn. He reported to whichever CID sergeant was on duty at the time, and they would already have allocated anything interesting to members of their own teams.

Paul was on what the police termed "restricted duties," which effectively meant he wasn't insured to leave the building. He was no one's problem and everyone's, all at the same time, until senior management could find a way of getting him off the payroll for good. The moment it had been confirmed that his gunshot injury had caused irreversible damage to the nerves in his left arm, all parties had known that Paul and Lennokshire Police would have to part company, but sorting the details of the severance was a prime example of heel dragging. Much of Paul's time was now spent at the front counter assisting the civilian staff there with any queries from people who walked in off the street.

Paul's future was largely ignored. He was getting used to that too. Paul had been a close ally and friend of George

Elms, a man currently awaiting trial for murdering at least six police officers in cold blood just a few months earlier. Some of the mistrust had rubbed off on him. A lot of people had liked and respected George Elms, but understandably they had backed away from him when he had been named as the suspect for the murders. Paul had known from the very start that George was innocent, and his confession at the scene of his arrest had done nothing to change his mind. Nor had any of the evidence he had managed to get his hands on since then. Paul was now filling much of his spare time at work unofficially investigating the murders of the six officers, particularly the shooting of Samantha Robins, his close friend and colleague. She certainly died at someone's hands and it was eating Paul alive that the culprit still roamed free.

'Ali? What's going on?' Paul tried addressing someone directly. He was standing at the front counter of Langthorne House. The civilian staff weren't likely to be with him until closer to their eight thirty start, and he had gone to see why the public door had been opened early, and men wearing Fire Forensic Examiner suits were walking in and out, carrying various pieces of equipment. Ali looked like she was in a hurry to leave.

'Paul!' she said, as though his question had brought her out of a trance.

'Yes, Ali — Paul! What the hell is going on this morning? You ain't even dressed right!' The CSIs wore blue polo shirts with their title on the breast, tucked into black combat-style trousers with loads of pockets, and patrol boots. Ali was in blue jeans and white trainers with a long sleeved T-shirt. She was a pretty girl, her Italian heritage evident in her brown eyes and long, dark hair.

Ali looked around her. 'I can't really speak, mate, not now.' She looked near to tears.

Paul cocked his head to one side as Ali went towards the door. He noticed that the backpack she was carrying by the top handle rather than over her shoulder was stuffed until the zip wouldn't quite close.

'Are you okay?'

'No. Not really, Paul.' Ali hesitated long enough to suggest that she wanted to talk to someone about it.

'You wanna pop in the office? I can pretend I care if you like?'

Ali gave him tired smile. 'I don't want to get you in trouble.'

'No one gives a fuck about me, Ali, or who I speak to.' Paul reached down behind the counter and pressed a button. It opened one of the two rooms that were accessible from the front counter area. The door swung outwards slowly. Ali watched it, seeming to run through her options. She stepped into the empty room.

A computer sat on a desk, its screen dark and the standby light blinking.

'We'll be okay to talk in here.' Ali had been peering at the sound-recording device in the middle of the table. The room was sometimes used for interviews where there wasn't the necessity to take the interviewee down to the basement for the full custody experience.

'I got suspended,' she blurted out.

Paul hadn't been expecting that. He sat back a little and let Ali carry on.

'About five minutes ago. I got a bollocking this morning from Helen Webb. She told me to piss off and write her a statement for PSD. But before I was even able to log in, someone from PSD came in and told me I was suspended on full pay. He said I would need to surrender my uniform as it was part of the evidence, and then I was to leave the building. He took my security pass card and told me not to go outside the county. Said I would be hearing from him.' Ali tapped her pockets and pulled a business card from one of them, laying it on the table for Paul to see. He leant forward and read, "Paul Adams, Professional Standards."

'Sounds like a right cock.'

'Yeah. I mean *Paul*, really.'

Paul smiled. 'Yeah. You can never trust a *Paul*.' He sighed. 'So what was the bollocking about? You must know something about it.'

'Oh, yeah, sorry. Haven't you heard about the fire?'

'There's been a fire?'

'Ah, fuck, I thought everyone knew. There was a fire overnight, last night. Do you know about the job from yesterday? The heroin that was seized from the bloke in the ditch?'

'Yeah, three bricks of the stuff. They reckon it's uncut, up to half a mill.'

'Yeah. Well, it's gone.'

'Gone?'

'Burnt.'

'Burnt?'

'Yup. It appears someone set it on fire last night.'

'Set it on fire? How the fuck did they do that? You can't even get into the safe for a dooby without the custody sergeant having to sign it out in his own blood, let alone moving three bricks of pure heroin.'

'But it wasn't in the inspector's safe. It was in my drying machine in the CSI office because the Tac team gorillas forced the bloke into a ditch full of water. Damn near killed him.'

'Yes, I did hear that. So the gear was in the CSI office, and what? You're the only one with access so you're guilty?'

'Yeah, except I'm not the only one with access. You know the door? It's a coded lock and most of the station have probably been given the code at some point. I just happened to be the twat opening the door this morning, and I put the fire out. Helen Webb's clearly pissed at the loss of evidence and she had a go at me. Suggested I had the dryer on too hot.'

'Is that possible?'

'No. It's six thousand pounds worth of technology, they don't set things alight. You can't set it to get anywhere near that hot and even if you could, a damp bag and an even damper brick of powder? Have you any idea how hot that would have to be? And you wouldn't get flames, you'd just get incineration.'

Paul held his palms up. 'Woah, CSI scientist. I take your word for it.'

'Someone set that fire. It has to be deliberate.'

'And they've seized your clothes? For what, accelerant?'

'Exactly. Who knows what they'll find on that uniform. You have no idea the places I go and the things I do in that.'

Paul couldn't help laughing. 'I bet.'

Ali laughed. 'You know what I mean.' Her laughter subsided quickly.

'I'll let you get away,' said Paul. 'The sun's up today — go put your feet up and try and forget about this shithole. Treat it as some extra holiday.'

'I should, you're right. Though it definitely doesn't feel like a holiday.'

'You've got nothing to worry about,' Paul added.

'I know that. I'm not pissed off because I'm worried about the investigation, it's the fact that they feel the need to investigate me in the first place. I'm kinda proud of my record here. But they just treat you like shit.'

'That is true. I saw the way they treated George Elms, and then Sam when they thought he was reaching out to her. We're all just something to be used when they think they need us, and abused when they think they don't.'

'George Elms,' Ali murmured. 'You still chasing shadows with that one?'

'Yup. And I won't stop chasing them.'

'Did you ever get the information you were after?'

Paul shook his head. 'No. Same response you gave me. But you at least said it wasn't worth your job.

Everyone else looked at me like I was something they had just scraped off their shoe.'

'The briefing was pretty strict. No information was to be released about any part of the investigation around those murders. I did a lot of the groundwork, but the results were fed to the supervisors and the senior investigating officer. It was clear that they didn't want us minions to know the outcome.'

'Langthorne doesn't want that particular series of crimes investigated,' Paul mused.

'Why would they? They have their man. He admitted it.'

'They don't have a single piece of forensic evidence that puts George as the killer. Certainly not beyond reasonable doubt, unless you can tell me any different?'

'Still pushing me, Paul. Even now!' Ali's smile was a little more genuine now.

'Like I said, I'll never stop chasing those shadows, Ali. I just want to know who killed my mate.'

'Sam?'

'He's still out there.'

Ali was silent, with a thoughtful expression, and then she breathed out. She reached out to the monitor, and spun it towards her.

'Pass me that keyboard.'

Paul did as she requested and as the monitor fired up, Ali started typing. 'They might have nullified my login already, in which case you're still on your own.'

Paul watched Ali's face as she began to type her password. 'Don't do anything that's gonna get you in trouble, Ali,' he said.

'What are they going to do? Suspend me?'

The screen showed a database program Paul didn't recognise. He could tell it was web-based from the surround.

'This is the CSI main database. All the findings from the shootings are stored on here under Op Tuscan. I'll send you a zip file of everything I have access to. There's a bit of a security glitch with zip files. Basically, there shouldn't be any record of me sending it or even of you receiving it, but the second you open it the system will log the computer location and give a good idea of who the operator is. How you find a way round that is up to you.'

'Thanks, Ali.'

'Don't thank me. Thank Helen Webb — she pushed me into this.'

Paul nodded. 'Helen is good at that.'

CHAPTER 10

The two-man interview team marched solemnly into the back office of Langthorne House custody suite at 09:00 a.m., twenty-two hours after their prisoner had been walked through the custody door. They had devised a strategy that was now in tatters. Their prisoner had been left overnight to sit and stew on his situation, he should have been chomping at the bit to confess all. Instead it was a different story that they had to report back to their boss, who sat waiting for them.

Detective Inspector Darren Arnold looked tense.

'Sorry, boss,' the lead man offered.

'I assume he told you he was delivering a large quantity of heroin yesterday and then gave details of where the rest is?' the inspector said.

'No such luck, boss. He went "no comment" to everything. Even when he was asked his name and date of birth.'

'And with no solicitor?'

'No solicitor,' the man confirmed.

'So a man with no record of dealing with the police at all, suddenly gets hit with three bricks of pure Class A on the passenger seat in his car, then acts the seasoned pro under questioning?' Inspector Arnold rubbed at his scalp.

'I wouldn't say he was quite the pro,' the lead man said, looking at his colleague.

'Nah, he weren't a pro,' the other responded, 'He's shitting himself. He's still convinced he's going to prison.'

'You could tell he wanted to talk to us. It was like he was taking advice from someone and taking it real literal, like.'

'You think he got briefed by the drug gang? If you get nicked, say nothing?' Inspector Arnold said.

'Yeah, and you never know, someone might just set the evidence on fire.'

Inspector Arnold puffed out his cheeks. 'It stinks, don't it?'

'Did we find any links with anyone here?' asked the man.

'Nothing I've been made aware of, but to be honest I doubt I would be the first to know,' said the inspector. 'This is being handled by the senior echelons.'

The men nodded.

'I have to call the chief superintendent. She wanted to know the minute you people came out of the interview.'

'Be nice about us though, yeah?' The lead man grinned nervously as the inspector got to his feet, his phone already at his ear.

'Can't promise it'll do you any good!'

* * *

Helen had been waiting for Inspector Arnold's call. 'Give me some good news, Darren.'

'I wish I could. No comment.'

'Shit!'

'Sorry, ma'am, the team tried their best. They reckon he was coached.'

'Of course he was.'

'Ma'am, I wanted to check with you. If this was any other case, I'd be releasing the bloke with no further action. We've got two hours left on his clock, a no comment interview and no evidence of the offence besides the statements describing brick-size amounts of an off-white substance. Unless you can tell me there's something salvageable from the fire that adds to the evidence?'

Helen leant back in her seat and grimaced at the ceiling. He was right, of course. The heroin had been incinerated. Even if they could prove what it was from any residue, the continuity was lost. Any number of people had been in that room putting out the fire, cleaning up the mess or just taking a look. It wouldn't take much of a defence solicitor to point out that they had lost their ability to confirm that their client was solely responsible for what had been in that bag. There was no reason to keep the man in custody any longer and no reason to bring him back.

'Kick him out. No further action.'

'Any consideration for surveillance? We might still salvage some intelligence, at least?'

'No. It crossed my mind but I'm more and more convinced that the bloke's just a stooge. By the end of the day they'll have some other gullible moron with bricks of heroin for a passenger.'

'Understood.'

Helen Webb's mobile phone suddenly burst into life. It was her other one, a pre-pay Nokia she kept with her at all times.

'I can hear you're a woman in demand, ma'am. I'll get it sorted here in custody.'

'Thanks, Darren.' She pressed the button hard to end the call. 'For nothing.'

The mobile phone was still ringing. The display showed "unknown number."

'How goes it? I take it you had a good result yesterday evening, Chief Superintendent?'

Helen immediately recognised Ed Kavski's voice.

'This isn't the best time,' she said.

Someone was tapping at the door.

'*Yes?*' she called out. Then into the phone, 'Ed, one second.'

Jean appeared round the door and mouthed the word "sorry." Her cheeks were red, and she looked flustered.

'It's fine, Jean. What's the matter?'

'Sorry, ma'am, it's the chief. He's here.'

'Here?'

'Here. Outside, waiting to speak to you.'

'Okay, Jean. Get the man a coffee will you, or something. I'll be right out.'

The door clicked shut. Helen lifted the phone back to her ear. 'Ed, this isn't a good time at all, you'll have to wait.'

'There's no need. Just confirm the job went down clean and you got your man.'

Helen knew exactly what Ed was after. He was making sure there were no loose ends, nothing that could get back to him.

'Yes, Ed. There were some complications, but we got the man.'

'And the gear?'

'I need to go now, Ed. The chief is outside my office door.'

'The chief indeed. Say hello for me, will you? Is my man bailed for the drugs to be tested?'

'Look, Ed, there were some issues. We got the gear, the chief will be happy with that. It should be enough to appease him for now, so job done. Thank you for your part.'

'What happened to my guy?' Ed's tone changed, he sounded suspicious.

'We're releasing him now. He won't be facing any further action from us. Look, I can't see how that's any of your concern anyway. I really have to go.'

'You're releasing him? Why would you do that?'

'These things happen, Ed. I can't talk.'

'These things don't happen!' Ed paused. 'Unless you lot offered him a deal? Got him to talk to you about where the shit was from and where it was going?'

Helen grinned. It was a bit of a turn up for the arrogant shit to be feeling the pressure for once. She could tell him the truth — Lennokshire Police fucked up big style — but he would revel in that. Then he'd swan off until he needed her again. Fuck him, he could sweat until *she* needed *him*.

'I wasn't party to the conversation, Mr Kavski. These sorts of things can happen, you and I both know that, but he didn't know anything about your organisation anyway. What could he offer in return?'

'Well, he must've found something.'

Helen's smile grew more mischievous. 'Or maybe he now needs to.'

She ended the call as the knocks at her door began to sound impatient.

* * *

Ed Kavski moved the phone away from his ear and looked at the screen. His jovial expression had morphed into a vicious snarl.

'No further action!' he said aloud. He had enough experience of policing, and of jobs like the one he had handed Lennokshire Police on a plate, to know what that meant.

He prodded at his phone again, moving through his contacts. 'Gee,' he snarled.

'Wassup?' Lee Chivers evidently realised that this wasn't a time for small talk.

'Your man, John, got me that driver?'

'With the sick kid, yeah.'

'Three kilos of heroin on his passenger seat.'

'Yeah, at least.'

'He's being released from Langthorne nick. They're kicking him out right now, no further action.'

'You lost me.'

'No further action, Gee. You ever heard of that before for a man with three kilos of fucking gear? No, you haven't.'

'What you saying?'

'What I'm saying,' Ed spat, 'Is that we got ourselves a fucking rat. That is what I'm saying. There ain't no other way he walks from there.'

'Piece of shit. I'll kill him.'

Ed gritted his teeth. 'Not before we find out what the cunt said. This is a problem. Think about what he knows, what damage he might be able to do, and find him. And you call me when you have.'

'Leave the cunt to me.'

Ed ended the call.

CHAPTER 11

'Sir!' Helen got to her feet as the chief walked in, clutching a clear plastic bag in his hand.

'Sit down, Helen, for fuck's sake.'

Helen did as she was told. She pulled nervously at her skirt. The chief remained standing.

'Having a bad day?' he said.

'A bad day?'

'I was just going to say that Langthorne has had better, but I can't quite remember when. What is it with this little corner of my county? I can't leave you alone for five minutes, it seems. I remember a night not so long ago when the previous area commander was found hanging by the neck using his own belt at this very police station. On the same night my predecessor was found in bits under the wheels of a car within a couple of miles from here. We had inspectors dead, PCs shot, a sergeant nicked, children in hospital, and no sign of any offender. A bloody disaster. All on your watch, Helen.'

He paused. Helen leant forward a little. 'You can't lay the blame for that at my door.'

'And then,' the chief ignored her. 'And then I get the top job, and I think I'll stick my neck out and let you sort the fucking mess out. Steer Langthorne back to calmer waters. I put you in the role of area commander. We spoke at the time. It wasn't a demotion, it was an opportunity to make good, to show me and the whole force that my faith in you was right, that you could lead this area out of its biggest ever disaster. And what happened then?'

Helen gritted her teeth. She knew what was coming.

'Six police officers dead in little over a week, murdered by the very man who had been in our custody, in the cells of this station no less, who we released so he could continue with his spree. Then more officers had to die chasing the fucker down.' The chief leant on her desk, his hands taking his weight.

'I am well aware of what happened that day,' Helen said, meeting his gaze.

'Well, of course you are!' The chief pushed himself back off the table. He turned and began to pace the office, coming to a halt at the slatted blinds covering the tall windows. He tugged at a cord to spin them shut.

'Of course you're aware, because you were very much involved, every step of the way, weren't you, Chief Superintendent? You were at the helm, where I put you, leading this division. With one of your members of staff torturing and murdering others. And how do you react when you get hold of him? You order uniform officers to shoot him dead! Fuck knows he might have deserved it, but the whole world was looking, Helen, the whole fucking world, and you were ordering a man to be shot and killed rather than face justice, the law of the land, what we all *swore* to uphold.'

Helen crossed her arms. 'I've already had your bollocking for that incident, for that whole terrible experience.' She felt herself losing control. She wouldn't sit there and be lectured again, not by this man.

'But they don't end, do they, Helen? Here we are again, another first-class cock-up.'

Helen came back at him. 'Where were you? When the whole world was looking, as you put it. Where were you? Well I know where you were — at just about the right distance away for absolute deniability. Sure, I have to accept the blame for what happened during that investigation, but you shouldn't be lecturing me, trying to make me feel small, you should be slapping me on the back and thanking me for being the fall guy, so you didn't have to be. You played that perfectly, *sir*. Yes, I made mistakes, but I didn't have the luxury of staying away, far enough from what was happening to scrutinise the actions of those directly involved. Where were you?'

The chief said nothing for a long time. His hands made fists then came open again. 'If you aren't capable of running your area, of running major incidents, if you require micro-managing from those above you, maybe this isn't where you should be. Maybe you need less responsibility. Maybe you're not as capable as you like to think you are.'

'So what do you want? My resignation? I came to you when George Elms was in custody and I told you everything that had happened. I told you immediately what I had said over the radio and I offered to step aside. And you persuaded me to stay, *you* reminded *me* how much pressure I had been under. You told me that those tapes were irrelevant, because George Elms wasn't shot and wasn't killed. And *you* told *me* that I should continue in this role, that the officers under my control needed stability, not change.'

'Why is there a quarter of a million pounds of evidence still smoking in one of your offices downstairs? I spoke to the fire brigade briefly on the way up here. They told me with absolute certainty that it was deliberate.' The chief threw the bag onto Helen's keyboard. She stared at it. It was a piece of clear, melted plastic sealed inside a police evidence bag.

'What is this?' she said.

'The container for the accelerant your arsonist used. Appears it had strong alcohol in it. They've obviously not been able to test it properly yet, but there's little doubt that this is what got that fire burning. And if you were still left in any doubt, the CCTV camera on the CSI's corridor has been moved to point directly at the ceiling and the last seven days footage has been wiped off the whole system.'

'Jesus!' Still stinging from the chief's attack, she now seethed with rage at the knowledge that one of her staff members had deliberately sabotaged her evidence.

'Jesus, indeed. He might just be the only person that could sort out this fucking mess. I've got officers down here who've lost it. They're stopping me in the corridors and in the canteen and they're telling me we're not doing enough for the fallen officers and their families. They're all still shell-shocked out there, Helen. I've never seen anything like it. You've got no hold on them at all. Morale is non-existent and I don't see anything that has been put in place to stop the next mad gunman going on his rampage.'

Helen stood up. 'It's going to take us all time to get over what happened. It's just a few months since six of their colleagues were slaughtered, and we were all given the benefit of listening to them die. You don't just move on from that. You don't just come back into work happy to get on with your job, happy to answer the next call. Not when you know only too well that those poor fucking saps were just answering calls when they got shot. They never stood a chance. *I* never stood a chance, nor did this police force. We just need a little time to heal.'

'This security guard. The same night as George Elms runs riot, this ex-copper gets beaten to within an inch of his life. His poor ex-police dog wasn't so lucky. The bloke has become a focal point for the whole force. He's seen as the survivor from that night, their little beacon of hope. But there's no suspect for it, and from what I understand there's no sign of one. I'm getting constant pressure, constant criticism, that we don't appear to have a clue what's going on. I spoke to you a week ago, and you told me there'd be a breakthrough by the time I came down here to open this arch commemorating the very officers that fell those few months ago. Perfect, I thought, my opportunity to stand in front of that increasingly angry, increasingly frustrated group of officers, who are very quickly turning their backs on their employers — on me — and tell them about this major breakthrough. That this attack on the police family will not be tolerated, that someone will answer for it. And you phone me and tell me that this won't be the case, but you *do* have a significant drug job. And this is what is left of it!' The chief gestured at the bag still lying on the keyboard. 'A piece of melted plastic. Well, let me tell you, this was a significant job, Helen, because it was the final nail in a long row of coffins full of my fucking officers.'

'You're sacking me?'

'If only. I've done my homework and that would appear to be more hassle than it's worth. Personnel insists that the tapes of you ordering that man dead would be the only sure-fire way of getting you out, but it wouldn't be clean. You'd be suspended, the tapes would go to the IPCC, the press would then have full access, and the force would get dragged through the mud once again. This force has taken an absolute battering. The only clean way for this to end, for us to be able to start rebuilding, is for you to resign, Helen. Walk away into the sunset. Your pension should still keep you in business suits and open-neck blouses.'

Helen slumped back into her chair. 'So those cowards in personnel are all briefed and ready to go, are they? I bet they can't wait.'

'No, actually, they won't be expecting your resignation, Helen, no one will. I can't be the one making that decision. However, I think that if you sit here and take a few minutes to have a look at what has happened with you over the last few years of your career, what has happened here on your watch, I think you'll take the decision yourself. As far as personnel goes, it will just be a nice surprise for them.'

Helen forced a kind of half smile. 'You talk about the force being dragged through the mud. It's you that would be under scrutiny. You're trying to save your own arse, not Lennokshire Police. Don't think you're fooling anyone.'

'I *am* Lennokshire Police, Helen. And you are nothing more than a fuck-up within it. You have your options: resign and walk away with whatever you can scrape together from your career, or stick to your guns and be publicly pulled apart, every part of your working life scrutinised until I step in and throw you out. By that time the media will be begging for it, and we can save the tax payer some money topping up your pension. Take that route and I will personally make sure you answer for conspiracy to murder.'

'You bastard.' But Helen knew she was beaten.

'Maybe. But I have to start protecting Lennokshire Police, Helen, something that you have failed to do on a massive scale. I will expect your resignation by tomorrow morning. An email will do. Fuck it, stick it on a fag packet for all I care, just make sure you make the right call. Save this force and save yourself, Helen. Who knows what grubby little misdemeanours you *have* managed to keep a lid on.'

Helen jumped to her feet and stood square to the chief, clenching her fists. For once in her career, in her life even, she couldn't find the words to express her rage. It took every ounce of her energy to stop herself from lashing out, and smacking that fat, spineless piece of shit right in his red face.

The chief took a step backwards. 'Oh, and Helen, your last duty will be to attend this memorial ceremony. Don't think you can let your force down one last time. I'll see you there.'

The chief slammed the door shut as he left. A meeting that had lasted just a few minutes had effectively ended twenty years of hard work, of building a career. Helen felt angry, upset, and empty all at once. But more than anything else, she just felt foolish.

She sat down, ignoring the desk phone that eventually stopped ringing, to be replaced by a gentle tapping at the door. She had nothing left to say to anyone.

CHAPTER 12

Barry Lance shuffled uncomfortably in the queue. He checked his watch again and sighed loudly. An admin clerk was conversing with the woman at the till about how this might be the sunniest September he could remember.

The man in front of Barry, interjected. 'Do you mind if I just get this?' He thrust a quickly cooling cup of tea towards the lady.

'Well, I'll leave you to it, Angie,' said the clerk, taking the hint and hurriedly walking away.

'Anything else?' she asked.

'And whatever this man is having, please.' The man gestured to Barry, who lifted his eyes in surprise.

'Oh, there's no need. I'll order in a second.'

'I insist,' the man said. 'I need a minute of your time, sir, if that's in order.'

Barry checked his watch again. 'I'm tight on time today.'

'Then let's speed this up. What are you having?'

'I'll have the scrambled egg on brown toast.'

The man smiled. 'And just the toast for me.'

Without a word, the woman walked to the kitchen area and out of sight.

'I'm Paul Baern, sir. I don't believe we've met.' Paul held out his hand.

'I know who you are,' Barry replied.

'Seems to happen a lot, that. I've started thinking that maybe it isn't a compliment.' Paul smiled.

Barry fidgeted uncomfortably and was relieved that his eggs arrived quickly.

'Scrambled egg on toast and plain toast.'

Paul thanked the woman and paid. He led the way to an area off to the right, against a window. There was no one else in that section of the canteen, the room as a whole was very quiet. Barry still felt uncomfortable.

'What's this about, Paul? Only I really don't have long.' He wasn't lying. He had a meeting with his team in ten minutes' time. After the last job, which had ended with their target unconscious in a ditch, he needed to have a debrief with them. The job had been far from clean. Mistakes had been made, and he demanded better from them.

'Just a few minutes,' Paul replied.

'You have two.'

'George Elms,' Paul said.

'How did I know that man was going to come up?' Barry cut into his toast.

'What's your opinion on him?'

Barry lifted his eyes to Paul's. 'You want my opinion on a man that killed six police officers in cold blood? Who then turned a gun on me and my men? He stabbed that girl more than thirty times, I hear. Do you really need my opinion?'

'I know he didn't.' Paul picked up a triangle of toast and bit into it. It gave Barry a chance to reply.

'He said he did.'

Paul took his time. 'There has to be a reason for that. Because I *know* he didn't.'

'Why would anyone admit to something like that?'

'Someone got to George. It wouldn't be difficult to work out what his weaknesses are if you wanted to manipulate him. If you knew him at all, you would immediately be able to identify them yourself.'

'So he's taking the rap for someone, is he? What about the evidence? He was with the girl copper when she died, the one who was tied to a chair, and when I nicked him he still had the gun that had killed her in his hand. That's a little bit more than coughing something you didn't do, I would say.'

'He had the gun that shot her. Not the gun that killed her.'

'I wouldn't shoot an unarmed copper tied to a chair with a gag over her mouth, no matter what *leverage* you had over me. Did you know she was pregnant too?'

Paul nodded. 'I didn't at the time, but yeah I know now.'

'Well, I would need a lot more convincing that he wasn't the one to fire the shot that killed her. Who did then?'

'This is the thing. This is the thing that keeps me going every day. That woman who was tied to the chair and shot twice was Sam, a good friend of mine—'

'George Elms was also your good friend, I understand,' Barry interjected.

'He was. But I'm not looking into this for him. He made his choice when he put his hands up to something he didn't do, because then everyone stopped looking for the person who did. Everyone except me. I want the bastard that killed Sam, and that killed all those officers, to answer for what he did.'

'And now you're talking to me? Like I might be able to provide answers?'

'Exactly.'

'I don't know anything more about the shootings than what I put in my statement, and I've not been involved in any of it since. You're asking the wrong man.'

'I've read your statement.'

'So you know I can't offer anything to back up your *mate*.'

'You said that you didn't feel threatened by George, even when he turned towards you with a gun in his hand.'

'My words were different. I said the man was confused, he was in a lot of pain. I think he was just turning towards a noise he heard. He probably didn't even know I was there. I also said that if he had seen that I was a police officer, then I believed he would have used the firearm against me and my team.'

'Yes, yes, I read that too, but you have to justify your own use of force, don't you? Not that you would ever struggle with that. He was a suspected murderer and he had a gun in his hand! A perfect opportunity to shoot the man, use your own brand of justice right there and then. There wouldn't have been any questions, would there? You would probably have been lauded as a hero. You must have been furious with George at that moment. We all were.'

'I don't like shooting people unless I have to.'

'Even a man that you believed had shot and killed six police officers in cold blood?'

'He's answering for that.'

'None of us thinks prison is any kind of justice.'

'He's in there as a copper. He won't be having a nice time, you can be sure of that.'

'I don't think you did *believe* he had shot anyone. I know you suspected it, we all suspected it, but you didn't *believe* it, did you? Not when it came down to it.'

'None of this matters.' Barry finished his scrambled egg. 'I've really got to get going.'

'Sir, there are people in the intelligence world who don't believe it either.' Paul was looking up at Barry, who had got to his feet and was pushing his chair back under the table.

'Is that why you bought me breakfast? To tell me that there are some people out there who aren't convinced that George Elms is guilty?'

'Not entirely. There's some work that needs doing, is all. There are some questions that need asking of some nasty people out there, and this is the bit I struggle with. I happen to know that your team are very good at asking questions so that they are answered. I can't get anyone into an interview room because while George insists he did those shootings, I can't really arrest anyone else for it.'

'You could if you had any evidence. And I would suggest that's where your problem lies.'

Paul smiled cheerily. 'I know what you're saying. Sometimes an investigation will get stuck between a rock and a hard place. That's when you need one of them forcibly removed. I don't have enough evidence to get someone else in to talk to me because I can't go out and ask the right questions of the right people. I'm grounded here.'

'I'm sure you know how my team and I get tasked. There are proper channels to go through. If you want someone found and spoken to, you put in a request and we do what we can to help. I don't accept jobs over breakfast.'

'Of course you don't.' Paul got to his feet. 'Sir, on that night a very senior police officer ordered you to murder George Elms. I've heard the tapes from the radio traffic, but there are also records of phone calls to you around the same time, from the same person, and I bet they were making the same demands.'

Barry had turned to walk away but now came back to where Paul stood. He lowered his voice. 'There are no issues over my actions on that night.'

'None at all.'

'Then you're speaking to the wrong person.' Barry turned away.

'Has she ever mentioned Ed Kavski to you?'

Barry slowed, and turned his head slightly.

'Did you ever wonder why Webb wanted George Elms dead?' Paul asked.

Barry walked away.

CHAPTER 13

'So you understand that you are being released, and this matter is now closed as far as we are concerned. However, you may be liable to be re-arrested if any new evidence comes to light. Does that make sense?'

Tony Robson looked up at the custody sergeant. The sergeant's stern expression didn't really suit him.

'It doesn't really, no. I was sat in that cell coming to terms with a prison sentence and now you're telling me I get to go, and you're done with me. Is that right? I mean, what changed?'

The sergeant leant on his elbows, his hands clasped together, and a genuine smile broke through.

'Maybe this is your lucky day.'

* * *

As the heavy metal gate clanked shut, Tony thanked the junior officer who had been tasked with escorting him off the premises. He watched as the officer walked back towards the entrance to the custody area. At no point during the nearly twenty-three hours he had been sitting in there, had he considered that he would just be turfed out and told to go home. He might have cried if it wasn't for his urgent need to get home and see his son.

He'd been kicked out of a side gate. The nearest taxi rank wasn't far, and it was a pleasant afternoon. The sun was starting to hang lower in the sky, earlier now as September neared its end, but it was still strong, and he walked right into it as he started towards the path. He closed his eyes against the warmth and a big smile spread across his face. Exhaustion and desperation gave way to relief, and a sudden feeling of hope that just maybe everything would work out okay for him and his boy. He didn't know how, but maybe their luck was starting to turn.

The path opened out to the wide expanse of Churchill Avenue. It was one of the main routes around the top end of the town, two wide, one-way roads feeding traffic in different directions with a ten-metre grassy expanse between them, dotted with benches, well-established trees, and colourful flowerbeds.

Tony was still smiling when the white Ford Transit van stopped a few metres behind him. Three men jumped out of the back, running as hard as they could towards him. The lead man was carrying a black sack made of tough plastic. Suddenly Tony's world went dark, the warmth of the sun extinguished in an instant. The bag tightened on his face, and pressed against his nose. His mouth opened wide and he sucked the bag into his mouth in his attempts to breathe. Tony brought his hands up to wrench off the bag, and received a punch in his abdomen. The street was busy, cars were passing but none stopped. Concealed by a solid row of parked cars, the men dragged Tony to the van. Blows rained down on him and he heard voices, threatening further violence. Tony was thrown sideways into the van, landing hard on the corrugated metal floor. He could see nothing beneath the bag, and, unable to breathe, he soon lost consciousness.

It was all over in less than ten seconds.

* * *

He awoke with a start. He tried to move his hands and feet but they were bound with duct tape, his wrists pinned behind his back around the back of a chair. His ankles were taped and crossed beneath the chair. He could taste something metallic that caused him to swallow repeatedly.

He was sitting in the middle of a large, empty storage area. The light grey corrugated metal walls looked relatively new. The concrete floor was scratched, with large, discoloured patches as if heavy objects had been dragged across the floor. At the far end was a metal silo. Tony could see some sort of vegetation falling out of the far side. The air was still, with a pungent smell of compost. A mini digger was parked up at the far end, almost against the metal wall, its long arm outstretched so the bucket was resting on the floor. Tony could hear the sound of larger diggers, but they were distant, their sound carried on the breeze that occasionally drifted through the high slit windows. These were positioned so that one end of the building had light while the other skulked in darkness. A pigeon fidgeted in the roof, directly above his head.

Tony's head hurt. His whole body ached, and the solid wooden chair wasn't helping. A thick spindle ran down the back, and it pressed against him.

Tony heard what sounded like a large door lifting in stages somewhere behind him. He didn't try and turn. He kept his head still, eyes forward, jaw clamped shut. Tony could hear the clang of a metal chain. The heavy tread of several pairs of boots made their way towards him.

'This is him, is it? Langthorne's latest rat?' Ed Kavski stepped around the prisoner. Lee Chivers stood beside him, with a third man somewhere further back. Tony could hear the rattle of the door being secured. The footsteps drew closer. Tony recognised "John," the doorman who had got him into this shit. He glared at John and waited.

Ed Kavski looked at John, who nodded.

'This is the guy I set you up with.' John was avoiding Tony's glare. Tony shook his head and turned his attention to Ed. It was clear that he was the main man. He was well-built, his arms strong and well defined. His hair was cropped close to his scalp and tattoos climbed from his torso up his neck and down both his arms. One of his arms wore a full sleeve of tribal bands and jagged lightning bolts.

'Do you understand your situation then, my friend? 'Cause it's only fair that you know what this is all about.'

'I don't believe we've met,' Tony said. 'And we're not friends. I wouldn't treat a dog the way you've treated me.'

'What about a rat?' Ed came closer and thrust his face towards the bound man. He seemed to be inspecting every part of Tony's face up close. His lips twisted into a smile. 'No one likes rats, do they?'

'I don't know what the fuck you're talking about.'

Ed stood up. 'That attitude won't get you very far, Tony. Let me tell you that straight from the off. Or at least it won't get you very long. You see, I have to look at what I know. You get nicked with three kilos of my gear, right? I know the system because I used to be part of all that shit, see. So I know that they don't let you walk for that, no matter what you say to them. That is, unless you make some sort of deal, unless they see you as some sort of opportunity. The sort of bloke that's not been in trouble before and doesn't really belong behind the door for moving gear around the county. The sort of bloke that will do anything to stay out, so he can look after his cripple boy.'

Tony struggled against the restraints.

'No need to get emotional now, Tony. You ain't getting out of them, mate, and even if you did, what do you fancy you're gonna do? You're not made for this lark, are you? That's why they got at you, isn't it?' Ed walked round behind the chair and spoke into Tony's right ear. 'That's why I can see a way out of this for you. If it was one of these blokes here that had turned, that had agreed to work for the coppers, against me, well that would be unforgiveable. I can't accept that from these blokes. But you? You're just trying to keep your son safe and maybe you don't know the rules.'

'I'm not working for anyone. They didn't offer me anything, they don't expect anything back from me — nothing at all. They just let me go.'

'They just let you go?' Ed faced Tony again. Lee stared intently at Tony the whole time. John was on his other side.

'They just let me go.' Tony swallowed. Even he didn't understand why they had.

'You see, that attitude gives me a real problem, Tony. If you were willing to talk to me, to tell me what was said, what was offered and what you told them in return, then we could start to work this out. But right now, every second you spend in my company is bad for me and for my boys here. It puts me at risk, and I don't take risks that I don't have to.'

'I don't know what else I can say to you. They said I was free to go. I was expecting to be sent to prison, and I didn't think I would be seeing my son again. Then the custody bloke told me to go home. I wasn't going to stick around and ask if they were sure.'

Ed's face twisted into a sort of smile. 'No, of course you weren't. Couldn't believe your luck, I bet. Except there's no such thing as luck when it comes to the filth. John here recommended you, so it reflects on him, too. The man went out on a limb for you. He said you were the sort of bloke we could rely on. So if that's not the case, if you're not going to talk to us about what went on in there, and what you said to them, then John here is going to have to be the man to put it right. To put you right.'

'No comment. That's all I said. Some inspector talked to me in the cell about my boy and he told me to say nothing in interview. I did what he said and the next thing I know I'm walking home.'

'What inspector?'

'I don't know. He said his name but I can't remember it. I wasn't taking notes.'

Ed screwed up his face. 'You want me to believe that some inspector that you don't even know took a risk like that for no good reason? Just to help you out? Now I *know* you're lying.' He spat, then nodded at John. 'Time to make it right.'

John took a step forward, and Ed and the other men seemed to melt into the background. His right hand had been behind his back and he brought it forward. He was holding a black pistol. He put the barrel against the side of Tony's head. He hesitated for a brief moment.

'Sorry, Tony' he said, and pulled the trigger.

CHAPTER 14

'Can I help you?' the assistant said.

Tan and Spray was a small shop just off Hythe's high street. It offered stand-up tanning booths in five-minute slots. The girl, tall, slim and blonde and barely out of her teens, lowered her pink smartphone ever so slightly and looked at him with a bored expression.

'I'm here to see Tommy,' said Kane Forley. 'He still works out of here, right?'

The blonde girl lowered her phone further. 'Do you need a go in a tanning pod?'

'To be honest, love, I'm not a massive fan of the orange look. I need to speak to Tommy. Can you let him know I'm on my way down?'

Kane started to walk round the counter, towards the rear of the shop, where he knew he would find a door to the basement. The girl stepped out and blocked his way.

'There's no one else here, mate. This is a tanning gaff. There's no one back there.'

Kane didn't hesitate. He slapped her face, a stinging blow with the back of his hand. She reeled and fell back behind the desk. She struggled to her feet just as Kane entered the back of the shop.

The door to the basement was flimsy, and Kane walked through, down a steep flight of stairs where the light grew progressively dimmer as he descended.

The door at the bottom was a different affair altogether. The hinges were covered with metal plates so the door couldn't be taken out, at least not quickly. Kane wasn't about to try. He knew that the man sitting on the other side was the biggest arms dealer this side of London.

He knocked.

Coming down the stairs, he had been well aware of the cameras. Two more pointed at him from above the door, which clicked and shivered. Kane pushed it open.

The door had swung away from him, revealing another corridor. It was all just as he remembered, right down to the white walls and the absence of natural light. The only light emanated from a door on the right hand side. Behind it sat Tommy Cotter, frowning.

'Tommy-boy!' Kane stretched out his hand. Tommy was sitting back, hands together, resting on his considerable stomach. His shirt was pulled tight over trousers that did little to hide his bulk. He didn't move.

'You didn't have to hit her,' Tommy said, his voice flat.

Kane jabbed a thumb backwards. 'The girl upstairs?'

'Jixy. She's a good girl — does her job right.'

'I'm sorry, Tommy. You're right. But she wasn't playing ball, you know? She wasn't being exactly forthcoming.'

'That is her job. That's what I meant by doing it right.'

'Sorry, like I said. I'll make it up to you.'

'Not to me. I ain't the one with a swollen face. You need to make it good with Jixy.' Tommy turned his attention to the numerous flat-screen monitors hanging on the wall in front of him. Jixy had moved to a mirror on the wall and was touching the side of her face. She looked upset.

'She'll be sweet. I'll make it good.'

'What are you doing here, Kane?'

Kane sniffed. 'Same reason I came here last time, Tommy. There's only one reason to come and see you, ain't there? No offence.'

Tommy was looking intently at Kane. It made him feel self-conscious. He wiped his brow with his sleeve.

'Last time you made a lot of noise with what you got from me. Seems you're a bit of a liability. You get caught, the attention on you bleeds outwards. The filth will want to know everything about you — who you are, what you have, what you fired and, most importantly for me, who the fuck you got the cannon from.'

'Tommy, spare me the lecture. I had it last time.'

'Sure you did, everyone does. It just seems that you didn't listen to me last time. You got lucky then. The cops fingered someone else for the jobs and you got to walk off into the sunset. I thought that was the end of you around here.

'You should be so lucky!'

'The Russian wanted you gone. He told you that and he told me that too.'

'I told him I had a job to do. I told him once it was done, I would go. It's not done yet.'

'What was it? Six coppers dead and a seventh doing the time for all of them? I'd say that was job done. Job well-fucking-done.'

'There's an opportunity. It's too good to miss!' Kane gave a series of rapid sniffs.

'What opportunity?'

'Lennokshire's biggest — the big chief.'

'What about him?'

'He's sticking his head above the parapet in Langthorne, later this afternoon.'

'So?'

'What do you mean, *so*? I want to shoot that head off, Tommy, like at a fucking funfair. He's the big man, the top dog. I take him out, that organisation falls to its knees.

That's exactly where they had me, Tommy, on my fucking knees. Eye for an eye, and all that. And it keeps them scared, see, 'cause they think it's over. They think that the big bad wolf's been caged so they can walk back out into the sunlight.'

Tommy Cotter was shaking his head. 'You're not serious?'

'Dead serious.'

'Why the fuck do it? I remember your whiney fucking story, the whole thing with the copper who stitched up your brother as a nonce so he hung himself. Your mum bit it too, couldn't cope with the shame. I sucked it all up and you had your chance for your sweet revenge and, fuck me, did you get it! I mean, it was beautiful. I'd take my hat off to you if I was wearing the fucker but this, this is stupid, man. Now fuck off, Kane, before I start believing you might actually give it a go. And don't you ever come here again high on coke and talking to me about business. This ain't how I operate, do you understand me?' Tommy Cotter's voice boomed out across his glass table and filled the space.

Kane took in Tommy's stern expression and looked aside, at the white walls, broken up by pieces of art in varying stages of completion. Tommy thought he was some sort of modern artist, and he took his work seriously. He was probably good. But he wasn't just that. He was also capable of cold and extreme violence and he possessed all the tools needed to carry it out.

Kane had never been good with his temper. He'd known it long before he had been diagnosed with mental health issues. Kane hadn't bothered with the medication, he'd always considered his temper to be an asset. When he lost it, he got his way, so why control it? But he had learned just enough to be able to hold himself back occasionally. He took a breath. Then he said, 'I have money.'

'Money is no good to me behind bars.'

93

'There's never any link to you, Tommy. The guns are clean, there's no connection.'

'There's you.'

'You think I'd talk about you? I know better.'

'You know nothing. The people I deal with all stand to lose something that's more important than their freedom — something they can't let go of. So when they're sat in front of some slimy detective being offered a fag and a free ride home, they know that their freedom won't be worth having if I take that something away from them. Most of the time it's their family, their kids. It could be their life savings, their career or their reputation, whatever. You're a bit different, Kane. The only thing you've got worth having is your freedom. There's nothing I can take from you that hasn't been taken already. Not only does that mean I don't have any control over you, it also means that you don't either.'

Kane sniffed. 'You know you can trust me. I never let you down last time, did I? I'm still the same man as I was then.'

'You're not, Kane. Look at you. You turn up on the very day you wanna take out one of the most senior coppers in the country, with coke all round your nostrils, tweaking out of your mind. When did you even decide to do it? This morning? The last time you walked through that door you were being backed by the Russian. I know for certain that he wouldn't be endorsing you on this.'

'How can you be so sure?'

'Because of all the reasons I just said. Because it's idiotic, and because he's still pissed with you. The man you set up to be nicked was supposed to die. I know you wanted the filth to be pulling the trigger, but that didn't happen and he's still breathing. And if he's breathing he can talk.'

'But I have the thing he couldn't stand to lose,' Kane said, smiling broadly and making gun shapes with both his hands, 'which means I have total control. Maybe I have learned a little something from you.'

Tommy shook his head. 'My answer's the same. You did a job and you did it well. If you had any sense you would be long gone by now, counting your blessings. To even be here in Langthorne is beyond stupid. You will get caught, or, if I'm lucky, you'll get dead. The way my luck is going at the moment you'll just get caught. And then I'll have to kill you myself.'

Kane's mood darkened again. 'You're not the only man who can make this possible.'

'I'm the only man who won't shoot you in the face the minute you ask. By all means, do me a favour and go ask someone else. Now fuck off before I decide I should shoot you.'

Kane met Tommy's gaze. He licked his lips. Then, without another word, he turned and made his way out.

* * *

Tommy watched his progress on the monitors on his wall.

Jixy was sitting on a high stool, still inspecting her cheek. Kane swung his fist and Jixy took the blow full in the face. She fell backwards onto the laminate floor.

Tommy got to his feet as Kane Forley left the building. He kept his eyes on the monitor as he scrabbled on his desk for his mobile phone.

CHAPTER 15

The weapon clicked. Tony squeezed his eyelids tighter and jerked back. There was another click.

'What the fuck?' John sounded confused. He pulled the trigger again, then turned towards Lee and Ed.

'I don't get it,' he said.

Ed Kavski didn't reply. He lifted his own weapon and pointed it at John's head. John started to say something as Ed fired. The bullet entered his skull and came spiralling out of the back of his head. Tony was splattered in warm blood and bits of brain and skull. John fell, dead before he hit the floor.

'Jesus! Fuck!' Tony shouted. The gathered men watched him as he leaned over to the right, away from John, who was slumped against the chair. He vomited.

Lee Chivers snorted, then he stepped forward and punched Tony, hard, in the mouth. The blow loosened teeth, and Tony's head hit the back of the chair. Lee brought his knee up into Tony's chest and the chair rocked backwards, onto the two back legs. It toppled, hitting the concrete floor hard. The wooden spindle was forced hard into his back, pushing the air out of his lungs.

Tony gasped for air, his mouth opened and closed like a landed fish. He tried to concentrate. He'd had the wind knocked out of him enough times to know what to do, but the position of his hands was further restricting his recovery. He focused on the high ceiling above him. Slowly the oxygen seeped back in.

Lee Chivers crouched at his side. 'So, Tony, this is the position we find ourselves in. You all tied up and beaten up on the floor, your boyfriend over there dead as a fucking dodo. Maybe this will convince you to talk to us about your little discussion with the filth.'

A baseball bat. It hovered above Tony's head, the end almost brushing his forehead. It was weathered, well used. Tony's eyes followed it as it swung back and forth.

Lee jerked the bat backwards and the heavy end made contact with Tony's side and the wooden arm of the chair. Tony had seen it coming and had twisted his body away from the blow as best he could. He still got a painful blow to his left hip, but the chair took the main hit and rolled sideways.

Lee circled Tony, a beast playing with his prey. He kicked out into Tony's midriff and Tony's lungs were again sucked empty. He was still on his side. Saliva leaked from the side of his mouth onto the cold, grey concrete. He kept his eyes tightly shut.

Ed Kavski's phone burst into sound in his pocket and he pulled it out, turning away to look at the screen.

'What the fuck?' He looked at Lee. 'Cotter. He don't phone for nowt.'

Lee shrugged. 'Call the fat fuck back.'

'Two minutes. Carry on with your conversation.'

Ed turned away and Lee glared at his back, his jaw tensed. He turned to Tony, who was staring right back at him.

The other man turned his attention to the ringing phone. Tony hadn't had long, but it was just long enough to take advantage of the distraction. When he'd fallen, the wooden strut running up the back of the chair had cracked, and he was now able to move his wrists. He tensed his shoulders and pulled his arms up. The wooden strut came away near the bottom. The spindle was shattered right through, leaving a sharp break and he took the top piece in both hands. He twisted it so the sharp, splintered edge dug into the tape stretched tightly between his wrists. He felt the tip of the spindle puncture the tape, but only slightly, nowhere near enough to be able to separate his hands. He would need a lot more time.

Tony offered up a faint smile. He hoped to get the man talking again, anything to delay him.

Ed swore loudly, distracting Lee.

'You're fucking joking!' Ed shouted. 'When was this?' He let out a sigh that became a groan. 'What else did he tell you? Anything else about what the fuckwit wants to do? The man's a fucking lunatic. He'll fuck everything up. I told him to stay away.'

Lee kept his eyes on his boss.

'You done with me now?' Tony called out. He was ready.

Lee moved his head slightly.

'I said, are you done with me, you ugly piece of shit? Is that all you fucking got, brave boy?'

Ed ended his call and spoke direct to Lee. 'I've gotta go. There's something I need to sort out. Get this done and then call me, we'll meet up. You're gonna be needed too.'

'You don't want to see how this ends?' Lee gestured at Tony with the baseball bat.

'I know how it ends. Just make sure it's cleaned up.'

Ed walked away, his phone in his hand.

Tony waited for him to leave and looked up at Lee, who shrugged.

'Just you, me and Poland then.' Lee gestured at the man still standing in the background. 'Old Poland don't say much — he still can't speak the lingo.'

Tony continued to watch Lee. He'd met plenty of people like him. He had seen a man build up to a fight so well that he'd won it before a single blow was landed. 'The show before the show,' Tony's trainer had called it. He'd described how a clever opponent could get into your head, fill you with doubt. It never worked with Tony, he would use it to fuel his anger.

'How about you let me out of this chair and chuck that bat away, boy? Even it up a bit, just you and me, and we'll see if you're still smiling then. That's what *men* do.'

Lee's grin widened. 'Why the fuck would I want to do that? We're not here for a dick swinging competition. You need to talk to me about what you said to the pigs, and then I need to decide what I do with you when you've told me. It's as simple as that, Tony.'

'We're done with that now. I've told you what happened, so you let me up and we'll have a conversation about where we go from here.'

'Seems to me we're far from done. John was a good man, he was loyal, but he was fucking stupid. People took him in too easy, he was a sucker, especially for a sob story about some sick kid. But he didn't think about the damage to us. You saw what happened to him. What do you think we'll do to someone that's been talking to the coppers? Someone who's struck a deal to save their own skin and needs to report back to them?'

'I've told you that's bullshit.'

'And we've told you why it ain't. You haven't said a single word that explains to me why they'd just let you go. With what they found on you, they should be sticking you behind the door for a fucking decade. Yet here you are, Tony. Here *we* are.' Lee's grip on the bat tightened.

'I can't tell you any more than I have, so you'd best do what you got to do.'

Lee smiled. 'It's gonna make a mess, Tony. You sure you don't want to just skip that bit and give me a different answer?'

'Fuck you.'

Lee's smile disappeared.

Tony's cheek still rested on the floor but he moved his eyes and his shoulders tensed in readiness. The Polish man stepped in closer. Lee had the bat in both hands. A baseball bat is a clumsy weapon, you need to take a long swing. Tony saw Lee's arms coming down in a long arc. It gave Tony enough time to make his move.

Tony pulled out his freed-up arms and wrapped them round the Polish man's legs. He pulled with all his strength, catching the man by surprise. The Polish guy fell onto Tony, shielding him from the strike. The Polish man took its force in his forearm, a bone cracked audibly and he collapsed over the upturned chair. Lee immediately looked to swing again. Tony reached out and took hold of the thick end of the bat. He wrenched it with all his strength, and it came free from Lee's hands. But the smooth metal slipped out of his grip and the bat spun over his head and slid away on the concrete floor.

Lee froze for a split second, but then swung hard with his right boot. Tony shot his arms out to absorb the kick and grabbed hold of Lee's foot. He jabbed hard at the pressure point in Lee's calf and Lee grunted in pain, he tried to pull away and was caught off balance. Tony did what all good wrestlers looked to do, he took the fight to the floor.

Lee immediately tried to get back to his knees but Tony took a firm grip round his opponent's throat, he squeezed hard. Lee's struggles were becoming weaker and weaker. His eyes bulged, and his face turned a dark purple.

Tony had forgotten about the Polish man until he felt the first blow strike the side of his head. Tony didn't immediately break off his grip on Lee, he wanted the bastard unconscious at least, but at the second hit he let go of Lee's scrawny neck and pushed him backwards. Lee arched his back and clawed at his neck, his breathing loud and laboured. Tony knew he would recover quickly but he had to deal with the immediate threat first.

The blows coming at him were slow and deliberate as the Polish man only had the use of his weaker arm. The injured arm hung limp and Tony grabbed hold of it and pulled, it caused him to yelp in pain but he didn't have the angle to pull him off his feet.

Lee thrashed around a bit and then got control of his breathing as he started to recover. Tony needed to deal with the Polish man quickly.

Tony's left hand slid behind the Polish man's neck. He moved his right hand behind his back and felt for the broken spindle. He pulled it out and thrust the sharp end upwards into the Polish man's neck, just above the Adam's apple. It went deep. The man rose to his feet, taking the spike with him, embedded in his neck. Tony let go and hot blood rained down on him, forcing his eyes to shut. The Polish man went to the floor in stages, the threat from him was neutralised. Tony turned his attention back to where Lee had been fighting for breath. But Lee was gone.

Tony rocked and twisted his body in an attempt to see all around him. No Lee, but Tony couldn't see behind him. He tried to free himself from the chair, running his fingers over the tape round his ankles, feeling for an edge to grasp and unwind it.

He heard the scraping of metal some distance behind him. Someone was picking the bat up off the floor. Tony fumbled with the plastic. He still couldn't feel an edge and he couldn't see the tape. Tony heard the bat hit the floor with a clang.

A scraping sound, then another metallic clang. Closer, another step and another clang. Lee was taking his time getting back.

Tony tried to breathe slowly, as he had been trained, but he flinched at each clang. His eyes stung from the blood, his vision impaired, it had made his hands slick too. At last he felt a raised piece of the tape.

The bat struck the floor again. It scraped back off the floor, it was closer and closer.

Tony now had the tape between finger and thumb. It started to peel away. He was careful not to let it fall from his grasp. He tugged it a little looser, and at last it started to come free. Tony was bent double, straining to free himself, his ankles started to feel a little looser. He needed more time.

The bat fell hard onto the ground. Tony felt the gravel roll against his head where it had been disturbed. Lee Chivers was upon him.

Tony was still groping round his feet. The last layer came away. He pulled his legs up towards his chest and grimaced as the tape tore the hairs from his skin. His left foot wriggled free and he kicked away the tape that was still around his other ankle. In a few seconds he would be free.

He heard the bat scrape as the hitting end was picked up off the floor. Tony's feet were finally free. He took his weight with his left hand, turned his head to see where Lee was. Just in time to see the glinting metal of the bat swinging down through the air, Lee's bulging eyes full of hate beyond it. For Tony the world suddenly went black.

* * *

His chest rising and falling from the exertion, Lee took in what he had done. He didn't know how many times he had struck the man at his feet, but it was enough. He was gone. Lee stepped back to take in the mess in front of him. He looked over to the fallen Polish man with the wooden spindle still sticking out from his neck and also over at John, and his opaque dead eyes. Lee wiped his sleeve across where blood had reached up to his face and took a deep breath.

The adrenalin ebbed away, to be replaced by doubt. Lee realised that he hadn't got the information his boss required, and to make matters worse, he'd lost a man. Not that Lee cared about that, but it was a lot to clear up. He was splattered in blood and brain matter, and holding a murder weapon in his hand. He'd sort himself out and get rid of the bat, then come back and clean the mess up properly. They had an agreement with the landowner, who knew better than to stick his nose in where it wasn't wanted. Lee had time to do a proper job with the clean-up.

Lee shrugged. 'Fuck it,' he said, and made for the door.

CHAPTER 16

Helen Webb snatched at the cup before the young waitress could put it down. The Grand Hotel was quiet. It was 11 a.m. and the only other customers were a small table of elderly women. She looked out of the window at the Leas, a grassy expanse that stretched for several miles along the front of Langthorne, just above the cliff. Helen had always found comfort and peace here. There was something about the smooth green lawn against the restless sea and the blue sky. It was simple, like a child's picture.

Helen sipped at her double latte. It was good, and she emitted a sigh. Coffee was one of her few pleasures, one of her luxuries, and the Grand did the best coffee in town. She had hoped that good coffee and a peaceful view might help her reflect on her conversation with the chief. Helen was getting used to having her back to the wall. She'd kicked her husband out of their home just a few weeks ago and had already started proceedings to make the split official. She had sat on it for a while, in order to let all the emotion drain away, and then she'd sorted everything out in a couple of days. Turfed him out, told her solicitor what she wanted, and signed an agreement that would see her two girls officially in the custody of her mother. Her husband had called her sudden efficiency 'cold,' but in truth it was more like numbness, the absence of any emotion at all. Now, in this new situation, she would wait for the same feelings of anger and betrayal to subside and then she would sort out the mess that her career had become.

'Fuck!' Helen's phone rang in her handbag. The elderly ladies glared at her disapprovingly. Helen was sure she had turned her phones off when she had walked out of the office. It seemed she had forgotten to turn off the one that connected to Ed Kavski.

Helen pulled the phone out of her bag. 'This is a bad time, Mr Kavski.'

'Are you still with the chief?' He sounded desperate.

'Nope. The chief and I have said all we needed to say to one another.'

Kavski didn't catch the irony. 'He's out and about today, right? Some sort of public engagement?'

'You know he is, I told you that. What do you care what the chief's doing anyway?'

'I don't, Helen, but there's someone out there who does and he's planning on ruining his day. And yours.'

'What are you talking about?' Helen picked up her coffee cup.

'One of my contacts has been in touch with me. I just put the phone down. He got a visit from a man who was looking to buy a firearm. He was boasting about how he had plans for the chief.'

Helen's back stiffened. The tension, which had begun to dissipate ever so slightly, was back in full force. She put down her cup, spilling coffee across the table top.

'You believe this threat is credible?' Suddenly her voice was hushed and she was checking round to make sure no one was in earshot.

'No doubt.'

'Did he say anything more about how or when?'

'No. I'm sure you know better than me, but he says the chief is in Langthorne today and he reckons he has an opportunity to take him out. That's all I know.'

Helen's scowl returned. 'And what do you care if the chief gets hit?'

'The same reason you do. If he gets to the chief and takes him out, there will be a lot of resources thrown at him and let me tell you, this is a man we would both rather just disappeared.'

'What does he have to do with me?'

'It's what he has to do with Langthorne. He could provide clues to issues you've already dealt with, issues that don't need revisiting. If this man rears his ugly head there are going to be questions — big questions — about Lennokshire Police. About you, Helen.'

Helen looked out at the Leas. Ed Kavski was genuinely rattled, even scared, and he was a man who didn't scare easily.

'Who is he?'

'It's best you don't know.'

'Oh, come on, Ed. Jesus! I'm not a fucking child! Enlighten me on what this has to do with me.'

'It has everything to do with you. That's all you need to know. This man is unpredictable, and that makes him very dangerous to both of us. He is the last man you want sitting in front of an interview team.'

'You mean he's the last person *you* want in front of an interview team.'

'Same thing.'

Helen suddenly felt a flash of anger as she decoded the message Ed was trying to convey. 'He knows something about George Elms, doesn't he?'

Ed hesitated. The pause was just too long. 'George Elms is behind bars. You did that, Helen, and it was right that—'

'Except it wasn't right, was it? George Elms is innocent, and this is the man who should be in his place?' All at once, Helen knew this was the truth.

'It's not as simple as that, Helen.'

'Jesus. *Fuck*!' Helen pushed her chair backwards and it fell over with a crash.

'Calm yourself, Helen. You have a job to do. You need to keep the chief safe over there. You let me deal with our mutual problem and we all get on with our lives. Simple as that.'

'Simple as that?' Helen shouted at the phone. She slung her bag over her shoulder and set off at a fast pace. She hit the wooden exit door hard with her palm and it flew back against the wall. The waitress watched her leave, shrugged and shook her head at the elderly women.

Helen Webb clattered down the steps, back towards the police station, still talking into her phone. 'How is anything simple? I pursued that man, hunted him like a fucking dog because you convinced me to, because I knew what he had done to my people, to my force. To me!'

'This ain't the time to be talking about fucking George Elms. The man's out of the way and you and your precious force are all the better for it. Now you need to protect your force again and make sure your chief don't leave the nick, apart from getting in his chauffeur-driven car to be driven home. This shooter isn't in a good frame of mind. He's lost it and that means he'll be sloppy, he'll make mistakes, and he'll end up caught or dead. And I can't guarantee dead.'

'Fuck you, Ed Kavski. We're done, this is all over. Take my advice and disappear.' Helen ended the call. She could see Langthorne House in the distance, looming at the end of a row of terraced houses that ran towards it in an unbroken line. She checked her watch. It was two and a half hours until she was due to head back to the Leas with the chief constable of Lennokshire Police. They would be at the opposite end to the Grand Hotel, at the site where a local artist had installed a polished metal arch in honour of the fallen soldiers of the Second World War.

The soldiers had believed they would return victorious, bathed in glory. Many had never come home. Today, this poignant gesture of remembrance was to be hijacked by the unveiling of a thin blue line running through the middle of the arch, representing the officers who had fallen while protecting Langthorne, seven decades later. Until just a few minutes ago, Helen Webb had convinced herself that the person responsible for their deaths was in prison. But now she was confused, and she knew it was too late to even begin to put things right. All she could do now was clear out her desk and try and cover all traces leading back to Ed Kavski and, also, the piece of shit that had really murdered those officers. She had to begin by keeping the chief out of harm's way.

Helen started walking again, as fast as she could manage in heels. She was almost running by the time she reached the car park of Langthorne House where she passed her ex-husband's blue BMW M3, which sat in her parking space. She'd got the car as part of the separation. She'd wanted it for no other reason than she knew how much he loved it.

Looking at her transport home, an idea began to form in her mind. The chief was going to end her career, but true to form he didn't want to get his hands dirty by sacking her. No one else would know of his plans, just like no one else knew of the threat against him. Almost without consciously deciding it, she suddenly found that she had climbed into the driver's seat and pulled the door shut. As the car started, Helen turned her own phone back on.

'Divisional Commander's Office, how can I help you?' Jean's harassed voice sounded from the car's speakers.

'Jean, I'm sorry but I've come over a little unwell. I'm going to spend the rest of the day at home. I'm sure I'll feel a lot better tomorrow.'

'Oh. You have this ceremony this afternoon, ma'am. With the chief?'

'I'll keep you updated, Jean. Sorry again.'

Helen ended the call and accelerated away. All her anger, any pangs of guilt she had felt at abandoning her post with critical information, had started to slip away. Just a few minutes ago, she had been hurrying towards her place of work where she was needed to keep the chief of police safe. Now, as she drove away, she was left with just that familiar numb feeling.

CHAPTER 17

'Sir? Are you feeling okay?' Emily Ryker leant forward. She was wearing a snug fitting polo shirt, skinny jeans and Converse pumps and the plastic of her security pass clanked against the desk whenever she moved.

Martin liked Emily. He had worked with her a few times since she had come to work in Langthorne, and he knew she was very smart. "She knows her onions," he had said to anyone willing to listen, and he meant it. Martin had been handed the unenviable job of being the officer responsible for missing persons in the area. He had quickly learned that the majority of people described as *missing* were in fact deliberately hiding, or at least avoiding their loved ones. Most of them were nothing but kids, and they all seemed to be drawn to the adult drug dealers and takers that operated in Langthorne's underbelly. Emily Ryker had a talent for flushing them out. Despite the short time she had been working in Langthorne, she had already become the go-to intelligence officer for anyone involved in the drug scene. This was the reason why Martin was sitting next to her now.

'I feel fine, thank you, Emily.' Everyone else called her Ryker. He was lying. He didn't suffer from hangovers, he was far too good at drinking for that. He just felt wiped out, massively fatigued and listless, and aching to have another drink.

'You look a little, er, stressed out, maybe?'

'Aren't we all?'

Emily smiled. She had big brown eyes which Martin considered quite spectacular.

'A cup of tea maybe? Or coffee? I was just going to have one.' Emily gestured over to the tea-making area.

Martin smiled. 'That would be nice.'

Emily stood and made her way over to the kettle. The intel office was a large one, housing seven officers along with their sergeant, all specialising in different areas. They were all out. Emily returned to her seat.

'What can I do for you then, boss? You still chasing missing kids?'

Martin flushed. He suddenly realised he hadn't really thought this through. He had been planning the conversation for a while and several times discarded it as a bad idea. It was still a bad idea, but he couldn't think of any alternatives.

'How could you tell I needed a favour?' Martin was trying too hard to appear relaxed. His snort came out wrong.

'Well, you're always welcome for a cup of tea, sir, but I assume you need my assistance for something?'

'No flies on you, are there, Emily?'

'Never sit still long enough. That's my way of dealing with them.'

Martin snorted again. 'Good advice.' He looked away, towards a whiteboard where mugshots were pinned in neat rows.

'You know a girl called Sally Morgan?'

'I know a shit called Sally Morgan.'

Martin recoiled ever so slightly. He hoped it hadn't shown. 'Druggie,' he managed.

'Yeah, she's in Peto Court with one of our big players.'

'Big players?'

'Yeah, fellow called Lee Chivers. We reckon he's pretty much running the show on the ground for the Russian.'

'The Russian?'

'Street name for the fellow who's been flooding Langthorne with Class A. No one knows his real name for sure. Chivers is like his enforcer. He doesn't get too involved with the dealing but he enforces debts and keeps a lid on the competition. Nasty bastard by all accounts.'

'You have a source on him?' Martin ran his tongue over his top lip. The intel team often had criminals who would reveal the movements of other criminals to them. It was common practice to use such sources and it was very much Emily's bag. She had a history of always having *someone* close, no matter who the criminal was, or how far up the food chain. She'd secured a lot of prosecutions that way, and without ever having to reveal her source's identity or use their evidence directly in court.

'We get a steady flow of intel on him, but haven't put him away just yet.'

'Is Sally the source?' Martin watched Emily closely. The kettle clicked off in the background and she went to make the drinks.

'What's your interest in Sally Morgan? She's a bit of a nobody really, a bit of a hanger-on. She sticks around to score off him. He beats the shit out of his women by all accounts. I know she's been knocked about by Chivers. He's a sick man, sir, the sort that enjoys hurting people, you know. Not the sort of bloke you would want to be anywhere near unless you really had to.'

'Had to?'

'Heroin,' Emily said. 'The things these girls will do for heroin.'

'It's a terrible thing.'

'So come on then, sir, what is your interest in the girl?'

'I know her father,' Martin replied, too fast.

'I see.' Emily had her back to him, looking down at the cups. 'What are you having?'

'Er, coffee please. Black.'

Emily made the drinks and set a cup down in front of him. She looked at him over the top of her own steaming drink. 'You know her dad well, then?'

'Yeah. I mean I used to, not so much anymore. He's at his wits end, though. He asks every now and then whether I know anything.'

'And do you tell him?'

'I'm not passing on anything I shouldn't.'

'I didn't mean it like that! I just mean, how honest are you? Because the truth would be pretty hard for the poor man to take, I would imagine. It would be difficult for any dad.'

'True,' he managed, and swallowed. 'Is she living with this Chivers fellow?'

'Last I heard. There are a couple of girls that are regulars. They both use and probably get passed around a bit. I've sent the tactical team out taking people's doors off with drugs warrants and she's popped up a couple of times. She was at an address in Dover Road recently when they went in. Basically anyone who's got something to do with drugs has something to do with her.'

'A user though, nothing else?'

'She got nicked for supply last year. Dealt to an undercover cop in an operation round Langthorne, but it was small-time. I think she was given five bags to sell so she could have one for nothing — the sort of arrangement they always get the bottom feeders on.'

'Bottom feeders.' Martin's voice was hollow.

'No better description, unfortunately. Shame really. I've spoken to her a couple of times and she seems like a nice enough girl. She told me to fuck off, but she's actually pretty well spoken.'

'You've spoken to her?'

'Yeah. We had information that she'd been sexually assaulted. I knew she wouldn't report it, but I tried to use it as a way of getting her on the books. Sometimes if you get them when they're still angry, when there's nowhere else to turn, they will speak to you.'

'Sexual assault?' Martin swallowed.

'We never bottomed it out. I had a good source, said she was in the unwelcome company of two men. It got rough too.'

'Lee Chivers?' Martin felt hot, so hot he thought he might combust.

'He set it up and took money for it. He was there but he wasn't involved, apparently.'

'How good was the source?'

'She was the other girl.'

'Jesus.' Martin lifted his mug, but dare not part his lips to drink. He used the mug to cover their trembling as he fought to control his emotions. He couldn't hide the tremor in his hands though.

'You sure you're okay? Did you know this girl too? Through your mate, I mean.'

'Only when she was much younger. Lovely kid, you know. I mean no one deserves that, do they? But she wasn't that type.' Martin raised his head, his eyes moist and deep. 'How does it happen?'

'I'm sorry it's not better news. Perhaps you should give a bit of a watered-down version to your friend, sir.'

Martin nodded. 'I will.' He left his full cup of coffee on the table. 'I'd better be getting back to work.'

Emily nodded. He was aware of her eyes following him as he stood and walked away. His steps were slow and deliberate.

'Sir!' Emily's voice stopped him as he got to the door. He leant on the frame, and gripped it hard to hold himself steady.

'I wish there was some way I could help her out, you know. Look after her.'

Martin smiled. It was an exhausted smile. 'If nothing else, Emily, this job has taught me one valuable lesson. You can't keep safe what wants to break.'

CHAPTER 18

'Yes?'

'Sir, it's the control room. Sorry to bother you.'

'It's no problem,' Martin lied.

'We've been trying to raise you over the radio, sir. I guess you're busy down there and not monitoring. Can you speak?'

Martin's heavy, tired eyes half-heartedly scanned the interior of his car. He couldn't see his radio and he was pretty sure he hadn't seen it all day. His head ached, a dull, irritating ache that gave everything a frayed edge. He'd retired to sit in his parked car for a few minutes. That had been thirty minutes ago, and with every passing minute his reluctance to return to the hustle of the police station increased. As the inspector responsible for the day-to-day running of three towns, he was at everyone's beck and call. There was always someone else's life to sort out, and no time to sort his own.

'Of course I can speak. What's the problem?'

'It's a high risk missing person, sir. Something you needed to be made aware of, is all.'

Martin did nothing to conceal his sigh. 'Okay. I'll be back at my desk shortly and I'll take a look. What's the call reference number?' Martin saw an opportunity to go back to his desk and close his door, make himself another strong coffee and read through the details of the missing person. It was a good excuse to be alone for a few more minutes.

'Two eight one of today,' was the reply.

'Got it. Briefly, what's the reason for the high risk?'

'The wife reported him missing last night. They don't live together but he was supposed to turn up to take their son out, and according to her he never misses an appointment with his son. It is very much out of character, and she also said that he got some bad news about their son at the hospital and she hoped he hadn't done anything silly. We got that all worked out though, sir. Seems our missing person was arrested for drug supply and was in your custody down there in Langthorne.'

Martin stiffened. 'Tony Robson?'

'Yes, that's him. You know about this already?'

'Well, no, but I reviewed him when he was in custody. I spoke to him for a little while. Why are you calling me if this has been resolved?'

'Oh, well the wife's called back in. Tony was released three hours ago and he hasn't made any contact with the wife yet, or their son. She's now convinced he's done something to himself. She says he spends every moment he can with their boy.'

'I'll go and have a look. The man went through a bit of an ordeal, he's probably just gone missing on purpose for a bit of reflection. Lord knows, we all need—'

'Sir, there's a little more on here.' The woman's voice cut in with sudden urgency.

'A man loosely matching the description of Tony Robson was seen being bundled into a white van by three men about the time of his release, and close to Langthorne

House. It wasn't long called in, sir, and there's no definite link, but they've linked the two calls.'

Martin's eyes opened wide and his shoulders slumped. What little energy he had, left his body in a sigh.

'I'll go and review it from my desk immediately,' he managed, already fumbling with the door handle.

Sergeant Jim Reeves was waiting in Martin's office when he got there. He had obviously been wearing down the carpet, and he stopped mid-step, his back half-turned as Martin bustled in. Reeves was known to be a bit of a worrier and he was visibly relieved at Martin's arrival.

'Jim,' Martin said. 'I imagine I know the reason you are here?'

'I imagine you do, boss. I've got my troops ready and waiting. I just need you to say what you need them to do for you.'

Martin slumped in his chair with another sigh. It had already been a long day. He felt the sort of exhaustion that overtakes you when you've been at the limits of your emotions for a prolonged period.

Martin was still angry. It was a smouldering anger that sat below the surface, nothing like the explosive anger that had him thumping the Volvo's steering wheel following his conversation with Emily Ryker. Martin knew he wasn't coping, and he knew how that generally ended.

'It's a high risk missing person. You've handled any number of these, Jim. The basic tasks for your staff are the same as usual.'

'I can't say I've handled too many kidnappings, sir.' Jim looked panicked.

'Do we know who's got him? What vehicle he was taken in? Do we even know it is the same person for sure?'

'No, sir.'

'Then the kidnapping isn't relevant. We need to stick to what we normally do, and make sure it's done to the best of our ability. Major Crime can handle the rest.'

'So you want me to get the normal details? Treat it like a normal missing person?'

'Yes.' Martin did nothing to hide his frustration. 'Get round to his wife and ask some questions. Get a proper search done of his home, see who he's friends with, who he's been talking to. The normal stuff.'

'The tactical team have searched his house already, sir. As part of the drugs job.'

'They searched his house for drugs. It's a very different search when you're trying to piece someone's life together, and besides, he lives separately from his wife. We need to speak to her and see how long that's been the situation. If it's a recent thing, he might still have stuff at her place. And she will still know a lot about his life, even if she says she doesn't. Shame the tactical team aren't available, I'd get them back out to do both addresses.'

'They are available, sir. They got in touch with me and said they were aware and were waiting to see if there was anything for them to do.'

Martin had been fiddling with his computer. He stopped suddenly. 'Are you sure you spoke to the tactical team? They definitely won't be available — they're doing personal protection on the chief at the Leas this afternoon, at the ceremony for the fallen officers.'

'Apparently not, sir. I spoke to their guv'nor, Mr Lance, who said they'd had a call from the chief superintendent who was running the event, and she'd stood them down.'

'Stood them down?'

'Yeah. Someone made her aware of our missing person issue and she reviewed the threat level for the chief and basically decided there isn't one. So she pulled his protection.'

'So Helen Webb knows about this? Normally she would take something like this over.'

'She's gone home, apparently she's not well. She said you were in charge.'

Martin gritted his teeth. 'Brilliant.'

CHAPTER 19

'He's back. Oh fuck. Sal. Sal! He's back!'

Sally Morgan had almost found sleep. She had only gone back to check that Lee hadn't taken out his frustration on her friend Lizzy in her absence. She had seen his truck was missing from the car park and gone up to pick up her stuff, to check on her mate and then she had meant to leave. But Lizzy had some weed, so she'd stayed for a couple of joints. She had no idea how long ago that was.

Sally was in Lee's flat, 49. It was on the second floor, and access to this floor was restricted to him and a handful of neighbours by an electronic key fob. He was gradually bullying the other residents and the live-in caretaker to get his floor cleared so he would have sole access and the perfect strategic position. No one knew for sure which flats he had control over. He used different ones to store any number of items, all of which were his "property," and included, or had included at some time, weapons, illicit drugs, sex workers, and recently, trafficked migrants. If there was money in it, Lee Chivers was on it. And his money was always near him.

Money was the only thing he didn't store elsewhere. It was kept in flat 49 until it reached amounts in excess of two hundred thousand pounds cash. Then he would conduct a frenetic operation to get the money out and distributed to a number of businesses, enterprises, and scams that would get the money back to him clean. Or, at least, with a paper trail legitimate enough to withstand scrutiny.

Lizzy and Sally were involved in this. They collected money from some of the small-time dealers in the area. Now, however, Sally was very much off the payroll, and it had been made clear that to return would be a very bad idea indeed.

Lizzy watched Lee get out of his truck and approach the communal entrance. Still she didn't move. The girls were fast running out of time.

'You need to get out, Sal!' Lizzy's eyes were wide, and she pushed Sally towards the door.

'I can't, it's too late! There's nowhere to hide out there!'

'Just get out. He can't find you here! You know what will happen.'

'Where the fuck are my shoes? I don't even have my shoes.' Sally gestured frantically at her bare feet, her mind still muzzy from the strong cannabis.

'We need to hide. Now! He thinks I'm out collecting his money, he can't know we're here! Maybe he's just coming in to get changed.'

'Fuck, *fuck*! There's nowhere here!' said Sally.

The girls surveyed the flat. It was a bedsit, dominated by a double bed under the window at the opposite end of the room to the kitchenette. There was a small bathroom near the front door and a single floor-to-ceiling cupboard opposite the entrance to the bathroom that housed the boiler and an ironing board. Nowhere to conceal two adult women.

'I'll go under the bed. You go with the money,' said Lizzy.

'What if he's here for the money?'

Through the flimsy front door they heard a male voice. It was Lee and he was shouting. 'What is it, Marco? This really ain't the fucking time, mate, you get me?' There was a short pause. The women stood, frozen at the foot of the bed, Lizzy looking at the front door, Sally facing her. Sally heard Lee's voice again, but quieter, further away, as if he'd gone towards the main entrance. She knew he wouldn't be long.

'Get right in there, the other side from the bag. He won't see you,' hissed Lizzy.

Lizzy had already dropped to her knees, assessing the space under the bed and Sally bent down to see if there was room for her too. There were suitcases lying end to end against the wall under the headboard, they took up nearly half of the space under the bed. Pairs of trainers were lined up at the opposite end of the bed. It would do. Lizzy moved some of the trainers, then slid herself under the bed feet first so she could lie flat and peer back towards the door. Her breathing was quick and shallow as she put the trainers back with shaking hands.

'There's room for me too,' Sally said

'We'll get caught. You need to go somewhere else, Sally.'

Sally let out a little whimper and stood up. She sprinted the length of the flat, grabbed at the bathroom door and darted inside.

Sally fell to her knees. There was just a flimsy wall between her and the outside corridor, and she could hear footsteps. Feet dragging. It was Lee's walk.

A key turned in the lock. Sally stood in the middle of the bathroom. She turned slowly, bracing herself for the violence that was now inevitable. She had no idea what to do, maybe she could rush him — use the element of surprise. She just had to get past him, so she could run.

She just had to get out.

Lee stepped inside. Then he turned to look back over his shoulder. Someone had shouted after him. He was carrying a long, thin object, wrapped in a black sack.

'The fuck you say?' Lee threw the sack into the flat. It bounced, sounding solid. Then he was gone, back out into the corridor. There were more shouts, he and another man yelling at each other. Sally heard scuffling, a sudden loud thud against the other side of the bathroom wall. The partition shook and Sally yelped. She put her hand to her mouth.

Sally looked down and saw her one chance. She dropped to the floor and tugged at a brown rug that ran alongside the cheap fitted bath. She folded it back and took hold of one end of the long plastic panel that covered the side of the bath. It gave just enough for her to be able to pull it away from the housing, exposing the space beneath. There were more thuds, scuffles and shouts from the corridor just a few feet from where Sally was trying to control her shaking hands.

Sally peered under the bath and immediately saw the bag containing Lee's drug money. It was blocking her way, big and heavy and made of a coarse, black plastic which caught when she tried to pull it out. She started to panic, and the final wrench drove the back of her hand hard into the base of the toilet. She clenched her teeth at the pain and stared at the bruise that was already forming.

She pushed her legs in first, then inched under the bath on her back. Her view of the door was partly obscured by the cracked white base of the toilet. She tried to fold herself around the bath indent and the supporting bars. Her buttocks and back rubbed against the rough concrete flooring. Her feet were scratched and scraped by the metal support bars of the bath. Tears streamed down her face. She needed a rest but she was out of time.

Lee was back. She heard him push the door so hard that it smashed into the wall. He strode into the flat, looking straight ahead. Sally was almost in position but the bath panel hung open. She was lucky. Lee stormed into the living area. And that meant Sally had a massive problem.

As quietly as she could, she slid herself into position. Her head was bent at an awkward angle, and the pipes coming up from the floor dug into her back and neck. The panel was still hanging wide open, the bag of money lying in the middle of the room. She had to get it back out of sight, but it would make too much noise.

Sally tried to control her breathing. She could feel her heart pounding. She was sure Lee could hear it. She prayed that he would put the kettle on, or the television, or that another fight would break out in the corridor, anything.

His phone rang. He swore loudly but it kept ringing.

'Wassup, boss?' His voice was flat, he sounded hesitant. 'What do you mean?' Sally could hear him pacing around the living area. This was her chance.

'I can't drop everything right now. There's still a little bit of cleaning up I gotta do from the job this morning. Look, I had to . . .'

Sally reached out for the bag. She couldn't quite reach the handle, and she dare not move out again. She took two handfuls of the thick plastic, and heaved. The bag moved, just a few inches, and it was the loudest thing she'd ever heard.

She took a firmer hold, tugged again and the bag shifted closer, over the blackened, exposed floorboards. As the bag inched towards her, the voice from the other room was becoming louder, the tone pleading. Sally tried to time the movements of the bag with Lee's words, but every sentence seemed to be the last. She edged the bag in. It fitted — just. Sally reached over it and hooked her fingers round the plastic edges of the bath panel, taking hold of the carpet at the same time. Panel and carpet moved back into place, though neither was quite flush.

Sally prayed.

* * *

Lizzy had her hand over her mouth. She lay under the bed, her feet flat against one of the suitcases. She had bent her legs as much as she could to try and stay as far away as possible from the end of the bed. Lee had stormed straight into the flat and she had watched him lean on the kitchen units, his sinewy arms taking his weight as he bent his head, his back to where she lay. Now he was on the phone and she could see his mood growing blacker with every passing second.

'Like I said, the fucker wasn't going to tell us anything and he was a threat to the both of us. He didn't know enough to hurt us but we both know he was sent back out to get information on us. To fucking rat on us. On you! You pay me to sort out problems like that, and you want a message sent out so people know it ain't gonna be fucking stood for.' Lee moved around the flat. His feet were centimetres from her head as he made his way to the window.

'I know,' Lee continued. 'Listen, don't think I don't know that. I just beat a man to fucking death with a baseball bat. I'm dripping in the cunt's fucking claret — now I didn't do that for me. I ain't taking that sort of a risk for me, yeah? I'll get this cleaned up like I said I would, okay?'

Lizzy's eyes widened as Lee's words sunk in, and her fear threatened to take her over. She'd known that Lee Chivers was capable of extreme violence, but this was something else. She could barely comprehend what he was saying. *Beat someone to death with a baseball bat!* She looked at the long, solid object wrapped in a sack, that he'd thrown to the floor when he first entered. It was damn near touching her head.

Lee moved to the bottom of the bed. Lizzy had her eyes scrunched tightly shut, but she could sense him near her head. She clamped her lips together so hard that it hurt, and held her breath completely. Lee hadn't spoken for some time and she wondered if he might be off the phone. She raised her head off the floor slightly, daring to open her eyes. She needed to know where he was. The heels of his boots were tan and so close she could read the word "Danner" written on the back in a darker brown. She was also close enough to see blood on his boots. Lee was facing his front door, feet apart. He sighed. Suddenly the bed springs came down on top of Lizzy's head through the cheap mattress. She flattened herself into the carpet.

'What the fuck?' The springs squealed as he stood back up. His feet pointed towards her. She could hear him pull aside the duvet and the sheets beneath it.

'No, not you.' Lee continued with his conversation. 'Look, I know it's a fucking mess, but you got to believe me. It don't change nothing.' He paced back to the kitchen area.

'I'll get back up there and it'll be clean as a whistle. Them blokes just have to fucking disappear. The Polish has got some family about but they all think he's been picking fruit in fucking Margate for the last three weeks. They know nothing about who he's been hanging with. John will be missed, sure, but he's always had his fingers in pies, running with people that could get him done. There's no reason for people to come knocking at my door. And if they do? So what? Some fucker I know got shot. You get rid of the shooter and your clothes, I'll get rid of the slugger and my shit and it's a standard clean-up at the waste site.'

Lee stopped talking. From where she lay, Lizzy couldn't be sure of his exact position, only that it must be near the bathroom. Sure enough, he spoke again but it was quieter, muffled as it came through the thin bathroom wall. She could hear Lee urinating. She felt able to take a few deep breaths.

* * *

127

Sally could now hear every detail. He'd pulled at the cord of the light switch and she had jumped so hard her foot had knocked against the bath and she'd silently grimaced in pain. Now Lee was inside the small room with her, everything he did seemed close and loud. She held the bath panel shut with the very tips of her fingers. She bit down on her bottom lip. The plastic was slipping from her grasp as her clammy skin lost its purchase. If she let go now it would swing open into Lee's leg.

He was still on the phone. Sally heard him undoing a zip. The panel slipped again and Sally hooked her fingers round it to stop it moving further. She bit her lip, her eyes tight shut. She couldn't pull the panel back in place, her fingers were in the way, their tips visible from the outside. She felt very vulnerable, exposed in the bright light from the naked bulb which ran down the centre of her face like a white scar.

Lee was so close to her. He was standing over the toilet, blustering, and swearing to himself. Sally dared to peer out. She could see Lee's boots with the baggy jeans falling over them, the edges frayed where they dragged on the floor. They were badly stained across the shin. Sally knew blood when she saw it.

'I'll sort it!' Lee shouted into the phone. Sally heard it crash into the bath above her head. It bounced a couple of times, then came to a stop level with her chest. Lee's legs disappeared and the light clicked off.

CHAPTER 20

'I didn't want to call at first, you know. I felt like I was maybe wasting your time,' Lorraine Robson said.

Martin gave her a warm smile. At the last minute he had decided to attend the missing persons call in person, partly because the area commander was aware of the incident, and partly because he wanted to be away from the office. This was the perfect excuse to be out, and out of reach.

Lorraine sat opposite him, on a single-seater couch. A woman constable sat at the dining room table, filling out the standard, and notoriously laborious, form for reporting missing persons.

'It's never a waste of time,' said Martin. 'You can never be too careful with this sort of thing. And he is your husband. You know better than anyone if his behaviour is out of character.'

Lorraine took her mug in both hands, her fingers barely visible under the sleeves of her hooded top. She was barefoot, the colour on her toenails flaking off. Her dark hair was tied back, but a fringe swept across her forehead. She had apologised for her appearance when she'd opened the door to the police officers.

'Ex-husband,' she suddenly said.

'Are you officially separated?'

'Separated, yes. We're not divorced.'

'Sorry, that's what I meant.'

'No, then. But Tony seems to think it's only a matter of time.'

'And you don't?' Martin usually hated asking people questions concerning their private lives. 'Sorry, I don't mean to pry. It's just that I had quite a long chat with Tony yesterday. I felt like I got to know him a bit, but that doesn't give me the right to dig into his private affairs.'

The woman shook her fringe. 'It's okay, don't worry. Did he talk about me then?'

'Well, your son mainly. We found something in common. I have a daughter, you see. She's much older, but we were still able to talk about the joys of parenting.' Lorraine and Martin looked up as a loud thud came from the first floor where the search team worked. Martin smiled. 'They won't be long.'

'We've struggled a little for our joys.' Lorraine looked around and made eye contact with the WPC who was waiting for something to write. 'I don't mean that Daniel's a bad kid. He's brilliant, he's always brilliant, I just meant—'

Martin held up a palm. 'I know what you meant.' Lorraine stopped speaking.

Martin looked around him. 'He hasn't moved out of here, has he? I mean, *he* might have, but it's still very much a house that both of you live in.'

'You mean all his stuff?'

'Yeah, I saw a few bits on the way in too.' Martin was big on first impressions. The house was on a road he knew well. He had lived there for many years, and had only moved eight years ago.

'I keep it here for Daniel. He's not taken the split very well, and he's holding on to us getting back together. I think if he saw me making it more final he would get upset again. It needs to be a slow process.'

Martin waved his hand. 'Like I said, we're not here to pry, but it can be important to get some idea of the circumstances. It's common for a separation or even an argument to be significant when looking at why someone suddenly goes missing.'

'We didn't argue. We don't. He hates it. He just walks away.' There was some bitterness in Lorraine's words.

'For long?'

'Not for this long, if that's what you mean.'

Martin shrugged. 'I don't mean anything. Is it possible that he's just gone away for a while, maybe to avoid an argument or a difficult conversation?'

'You mean about Daniel?'

'Yes. This is a massive thing for you both.'

Lorraine sipped at her coffee. 'I didn't get that impression. I only saw him briefly, when he dropped Daniel back. He was a little rushed to get away, we talked about what the doctor had said but not much more. I could tell that he didn't want to stay. That's not unusual for him. When something upsets him he goes away, gets his head round it and then he'll talk.'

'Was he upset?'

'Of course. I mean he wasn't in tears or anything. He doesn't cry — certainly not in front of me. He used to be a wrestler — amateur, but he probably could have gone pro. Anyway, he's never been the sort to show emotion.'

'And was that the last time you heard from him? Even a text or a Facebook post might be of interest.'

'Tony doesn't do Facebook,' Lorraine scoffed. 'No, that was the last I heard from him which was definitely out of the ordinary. He always contacted me at night, to speak to Daniel before his bedtime, but also to ask after us both. When I didn't hear from him I sent him a message. When he didn't reply, that was when I knew something was wrong.'

'Was that when you called us?' Martin looked over to the female officer, who was scribbling furiously.

'I called the doctor first. We have a good relationship with him. I called him straight after Tony left — to get it from the horse's mouth, you know? Then I called him again when Tony didn't reply. I didn't know what to do. I figured since Doctor Ngaye was one of the last people to see him, maybe he could tell me something I didn't know.'

'And did he?'

'No. He said that Tony hadn't taken it well at first, that he was upset and angry, which was perfectly understandable. He said that by the end he was actually starting to sound positive about raising the money he needed to sort it all out.'

'He mentioned that. Three grand a month.'

'Yeah. Or our son dies.' Lorraine rubbed at her face and sniffed.

Martin watched her intently, guessing that it wasn't yet quite real for her. She still hadn't come to terms with the fact that things might not work out okay.

'So as I said, you know Tony best. If he's under a lot of pressure all of a sudden, where does he go and what does he do?'

'Well, what he did this time is get himself arrested. You could have knocked me down with a feather when they told me that. And they didn't say what for, either.' Lorraine looked at Martin. 'Can you tell me anything about that? About what he was arrested for?'

Martin shook his head. 'No. It's for him to tell you. We can't give that out, even to the spouse. But I can tell you that he's no longer under investigation. He was released with no case against him.'

Lorraine shrugged. 'I guessed he had been fighting. He has a temper — never with me or Daniel — but he can go. I suppose you need to have one when you're competing in the ring.'

'It was nothing to do with fighting.' Martin looked over to the officer who was busy filling in the form. 'Is there anything else relevant you think we need to know? Something we haven't talked about?'

'Something's wrong. I know something's wrong, Inspector, because he didn't even send a message that he wouldn't be picking Daniel up. We've had our problems you know, times when the last thing we wanted was to talk to each other, but we always communicated over our son. Tony had never once let him down, in any way. He was our one constant and he is Tony's whole world.'

Martin nodded. He felt like he understood. 'This is a whole new level of stress though, Lorraine, and getting himself arrested was certainly out of character.'

'We've had a lot of stress, and this has been a massive setback,' she conceded, 'But I do know Tony well and I know that he would come and speak to me about this sort of problem, and we would sort it out together. I can't believe that he would just disappear like this and not talk to me. And even if he had, there is no way he would do this to Daniel — no way.'

'Pressure is a strange thing. It manifests itself in different ways in different people. Sometimes people just need some space. I know that's my first reaction when I feel like I'm under stress.'

'You're not Tony.' For the first time Lorraine spoke sharply.

Martin sat back in the chair and put both his palms down on the arms. 'You're right. I'll let my colleague run through the bits on our form that I've missed out, make sure we get all the information we need, and I'll keep you up to speed with what comes of it.'

Lorraine stood up and gestured at her cup. 'I'm going to need another one then. Do you want one?'

Martin smiled and passed over his mug. The woman constable declined and Martin knew she was looking at him. As soon as Lorraine was out of the room, she said, 'Sir, does she know about the abduction?'

Martin spun round to face her, his voice hushed. 'No. We don't know for sure that it was Tony. She doesn't need to know anything about that until we are sure.'

She nodded. 'Okay,' she said without conviction.

CHAPTER 21

Lee Chivers was furious. His phone crashed into the bath and he became a blur of movement and noises, grunts and shouts, as he punched doors and walls and brought his fists down so hard on the kitchen worktop that the plates in the cupboards rattled. It ended with him tearing off his clothes and throwing them into a pile in the middle of the room, where he stood naked, breathing heavily.

He marched back into the bathroom. Lizzy watched him go and let herself breathe again. She had been holding her breath, waiting for him to rip up the bed and stamp on her head in his rage. In the bathroom, he snatched his phone from the bath and turned the taps full on. He left it filling, striding back into the living room and prodding his phone angrily. He lifted it to his ear, talking to himself as he waited for the phone to connect. 'It's gonna get fucking hot round here. Time to get rid of the fucking money.'

Then Lizzy's phone erupted in a loud rendition of "Shake it off," by Taylor Swift.

It was in her back pocket. She reacted as if she had been stung, pulling the phone out and pushing it face down into the carpet, her mind racing.

'What the fuck?'

Lizzy's head was pressed against the floor. Lee's feet appeared at the side of the bed. His knees bent and they splayed slightly. In seconds she would be discovered, and then there was only one outcome. In a last desperate move, she pushed her phone a few inches away from her hand, closer to Lee, and the edge of the bed. She didn't move, didn't dare breathe. Her mind teemed with options. Maybe she could crawl out of the end of the bed and run for it — she had a clear path, with Lee standing at the side. But she wouldn't make it. She was so rigid with fear she wasn't sure she could even stand up. She remained with her eyes on Lee's feet, her hand still outstretched, resigned to her fate.

Lee's knee came down. A hand appeared, palm down on the carpet, and moved around under the bed, feeling for the phone that still blared, "Shake, shake, shake, shake, shake, shake it off, shake it off!" She watched his hand get closer. His fingers almost touched hers as he felt around. Then he put his hand on the phone, and pulled it out. His knee was still planted on the floor.

'Stupid fucking bitch!'

Lizzy closed her eyes as her phone clattered against the far wall, breaking into pieces. *This is it*, she thought, *This is when he looks back under the bed and finds me lying here. He'll realise I know that he murdered a man in cold blood. And that he fucking enjoyed it.*

Lee got back to his feet and strode into the kitchen. Lizzy heard cupboards open and slam shut. She dared to open her eyes, and watched him go through to the bathroom.

* * *

Sally had heard Lizzy's phone ring. She pushed the panel open, convinced he had found her friend lying under the bed. She would have to try and do something. Then, when the phone had bounced off the wall and she hadn't heard any screaming, she had hurriedly pulled the panel back, but it still wouldn't fit into place. She was holding it shut when Lee stomped into the bathroom and pulled at the light switch. He had his clothes in his arms and he threw them into the water. He stood over the bath for another thirty seconds before he left the room and Sally could smell bleach mixing with the rising steam. She realised she had another problem.

The pipes that fed the taps were still digging into the back of her neck. The pipe that supplied the hot tap was old, with no lagging, and it was warming up. If she didn't move she would soon be scorched. She pushed herself away from the wall with her shoulder to try and put some distance between the skin on her neck and the pipe, but it was no use, her body rocked back into the hot pipe. Sally was jammed up against it, with no room to move away, not without completely changing her position, and she couldn't do that without pushing the panel open.

She thought fast. With her left hand still holding the panel shut, she moved her right hand to the bag that lay along the front of the bath. Her finger and thumb found the zip. Mercifully, it was at the end of the bag closest to her, and she was able to tug it down far enough to reach inside and grab a thick wad of notes. The pipe was starting to burn her neck. She let out a whimper, and beads of sweat erupted on her forehead. Some of the notes fell from her fingers, spilling in front of her. The rest she held to her neck. It took all her strength to push her head forward, thrusting her forehead into the plastic of the bath. She managed to wedge a few notes between the scorching metal and her neck, enough protection to buy her a little time.

* * *

Lizzy dared to open her eyes. She could hardly believe she was still breathing. She could see bits of her phone littering the floor at the far end of the flat. She saw Lee's feet emerge out of the bathroom. He walked to the bottom of the bed, his hands reached down and her mind raced. *'The bastard, he knew I was here all along and he's just playing with me.'* But the hand gripped the object in the black sack. Lee lifted it up out of her sight, and she heard the sound of material ripping. The sack fell to the floor in front of her and she watched him disappear back into the bathroom.

She heard something heavy drop into the bath. The water stopped running. Lee reappeared, he was swearing to himself. He went in and out of the bathroom, getting dressed. He put on a pair of blue shorts and slip-on shoes. She could see his lower half, the visible skin on his legs was scrubbed red. He moved to the front door, leaving the keys to his truck lying in the kitchen. And then he was gone.

* * *

Neither of the girls moved. They didn't dare. Eventually the burning at her neck forced Sally to push at the plastic panel. She struggled a little to get to her feet, stiff from lying in one position. She rolled the carpet flat and straightened it. Her hands were shaking and her feet still bled freely. There was no time to tend to them — Lee could come back at any minute. Sally burst into the living area.

'Lizzy?' she hissed, afraid to speak aloud.

'Yeah, yeah, I'm here.' She scrabbled out from the under the bed.

'We need to get the fuck out of here.'

'Yeah, now! He killed someone, Sally! Fuck, he *killed* someone!'

'I know, Lizzy, I heard.'

Lizzy got to the front door before Sally and sprinted past her. Sally pulled the door shut and followed. As Lizzy ran past, a door to another bedsit opened and a bleary-eyed, obese man watched them go.

* * *

Lee was two floors up. He'd gone to see Mick, the caretaker, in order to bark some orders at him, ignoring the disapproving stare of Mick's Thai wife. She had never liked Lee. She had once goaded her husband into standing up to him, but the head injuries Lee had inflicted had put him in hospital. She didn't try again.

Lee told Mick to reset the key fob passes on the doors so that the cops couldn't use theirs. On his way back down the stairs, Lee nearly collided with a fat man coming from his own floor.

'Everyone's in a rush today, ain't they?' said the man.

'What's that you say?' Lee stopped and looked the man up and down. 'You got something to say to me, fat shit?'

The man sniffed. 'Nah, nah, man. It's just I saw your two fucking women running past me door, I thought they were back.'

Lee came closer to the fat man. 'What you mean, "your two women?" What women?'

'I don't know, Lee. You know, your two women. They're always down there.'

'When d'you see them?'

'Fuck me, Lee, they were just here, I thought they were with you, like. I thought they were staying in your place.'

'Running?'

'Running, yeah, running. Down the stairs and off like, you know? I thought they'd come out of your place, that's all. I didn't talk to 'em or nothing.'

Lee turned and strode back into his own flat, and into the bathroom. He tore at the carpet and pulled the bath panel away, holding his breath.

The bag was there.

He pulled it out from under the bath. It was partially unzipped and wads of money spilled out. It looked like it was all there. He peered back under the bath and saw that some notes had come loose, three twenties at the tap end of the bath and another four folded together and stuck between the two water pipes at the top.

Lee thought for a moment. He left the bag and made his way over to the bed. He knelt and peered underneath. His suitcases had been pushed back and the dust had been disturbed.

'They were here,' he said to himself.

Lee looked over to where he'd thrown Lizzy's mobile phone. The pieces were gone.

'Both of them.'

CHAPTER 22

Lizzy had been leading the way down an alley between some rundown hotels. It was the best way to get some distance between them and Peto Court while keeping out of sight, but there was another reason why she had chosen this route. There was someone she needed to contact. And for that she would need to be on her own.

'We need to split up,' Lizzy said. 'Lee thinks I'm out collecting cash and he thinks you've fucked off. He's gonna be suspicious if he sees us together.' Lizzy pulled out the remains of her phone from her pocket. She fingered the touchscreen and sighed. 'It's fucked.'

'Wait — did you pick that up from Lee's place?'

Lizzy looked at Sally. 'Yeah. Why?'

'You fucking idiot! When he sees it's gone, he's gonna know someone was in there!'

It took a second for Lizzy to register this, then her expression changed from annoyance to panic. 'Shit! He's gonna kill us!'

Sally shook her head. 'He was always going to, at some point or other. The bloke's fucking lost it. We can't ever go back there anyway. I couldn't, not after what we heard in there.'

'We should still separate, though. Just for a little while, at least. He'll be out looking for us and we'll be a lot easier to find if we're together.'

Sally seemed uncertain. 'Okay . . .'

'It'll be okay, Sal. We just need to keep our heads down for a bit. Think this shit out, work out what we do next.'

The girls had been walking fast and were now halfway along the coastal path, a grassy oasis that ran the length of the lower Leas. It ran between the beach and the cliff. The two women arrived at a place where flowerbeds gave way to a grassy clearing shaped into an amphitheatre. The lawn was terraced, forming natural seating that sloped back up into the cliff. The entrance to the zigzag path was easy to miss at the back of the seating area but Lizzy knew it well and she made straight for it with Sally still behind her.

'We'll split up here. You can either go up the path or carry on towards Sandgate. I'll sit and wait here for you to get a little way and then I'm going up the path,' said Lizzy.

Sally nodded. 'Okay. I'll just head up the path. I need to get some shoes, so I'll go into town'. She plunged her right hand into her pocket. 'Lizzy, here, take this, get some food and wherever you're going, take a taxi.'

Lizzy peered down at the wad of twenty-pound notes and hesitated. She knew what stealing from Lee Chivers meant. Then she snatched at the money. It wasn't going to make any difference now.

Lizzy watched Sally until she was out of sight. A well-dressed couple with a pushchair had looked Sally up and down as she passed, noting her greasy hair and dirty face, the sunken cheeks smudged with tear tracks. Her oversized hooded top was filthy from the grime under the bath, as were her skin-tight jeans. Her bare feet were scratched and bleeding. Lizzy didn't think she looked nearly as bad. The last thing she wanted right now was to attract anyone's attention.

The zigzag path had seven levels, cutting back on each other in hairpin bends. The third turn from the top was partly dug into the cliff face. It was hidden and sheltered. Lizzy checked around her. There was no one nearby. She entered the covered area, and instantly the air was cooler. She stood up on a bench that faced out to sea and pushed her hand between two rocks behind it. She drew out a packet of cigarettes, still sealed in their plastic wrapper, and a Nokia mobile phone in a weatherproof case. She quickly pushed the cigarettes into her pocket and stepped down from the bench. She checked around her again, then continued her walk up the sloping path towards the Leas. Before she reached the top, she was already calling the only number in the contacts list.

'Hey.' The call was answered on the first ring.

'I need to speak to you.' Lizzy's voice trembled.

'Okay, when?'

'Now. It has to be now.'

There was a hesitation, but only slight. 'Sure, okay. Usual place?'

'Yeah, ten minutes.'

'I'll be there.'

Lizzy ended the call. She felt in her pocket for her own phone. The screen was broken but she could still make out the number for Lee Chivers. Her finger hovered over his name. She didn't know if this was a good idea, but she sure as hell didn't have any others. She took a deep breath. She had to be calm for this to work. Her finger tapped his name.

'Lizzy,' Lee answered. He sounded calm.

'Lee, what the fuck's going on? I just seen Sally. She turned up in the town after her issue the other night and like gives my phone back, fucking smashed up. I just about managed to call you. She said something about staying the fuck away from you and then she left. Her feet were all cut, she ain't got no shoes and she looked a right fucking state. Oh, and she gives me like a hundred quid?'

Lee didn't reply. Lizzy gritted her teeth.

'I ain't seen her today. She say where she was going?' he said.

'That's the thing. She said about going to the cop shop. I told her to be clever, you know? You don't just go talking loose round the filth, but she was upset. I ain't seen her like that before.'

'When was this?'

'Like, ten minutes ago.'

Another pause. His tone remained flat. 'Where you at?'

Lizzy thought fast. 'You know where I am. I'm out collecting your money.'

'You lying to me, Lizzy?'

'No. Fuck no. What is it with you people today?' Lizzy's voice broke a little.

'The shopping list — you got it?'

Lizzy swore silently. 'Okay, fine, you got me. I been busy this morning, I had to go see my ma. Don't be fucking pissed at me, all right? I'll get it done.'

The shopping list. It was still in Lee's flat on one of the kitchen counters. It was in code but Lizzy knew how to read it. It was a notebook, listing who owed what for drugs.

A longer silence. 'So, you coming back for it?'

'Yeah, I'll have to,' Lizzy said with her eyes shut. With his attention diverted to Sally, she had planned on giving herself a bit of time, some breathing space so she could plan her next move. But now she faced having to go right back to him to keep up the façade.

Lizzy stopped walking. Her head slumped forward. Lee would know that someone had been in the flat, she had made sure of that, but he couldn't know there had been two of them.

Lizzy had concocted this idea when she'd been lying under his bed, looking out at his bloodstained feet and the

144

pieces of her phone. It had seemed like a good idea at the time.

'You coming back now?' His voice was a little more insistent.

'Yeah, I'll be half hour or so though, yeah? I'm the other side of Langthorne.'

'See you then,' Lee replied. 'Say hi to your ma.'

CHAPTER 23

Sally bundled through the pharmacy door. She had been a daily visitor at this particular chemist's shop recently. Her eighty mil script of methadone was part of her probation order and was supposed to be a substitute for the heroin and an effective way of weaning her off it altogether. It had worked for a couple of months, but then she'd been tempted to top up, just one bag, later in the day. That bag soon became two, and then she dropped the methadone altogether. Soon she was back to the levels she had been at when she first got into trouble.

The woman behind the counter recognised her immediately. 'Sally! How have you been?'

'Fine.'

The woman's smile faltered as she took in Sally's appearance, the dirt and the bruises. The bare feet.

'How can we help you?' said the woman.

'I just need some Sudocrem and some baby wipes. And some socks.'

The assistant came out from behind the counter. She was watching Sally move around the shop. Sally thrust her hands into her pockets, she wasn't about to draw attention to herself. The woman returned with the smallest size tub of the cream, some wipes and a pair of men's socks. 'You'll want them loose,' she said.

'How much?' Sally said.

The woman waved her away. 'Don't you worry, Sally, it's on us. I just want to see you get yourself sorted out.'

Sally offered a tight smile, mumbled some words of thanks, and left the shop.

Sally found a bench on the other side of the road, beside a ruined church. She ripped open the wipes and dabbed at her feet. The coolness was a relief and the cream was cooler still, so she dabbed it on thick. She paused for a few minutes, with her feet on the edge of the seat and her chin on her knees watching the traffic snake past.

A woman of about Sally's age was playing with her child. She leant over the buggy making silly noises and smiling. Sally found herself smiling, too. The woman caught sight of her, and her face hardened. She straightened up and pushed her child away. Sally's gaze moved to the figure of the assistant, standing at the door of the chemist's shop, watching her. As their eyes met, she turned away and moved further back into the shop.

Sally pulled the socks on and got to her feet. The sooner she got out of this town, the better.

The sports shop had someone to greet customers, a young lad of barely twenty, with a boy-band quiff. He neither greeted her nor disguised his contempt.

An older man bustled out from behind the counter, a frown on his face. 'We don't have any toilets.'

'I don't need the toilet.'

The man stepped in front of her, blocking her entrance, and looked her up and down. 'What do you need then?'

'I'm not wearing any shoes,' Sally stated.

'Okay.'

'You sell them, right?'

'Well, yes.'

'Then how about you get me a size five in the pink Air Maxs over there.'

* * *

'So what did you need to see me for that couldn't wait?' Emily Ryker gave an encouraging smile. They were in the Burlington Hotel. It opened out onto the Leas like a smaller, shabbier Grand. Emily thought the Burlington was all the better for being slightly run down. She had a good relationship with the owner and it suited her needs. Where else would open the basement just so she could sit in a dark corner with a mug of strong, instant coffee for herself, and a McDonald's for her guest?

'I can't eat that.'

Emily looked puzzled. 'You're turning down a McDonald's? Now I know there's something up.'

'He's killed someone.' Lizzy put her hand to her mouth.

'Lee has?' Emily wasn't smiling any more.

Lizzy's hand was still at her mouth. She jerked a nod.

'You want to tell me about it?' Emily shifted her position, the coffee forgotten.

'Not really, no.'

'So what do you want?'

'I need to be safe, Emily, but I know you can't do that. I just thought that if I told you about it and then he did something to me, you would know. And then the bastard wouldn't get away with it.'

'Woah! Hold on there, girl. There are things I can do, you know. If you're telling me there is a genuine threat to you and that he's killed someone, then I have a duty to make sure you're safe. If you're a witness for us we can move you out of the area, place you under police guard, put you somewhere he will never find you.'

Lizzy was shaking her head. 'I can't run. Not from him, I know I can't, and I can't be no witness. You can't use me for that. I won't say nothing on paper. That's why I came to see you, because I knew you wouldn't make me.'

Emily touched her nose, a nervous habit of hers. 'Jesus, Lizzy, I just want to keep you safe. Look, tell me what's happened, off the record, yeah, and we can go from there.'

Lizzy held her packet of cigarettes and opened it, her hands shaking. She offered the packet to Emily.

'No thanks. You know I don't smoke anymore.'

'You brought a lighter though, right?'

'Don't I always?' Emily took out the lighter, with a quick look around for the hotel staff. They knew to leave her alone when she was in here but she didn't want to be pissing anyone off with the cigarette smoke. There was no one about.

'Thanks for these, by the way.' Lizzy narrowed her eyes against the smoke.

'You're welcome.' Emily had been running sources for long enough to know the value of a packet of fags.

'He came back to the flat earlier. We saw him out the window.'

'We?'

'Yeah, me and Sal. She's been staying for a while. She'd had a bust up with him last night, a baddun, taken a bit of a beating, and he'd told her to do one.'

'What was it about?'

'She'd just come out of the nick, like. Your lot lifted her for a bulk choring, and he was pissed with the attention that put on her. Another copper on another day would have searched where she was living, see. I mean, she didn't give his address, she ain't that dumb, but he said it could've happened. He uses stuff like that to start riots when he's in a mood.'

'I know the sort.'

'So when she left he was still angry, like proper angry, and I was still there so she came back this morning to check I was okay. She lost her phone ages ago, so she

149

couldn't call me. I let her up 'cause I knew Lee was out and he don't come back much during the day. She was only supposed to stay a bit but we had some weed. She brought it round, she wanted to say thanks, see, 'cause I called some bloke up who came and got her. Sorted her out for the night.'

'Bloke? What bloke?'

'Someone had written a number and "Dad" on her papers from the nick. I thought it was her dad like, obviously, but she'd said he was dead before. Could just be some old fucker she's sucking off for dark money.'

'Okay.'

Lizzy put her head in her hands, the cigarette between her fingers. The smoke drifted up through her hair. 'Jesus,' she muttered.

'Take your time, Lizzy.'

'We hid. You can't get out of that place, can you? Can't get round someone that's coming in, and no fucker'll help. I was under the bed and Sal got into the bath bit. She got hurt squeezing herself in. He came in and he was *so* angry. I mean I've seen him lose it, I know he can be horrible, I know what he can do, but this time he was . . . different.' Lizzy let out a little sob.

Emily waited for Lizzy to continue. She wanted nothing more than to start firing off questions, but she knew better.

'He was on his phone and walking around his flat, like. I'm so fucking quiet, I ain't breathing, under the bed, just a few feet from him. I guessed he was talking to the Russian 'cause of how he was, you know? He's not scared of no one, but he talks different to him. He talked about some man, a man he had killed, and he was covered in blood. I could see the bottom of his jeans and they were covered in blood. Oh fuck!' Lizzy broke down and sobbed. Emily moved round and hugged her, burying Lizzy's face in her top, murmuring that everything would be okay.

'He smashed his head in with a baseball bat. He said something about a dump or waste site or something like that I think. I was trying *not* to fucking listen, but he kept calling him *rat*, he must've said it like ten times.' Lizzy pulled away. 'Jesus, Emily, if he'd found me under that bed he would have killed me on the spot. The fucking bat was on the floor of his flat wrapped in black sacks. He woulda taken that out and it would be my head caved in and my blood all up his fucking leg. Fuck, Emily. Oh, fuck!'

'All right, calm down, Lizzy. We'll talk this out, see where we go from here. You're safe now, hon, you're safe now.' Emily returned to her seat, where she sat with her hands together, waiting for the tears to stop.

'I will have one of those fags,' Emily said. Lizzy pushed the packet of cigarettes towards Emily. Emily still had so many questions, and she needed the answers fast. She had a dead man who needed finding and now she knew who was responsible. This was big news and her mind was reeling. Emily lit the cigarette and took a long drag. The tobacco did its work, focusing her mind and calming her thoughts. She wondered why she had ever quit.

Lizzy checked her phone. 'I got to get going, Emily. I can't be staying here. I got shit to do before I'm missed.'

'Lizzy, we need to talk about how we keep you safe from now on. I want you to think about me writing this stuff down in a statement, so we can go and get him nicked—'

'No, no, no! You told me we're off the record. I can't grass, not about this. I'll be as dead as that poor fucker.'

'And if you go back to him, who's to say you won't be dead too? You tell us what you heard and then I can deal with Lee. I can sort protection out for you because you're a valuable witness. It's the way it works.'

'If I need to, I'll get away from him. He can't hurt me then.'

'You just disappear, do you? And he won't think that's suspicious? If he thinks you have any idea what went on he'll always see you as a threat. Whether you grass or not, he will treat you like you did already. And the stuff you need to live your life, you can't get that without talking to people who know Lee, who work for Lee and who are fucking terrified of the bloke. If Lee Chivers wanted to find you, he could do it in hours.'

'He'll go for Sal first,' Lizzy blurted out, and looked down at her hands.

'For Sal? Why her first? So she got out too?'

The tears streamed again, and Lizzy could only manage a nod.

'What did you say, Lizzy? Does he know Sal was there?'

'I know what I'm doing,' Lizzy managed finally. 'She's got places she can go, people who care about her, she really can disappear. I got none of that.'

'So what, you threw her to the wolves? Is that it? Fuck, Lizzy, where is she now?'

'She's safe, I swear. But what about me? I got no one.'

Emily waited for the sobs to stop. 'You've got me, Lizzy. I'm here, aren't I? But you need to help me sort this out.'

Lizzy was already shaking her head, 'I ain't grassing, you get nothing out of me. You always said you never needed no statement from me, you said I didn't have to put my name to any information. I know people still got raided 'cause of what I told you, they still got nicked, still got banged up. What do you need me for this time?'

'This is totally different, Lizzy. This is murder, and you're at risk because of what you know, more at risk than you've ever been. There's all sorts of legislation round intelligence like this. I can protect you.'

'Fuck if I ain't heard that before. I got to go, Emily, I got to be somewhere. Listen, you know what's happened and you know where to find the man what did it, so do what you need to do. That's how you keep me safe.' Lizzy got up to leave.

Emily stood up too and blocked Lizzy's exit. 'You're just going to go back to him, aren't you? Back to his flat where he's cleaning up the blood of the man he murdered. How long do you think you can survive in that environment? How long before he's cleaning your blood off his hands?'

'Find a way of getting him nicked that don't involve me. Then he can't touch me, Emily. Now you got to get out of my way or you won't be seeing me again.'

Emily stepped aside. Lizzy walked away. 'You know where I am if you need me, Lizzy. Day or night.'

Lizzy pushed the door open and didn't look back.

CHAPTER 24

John Stone, the chief constable of Lennokshire Police, was enjoying the sun on his face. Although initially he had been furious that Helen Webb had slipped off home, claiming to be ill, he was now happy that at least he didn't have to concern himself with her issues. It was bad enough being here at all. Helen had stood down most of his protection team after she had reassessed the risk level. Again, he had been upset that she had done so without consulting him but he now stood in the sun, just happy that the occasion might not be the claustrophobic experience that often comes with a public appearance of the chief of police. He didn't need any reminder that he wasn't popular in this town, but with the September sun warming his face and the view from the top of the Leas down to the calm blue of the English Channel, he felt almost relaxed.

John Stone did his best to project a warm smile as a woman holding the hand of a squirming toddler approached him. They both looked very unsure of themselves. The chief was accompanied by Elena Maxton. She was the first female sergeant he'd been able to find to replace Helen. This was for the "woman's touch," as he'd described it.

'Sir, this is Amanda Cutter, Ian Cutter's wife,' Elena explained. 'And their granddaughter, Ellie-May.'

The chief put his arms out to Amanda but abandoned the embrace halfway, opting for a limp handshake.

'Of course. We met briefly at Sergeant Cutter's funeral.' He ignored the child.

'He was just Ian to us,' Amanda said curtly, her face reddening a little.

'To me too,' the chief replied, maintaining his smile as best he could. 'How are you? I can only imagine how hard it has been.'

'Yes, you can. That's all any of you can do. All the people that persuaded him to return, that wouldn't let him walk away from the job, all you can do now is *imagine* how difficult it is for his widow, for his family and the grandchildren that he leaves behind.'

'He was one of the good ones, a very talented man, and you're right, we don't let them go easily. I'm so sorry, Mrs Cutter, for what happened and how it happened.'

Amanda let out a sigh. 'I always said the job would kill him. I thought it would be the stress. I mean he was too old to be front line and he knew it, he knew to let the younger ones go out and do the rough stuff.' Her eyes were puffy. 'He made it, though. The tough old bugger got right to the end of his career. We'd been making retirement plans for years. I teased Ian before he went to work that last time that this was the reason he'd gone back, so he could put off having to travelling round Europe in a campervan. He will never have to do that trip now.'

'I'm so sorry,' the chief said.

'There's no need. He was to blame. The silly old fool should have walked away, but he couldn't. It was inevitable, really. He was only ever going to come out of there in a box.'

Silence. The chief shifted his feet and Elena intervened. 'Well, sir, we should get round the rest of the people, and I'm sure Mrs Cutter would like some time on her own.'

The two women shared a curt nod. Elena and the chief walked away.

'She's a bitter old fossil,' the chief hissed. 'No one forced that man to come back to us, did they?'

'Well, to be fair, sir, she did say that. She's just angry. You work all your life to enjoy your retirement and then it gets snatched away, just like that.'

'I suppose so. See? That's why you're here!' The chief grinned, already on his way towards the next group. 'Come on, Elena, get me round the rest of these people.'

CHAPTER 25

'That's Lizzy MacDonald.' PC Cavan Kendall punctured the silence in the Ford response car. He sat in the passenger seat with a Costa Coffee cup between his thighs.

'So it is. She looks in a hurry,' Constable Steve Goddes replied. He was in the driving seat.

'She's probably wanted. Usually is.'

'Fuck's sake, Cavan. I just got this coffee, can we not just sit still for five minutes?'

'You love working with me, Goddes, you know you do! You stay there and do some radio checks. I'll go speak to her.'

Cavan stepped out of the car and fixed his hat in place. Lizzy was walking towards him, her head bent.

'Hey, Lizzy! Long time, no see,' Cavan called out.

Lizzy lifted her head and walked towards him. 'I been keeping me head down, ain't I? Not been giving you any cause to stop me.' Lizzy was sweating, her voice was a little shaky, and her eyes darted about.

Cavan took a small step backwards. 'So what you up to?'

Lizzy looked blank. Cavan had a strong Irish accent and he was aware that he sometimes spoke too fast for his

English listeners. He repeated the question more slowly. 'It's the accent, right? I speak too fast. I'm sorry.'

'My aunt was Irish. Limerick.'

Cavan beamed. 'Best part. I've still got family there.'

'I remember. We've had this conversation before.'

'I remember too, I didn't think you would though! You'd had a few then, girl.'

Lizzy shrugged. 'So am I in trouble or something?'

'I don't only speak to people when they're in trouble, you know.'

'Nah, sometimes you stop people and just hope they're in trouble. Your mate over there, he's not checking me on your radio then, no?'

'Old habits.' Cavan smiled. He had piercing blue eyes beneath a crop of dark hair and a neatly trimmed beard.

'You're one of the decent ones,' Lizzy allowed. 'Nick me in a heartbeat, but you always let me have a fag before getting in the car. For a copper, that's about as decent as you lot get.'

'How's your fellow?'

'My fellow?'

Cavan gestured at the entrance to Peto Court, less than ten metres from where they stood.

'You still with the fellow from in there, right? The guy who'd slapped you around the last time we met. I talked to you about getting safe and you told me you would. I guess you didn't make it yet.'

'I never said I needed to be safe.'

'You didn't have to. You had bruising on your arms, red marks round your neck and I'm naturally suspicious.'

Lizzy shrugged. 'We all have our own lives.'

Cavan suddenly turned his attention to a voice that erupted through the earpiece he wore that connected to his police radio. He pressed a button clipped onto his stab vest and said, 'Go ahead, mate.' He looked at Lizzy, and said, 'Excuse me a minute, Lizzy.'

'Mate, still doing checks over here but it looks like she's wanted on a warrant. Failing to appear over in Canterbury after a shoplifting offence. There's some confusion 'cause she's been nicked since the warrant was issued but it doesn't look like that was dealt with, for whatever reason. I'm just getting it clarified but don't let her go.'

'Okay, mate, no worries.' Cavan turned back to Lizzy. 'My mate's telling me there's some issue with the computers up there so it's taking a while, and he's reminding me that my coffee's getting cold.' He smiled again.

'I'm not stopping you drinking it.'

'I don't mind, Lizzy, it's always a pleasure to speak to you.'

'I can't go, then?'

'I'm sure you don't mind standing with me for a minute, do you? Have you got somewhere to be?'

'No.' Lizzy shrugged again. She folded her arms across her chest and her gaze drifted towards Peto Court, just behind her. She started, and her eyes widened. Quickly she turned them back to Cavan.

'You okay, Lizzy?'

She gave him a little nod.

* * *

'Fuck!' Lee Chivers' voice echoed round the concrete stairwell. He'd stepped back from the window, but Lizzy might have seen him. The stupid fucking whore was probably spilling her guts to that pig out there, and now he would have all sorts of problems. Even if she wasn't, the fact that a copper had stopped her by Peto Court was bad news, especially given what he had in mind for her. Lee shook his head and gritted his teeth. Fuck it. It wouldn't matter, they knew she lived here anyway. It would always be the first place they'd come to look for her. He just needed to be sure they didn't come looking for as long as possible. And that when they did she was well hidden, or what was left of her. Lee startled to bristle with excitement. He'd prepped the flat, planned where he'd be standing when she entered, played it out in his mind, and now he was looking forward to his moment.

* * *

Lizzy's attention was suddenly elsewhere. There was no further talk of Limerick and how he'd allowed her to smoke a fag. Now she was agitated, fidgety, and scared. At first Cavan thought that maybe she had worked out that she'd missed a court date, and knew there would be a warrant out for her. But then he'd nicked her a couple of times in the past, and that hadn't scared her.

But now she was definitely afraid. Very afraid. Cavan shot a glance back towards the marked Ford, and his mate.

'Let me just check if he's done, Lizzy. He seems to be taking his time back there.'

Lizzy nodded absently, her attention on the block of flats.

* * *

Lee was still there, standing bent forwards facing the painted stone wall, one hand upon it, holding his weight, while the other held his phone to his ear. It connected to Niall Webster, once a talented self-employed brickie who had all but lost the battle with his alcohol addiction and now passed a squalid existence in the corner bedsit on the bottom floor of the building.

'Yeah.' Niall's voice was deep and rough, as though he'd just been woken up.

'Webby, it's Gee.'

'What you need?'

'You in your flat?'

'Yeah, 'course.'

'Lizzy's outside with the filth. When they fuck off, I need to make sure she don't do the same. I need to talk to her, see.'

160

'I get you. But fucking hell, Gee, it kills me getting in and out that fucking window.'

'I need this, Webby.'

'I'm on it man, fuck's sake, I'm on it.'

Lee cut the call.

* * *

PC Steve Goddes finally got out of the car and Lizzy turned to stare at him.

'Hey, Lizzy, you okay?' Steve asked. She didn't reply. He looked beyond her and frowned at Cavan, who shrugged. Like Cavan, Steve had met Lizzy before and neither of them had seen her react like this.

'What's the craic then, mate? Anything outstanding for Lizzy here?' Cavan already knew the answer.

'The W needs sorting,' Steve replied. "W." was police-speak for warrant. It was pretty obvious, but it served to give officers a few seconds to get the cuffs on before the subject worked it out.

Cavan kept his cuffs in his pocket for now, but he stepped a little closer to Lizzy and she returned her gaze to him.

'Lizzy, mate, we've done all the radio checks, and it seems there's a warrant been issued for you. It's for failing to appear at court, I think, but we can get that clarified back at the nick. You're going to have to come with us for now, though.'

Lizzy burst into tears. The tension drained from her face and she slumped forward, her head and arms seeming to hang from her shoulders. The two officers again exchanged glances.

'You okay, Lizzy?' Cavan asked. 'You know how this goes, worst-case scenario, you get to stay in overnight and you're in court first thing in the morning. It's no big deal.'

Lizzy didn't reply. Her body was convulsed with huge sobs.

Steve moved in behind her and took hold of her arm. As he heard the cuff ratchet shut, Cavan was sure he saw a smile on her face.

Then, just like that, she switched again. 'I can't be nicked!' Lizzy suddenly screeched and she pulled back as Steve Goddes took hold of her other wrist. 'You ain't fucking taking me nowhere!' Steve took a firmer hold of her flailing right arm and pushed her down. She dropped to one knee, screaming out in pain.

'Calm down, Lizzy, for fuck's sake.' Cavan put a hand on her shoulder, and she relented enough for the other cuff to be applied, but she was still vocal. She swore loudly. In any other area, every window would be twitching by now as residents looked on curiously, but here, in the streets surrounding Peto Court, no one gave a second glance.

Lizzy was still bent forward, as Steve held the rigid black plastic that bridged the cuffs. The two officers looked down at her. She quickly calmed down.

'You have no idea,' she said. 'Look, I'll come in myself tomorrow morning, no problem, I swear down, I'll come in, you don't have to do this.' She shook her head.

'Come on, Lizzy, you know we can't ignore this. Let's get you to your feet.'

Lizzy scrambled to her feet and walked towards the police car between the officers. Cavan saw her smile again. He looked beyond her, over to Peto Court where something moved at an upstairs window. A shadow? Anyway, it was nothing he could make out and he turned away.

* * *

Lee Chivers slapped the wall. They were taking her away! He felt as though he would combust with the frustration. He went to the top of the stairs that led down to Lizzy and the coppers and stood still, holding the door open, going through his options. He longed to sprint

162

down the stairs, baying for a fight. He sighed. He would have to be patient. Lizzy would have to wait until tomorrow. There was plenty that needed to be done before then, anyway. He still had to clear up his earlier "work," and he had another thieving whore to find. He would take his time when he found that one.

Lee took a last look out of the window. He could see the coppers, both standing still with their hands to their radios. Lizzy wasn't yet in the car. She was facing Lee again.

She looked worried.

* * *

Both the men's radios erupted at the same time. All three fell silent as the men listened. The second copper wasn't wearing his earpiece and Lizzy could hear the hurried transmission.

'*Shots fired, shots fired,*' someone shouted excitedly, then there was a silence and the two officers exchanged glances. The radios shook again. '*The Leas, Langthorne, shots fired, we have officers down, I don't know how many, the chief's been hit up here, we need a medic on the hurry up.*'

Cavan's hand went to his belt, and Steve Goddes broke into a sprint towards the patrol car.

Cavan grabbed at Lizzy's cuffs again. She squirmed in pain as they were hastily removed. 'You'll come in tomorrow, Lizzy. Go to the front counter and tell them there's a warrant, yeah? We need to go.'

Lizzy said nothing as the copper undid her cuffs. He had to bend to retrieve them when they fell to the ground. The patrol car revved hard behind him and Cavan ran round to the passenger side as the blue lights flickered on.

Lizzy watched the car race off. It passed a figure standing motionless on the pavement that ran alongside the building. Even at this distance she recognised Niall Webster. He put a cigarette to his lips without taking his eyes from her, and she knew immediately why he was there. She had heard Lee give this order to Niall once before when someone had tried to leave the building. No one left until Lee Chivers said they could leave. The cops had given Lizzy a way out, she had given Lee a show so he'd think she was resisting, and it had all been for nothing. The moment she'd seen him waiting for her she knew she'd made a big mistake. Now she was going to have to go in there and face him.

* * *

Lee's confused scowl was soon replaced by a broad smile. He watched Lizzy starting towards the entrance to Peto Court and ran to the door of his flat. As he pushed it open, it snagged on the large tarpaulin sheet he had laid out on the floor in readiness, and he had to push it with his shoulder. He made one last check that his tools were correctly laid out on the floor, smoothed the sheet back down, took up his position and waited.

CHAPTER 26

PCs Goddes and Kendall were the first to arrive at the scene. They saw people running away from the memorial arch, which was at the top of the hill where the Leas began. There was a McDonald's on the corner on the right side. The restaurant had been busy with teenagers and families, and it was emptying fast onto the pavement where most people took a sharp left away from the Leas and back towards the town.

Steve Goddes brought the Ford Focus to a sharp halt. The Leas had a one-way road that ran parallel to the walkway. Both men had understood that this would be shut off for the ceremony, but it was still open to traffic when they arrived. A crowd of officers were in a huddle to the left, all wearing dress uniform. Someone in black boots was lying on the ground, Cavan Kendall couldn't see who it was. A suitcase-sized medical bag obscured his view, spewing tubes, oxygen masks, and other items. Whoever this was, they were obviously seriously injured.

A second huddle of officers in formal dress was kneeling around another figure who lay prone on the ground. His shirt had been torn open, and a man in civilian clothing was applying pressure to an open wound in his abdomen. Cavan could see the fallen man's head rock slightly as they thumped at his chest. Another officer stood by, wide-eyed and helpless. When he saw the marked car, he ran across and leaned into the driver's window.

'It's fucking carnage.' Cavan thought he recognised the man from force headquarters. He wore sergeant's stripes on his dress uniform.

'A motorbike came past. We all had our backs to it, then suddenly the rider just started firing across here.' He pointed to where the group was frantically working. 'The chief's taken a hit, he's bleeding heavy. They're getting it under control I think, but it looks bad. The bike stopped just over there.' He pointed behind the Ford Focus. 'Marjers saw him shooting and ran at the bloke, he got hit but the bike started to move and Marjers was still able to knock him off. The rider fell into the car, pretty fucking hard but not hard enough.' Cavan looked back at the parked car next to where the second officer lay. It was a saloon and he could now see that it had scrapes on the boot lid and the glass of the rear windscreen was cracked. 'He came off his bike and went almost right through the window. I thought we'd got him, but he climbs off the car, shoots a couple more times and gets back on his bike. It was on its side and stalled but he got it going.'

'How long ago did he drive off?'

'A few minutes.'

'What sort of motorbike?'

'Sporty. Mainly black, fuck-off scrape down the left side.'

'We're no use here, are we?' Steve Goddes had already selected first gear.

'No. The ambulance should fucking be here by now and we're just plugging until they turn up.'

Steve nodded and the Focus lurched forward. As he sped away, the blue lights of an ambulance appeared in his rear-view mirror. He had to brake hard again as a girl hurrying away from the scene ran into the middle of the road.

Steve started the siren. 'There's two ways from here. He's going to want to get out of Langthorne, so he either goes the way he's facing, towards Hythe, or he goes round Langthorne's one-way system and out the top of the town to the motorway.'

'I would do Hythe on a motorbike. You would have to know that a lot of police resources will come down the motorway and he'd have to go back on himself to get there. He's going to want to put as much distance as possible between himself and us, and fast.'

'Hythe it is,' Steve said. 'Now get on that radio, Cavan, best we tell them what we're doing.'

* * *

Two members of staff stood close to Sally as she looked at herself in the mirror, down at the matt black Nike trainers, which had a flash of pink down both sides. She liked them. She couldn't remember the last time she had been able to choose new trainers and she had taken the opportunity to try on a few pairs, with the bonus of upsetting the shop staff. She had milked this, walking the length of the shop more times than she needed to, despite the twinges of pain that came from the new trainers rubbing against her scratched feet.

'I'll take these ones,' she said.

'In the box, or—?'

'No. I'm done with barefoot for now.' She pulled out the wad of notes and looked at the salesman. He stared at the cash. 'Payday,' she said.

'Okay. Ninety pounds then, please.'

Two loud gunshots rang out.

Everyone in the shop stopped what they were doing. The noise had come from outside the store. People ran past. More bangs added to the panic. A couple ran down the stairs from the top floor clutching a toddler, and there was a sudden rush for the door. Sally didn't move. She looked through to the very back of the shop where a fire exit door was just visible among the rails of clothes. She made her way towards it, moving against the tide of people leaving the shop. She pushed the metal bar and stepped out into the sun.

The scene was no calmer here. The shop backed on to the Leas and in the distance she could see people on the ground, and people running away from them. She turned right and joined the throng, jumping out of the path of a police car that came up behind her, its siren blaring.

CHAPTER 27

Lizzy felt the temperature drop as she stepped out of the September sunshine and into the damp interior of Peto Court. She couldn't remember even getting to the door but somehow her feet had carried her inside. As soon as the police car drove away, Lizzy knew that any chance of leaving Peto Court had gone. The police had driven right past the man whose job it was to make sure she didn't get away. She had no doubt there would be others and, sure enough, as she stopped at the heavy metal door and fumbled for her fob, the door swung open for her. She recognised this man too — John somebody. He was a big man, was John, round the middle mostly but across the shoulders too. He would be too strong for her.

'You walking with me, John?' Lizzy asked, her throat dry. He shrugged and gave a grunt as he stepped in behind her. She found the bottom tread of the solid steps. Her hand moved to the cold metal of the banister and she slowly mounted the steps to the first floor.

'We gotta keep moving,' said John.

'Sorry.' Lizzy tore herself away from the window, and the sunlit pavements and leaves that had drifted from the trees on the way up to the Leas. She liked it up there, it was peaceful and calm.

She went up the next flight of concrete steps to the second-floor landing, where she used her fob to open the communal door to the corridor. More windows ran along its length. Lizzy looked back briefly to where a forlorn-looking John had stopped as the door closed behind her.

The door to flat 49 was partly open. She stopped and hesitated, thought about knocking, and then about her story. She had done nothing wrong, she had just been approached by Sal and given some money. The story went that she had no idea about the poor sap beaten to death by the man waiting for her inside the flat. Lizzy took out the wad of notes she had been given by Sal. It was her trump card. Her only card. She knew she was going to have to play it straight away if she was to stand any chance at all.

She took a breath, then stepped through the door, already calling out. 'Lee, what the fuck? I just got walked up here by fucking—'

Lizzy stopped just inside the door. It took her a few seconds to process what she saw in front of her. She put her hand up to her mouth. Lee Chivers shut the door.

'I've been waiting for you, Lizzy.'

'What's going on, Lee?' Her voice lacked all conviction. She knew exactly what was going on. She forgot her story and closed her eyes.

'Open your *fucking* eyes.' Lee's tone dripped with barely controlled rage as he pushed her head with his. Lizzy had to take a breath to steady herself before she could comply. Her eyes opened, and she peered round the interior of the flat again. Her worst nightmare was laid out in front of her, with a tarpaulin sheet to catch the mess.

'Oh, Jesus,' she whimpered.

'What do you see, Lizzy? Tell me what you fucking see.'

'You don't need to do none of this, Lee. I came here to talk to you, to sort this out. I don't know nothing about what's going on. Sally was acting weird, now you're acting fucking psycho.'

Lee tightened his grip on her arm, bearing down on a pressure point in the centre of her bicep. The pain was so severe that she screamed and bent double. Lee pushed her to her knees.

'What do you see, Lizzy? You know I don't like asking questions twice. *What* do you *see?*' He stooped over her, his grip still tight on her arm, his mouth so close to the top of her head that she felt his breath in her hair.

Lizzy looked round the room, her eyes wet, her tone resigned. 'It's the flat, Lee. It's the flat. You've moved the stuff round a bit.'

'What stuff, Lizzy? Come on, you can do better than that!'

She could sense just how much the bastard was enjoying this. He fed on fear, and right now he was having a feast. She took a deep breath. 'You've turned the bed up on its side, it's against the wall now, which has made a space, and you've put a sheet of plastic down on the floor.'

'You know what that's for, Lizzy, right?'

Lizzy's head suddenly felt heavy. She squinted down at the end of the sheet. Lee pushed her forward, and Lizzy fell, face down, hitting her nose on the coarse plastic. The tears kept coming.

'Tell you what, Lizzy, let me tell you what I see.' Lee grabbed her by the hair and jerked her head up. 'It's fucking rude to ignore someone when they're speaking to you, Lizzy. You don't want to be rude to me, trust me on that. You look at me when I'm talking to you.'

He let her head go. She moved her legs under her and raised herself slightly. Lee paced to the other side of the room, where he turned to face Lizzy. He leant back against the windowsill. A breeze pushed the net curtains so that they moulded round him.

'I see a plastic sheet. I see a hammer. There's a scalpel, a cleaver and a disc cutter too, but that's for later. Do you see them? Loads of tools.'

Lizzy slowly turned her head from side to side.

'But what I really see in my flat now is a *lying* fucking rat, Lizzy, that's what *I* see.'

Lizzy attempted to look puzzled. 'What are you talking about, Lee?'

'Don't!' Lee pushed off the windowsill and took a few steps towards Lizzy, stopping just short of her. His right hand shot out and grabbed her chin with thumb and finger, twisting her mouth. 'Don't lie to me here. Not in my place. It's one thing to lie to me on the phone, but don't you dare come to my flat and lie to my fucking face. Do you hear me? That sort of thing makes me very upset.'

'What do you want from me?' Lizzy pulled her head back and Lee let go.

'I want you to tell me what you think you were doing hiding in my flat,' he said. He stood up and walked away from her as he spoke. 'Snooping on me when I was talking about my business. I want to know what you did today when you left here. Most of all, I need to know where that bitch Sal is.'

'I told you what happened, for fuck's sake. Sal found me. She told me to stay away from you, she gives me my phone back all smashed to fuck and then gives me this.' Lizzy held out the five twenty-pound notes.

Lee leaned back on the windowsill, arms crossed. He glanced briefly at the money but made no attempt to take it. Lizzy threw it towards him and the notes fluttered to the floor.

'You know I ain't interested in taking your money. I get what I get. I knew Sal got it from you — where else would she get it?' she said.

Lee paced over to Lizzy and squatted in front of her. He looked into her eyes for a long moment. She trembled, unable to tear her eyes away.

'Tell me you and Sal weren't in my flat earlier today. Tell me you weren't hiding under the bed, under the bath. Tell me now, Lizzy. This is your chance to fucking *tell* me.' His look seemed to increase in intensity. Lizzy had backed herself into a corner. She couldn't change her story now, after what she had heard. And she knew what it meant if he knew she had heard it.

'I don't know what you're talking about, Lee. You're scaring me now. You know I wouldn't lie to you.'

Lee straightened up and stepped past her. He pulled the door open so hard it slammed against the wall and he was out of the flat before she had even turned round. There was silence. Lizzy wondered if he'd gone, if she might have a chance to get away. She heard a loud crash, further along the corridor, hard enough to shake the floor. Lizzy hesitated. She slowly got to her feet as she heard another crash, this one further away. She heard a muffled shout, another bang, and some scraping. Lee came back in, pushing the man before him, the man from flat 59. Lizzy recognised him immediately. Her hand went to her mouth and she gasped. She had been found out.

Frank had lived in Peto Court for two months. He'd been kicked out of his nice home by his wife, who had finally tired of the drinking, which had got worse since he'd been laid off from his job as a long-distance haulier. He looked utterly bewildered.

'Lee! What the fuck? I'm down there minding me own business. What d'you want with me, son?'

Lee ignored his protests. He looked at Lizzy, and she looked right back, unable to break the stare.

'You gonna tell me that this man is a liar? That has consequences, you know, Lizzy. Is this man a liar?' Lee prodded Frank in the back and he stumbled forward.

'Don't do this, Lee,' Lizzy said.

'What the fuck, man?' Frank looked at Lee.

'Face her!' Lee shouted.

Frank gave Lizzy a questioning look.

173

Lee bent down and picked up one of his tools. It was a Stanley knife. The blade stuck out an inch or more and he held it in his right hand, close to his hip, where Frank couldn't see it.

'Is this man a liar?' Lee said again.

'Please, Lee,' Lizzy begged.

'Were you here today? Earlier? Without me knowing? Were. You. Here?'

Lizzy knew what her answer meant. It was her or Frank.

'No,' she said so quietly that Frank had to lean forward to hear.

'What did you say?' Lee hissed.

'I said no, Lee. I told you, I wasn't here. I don't know what you're talking about.'

Frank had opened his mouth, but his words became a guttural cry as the blade slashed him across the back from his shoulder blade. Lee took hold of Frank's wrist and pulled it down. Frank bent forward. Lee kept up the pressure and Frank dropped to one knee, his eyes tightly shut.

'What happens now, Lizzy? You tell me.'

Lee still held the blade in his free hand. Lizzy looked down at Frank. He was breathing heavily and his T-shirt, slick with blood and sweat, stuck to his back. Lee brought the knife back up and pushed the point into the base of his neck. Frank yelled.

'Shut the fuck up!' Lee warned, tightening his grip.

Frank was shaking. Sweat dripped from his top lip and nose and gathered on the plastic sheet.

'This is it, Lizzy. This is the man's spinal cord. We got something special you and me, ain't we? We've been round the block together. If you lied to me 'cause you thought I would get angry, take it out on you like I'm taking it out on Frank here, then I get that, but this is it. This is where you tell me you lied, and not this shit excuse for a fucking bloke, 'cause he don't mean shit to me and I will slice his spine here and now. On your say-so.'

'Fuck, Lee!'

'Tell him,' Frank pleaded. 'Jesus, love. Tell him I saw you with the other girl. Tell him what I saw.'

Lee stared at her. 'On your say, Lizzy.'

Lizzy rubbed at her face. 'Fuck, Lee. I was so scared you would be mad. It was Sal's idea 'cause she knew she wasn't supposed to be here. I just wanted her to get her stuff together so she didn't need to come back, that was all, but we panicked.'

Lee released his hold on Frank, who slumped to the floor, hitting his face on the plastic. He didn't move.

Lee stepped over him towards Lizzy, who had closed her eyes, her whole body braced. She felt a light touch on her shoulder as he passed. She waited another second then dared to open her eyes. Lee was back leaning on the windowsill.

'Get the fuck out of here, Frank.'

Frank groggily rose to his feet.

'I said fuck off.'

Frank staggered a little, his right hand on the wound on his back.

'And, Frank!' Lee called out.

Frank stopped and turned back, his eyes on the floor like a scolded child.

'This was a misunderstanding in here today, yeah? I'll get you a good beer for my part. Let's not make it any more than that, alright?'

Frank nodded, and stumbled back into the corridor.

'Did you get your phone working?' His tone was conversational. He suddenly sounded like the Lee she was used to hearing.

'It's working,' she said warily.

'I need to talk to you both, Lizzy. About what you heard. I was pissed that you lied, but we're past that now. I tell you everything anyway. Fuck, I probably would have spoken to you about it all when you got back. But Sal, she's *your* mate, Lizzy, you brought her here and she'd already outstayed her welcome. She's the reason for all this fucking about today, Lizzy.'

Lizzy felt able to turn around. Her guard dropped a little. He trusted her, he'd told her that before, and his concern was about Sal.

'What do you want me to do?'

Lee smiled. 'I need to speak to you both. But I know she won't speak to me, not today anyway. We need to talk about what I said. You both heard me talking on the phone, and I reckon you've got it all fucked up. See if you can get her to meet you, Lizzy, and I can be there too. We'll square this and then me, you and, fuck it, maybe even Sal can have a fucking joint or two and laugh it away, yeah?'

Lizzy sniffed. 'I ain't got no way of talking to her, Lee. She's got no phone and I don't know where she was going. She's got some place she goes when she wants to disappear and I don't know where it is.'

'Her best friend in the world don't know where she goes? That don't sound right now.' Lee was still smiling but his tone had hardened.

'I don't. I mean, she's pretty fucking tight about her shit, you know?' Lizzy paused, thinking. 'There was a number, a landline number. It should still be on my phone. It was local. She might be there.'

Lee nodded. 'Good. Give her a call and get her to meet up with you. Don't mention me, Lizzy. I'll be a surprise, alright?'

Lizzy nodded. 'I'll see what she says.'

'I'm relying on you, Lizzy. She listens to you. This is best for all of us.'

Lizzy smiled at him. 'I'll give her a call.'

'Fuck that! Let's have a burn first, shall we? Chill us both out.'

Lizzy nodded again, with more enthusiasm.

CHAPTER 28

'Sally Morgan!' a woman called out to her.

Sally slowed her pace a little.

'I know who you are, Sally, and I know that right now you need my help.'

Sally turned to look at the driver, who seemed vaguely familiar. She kept walking, facing forward again.

'Are you talking to me?'

'We've met before. You got beaten up. I know who did it and I know why — because you wouldn't sleep with those men he brought to the flat. I wanted you to tell me about him, what he was doing, and you refused.'

Sally suddenly remembered. 'I don't talk to coppers.'

'We both know that isn't true, don't we?'

'What does that mean?'

'Listen, Sally. You'll be dead by the end of the day if you don't get in this car right now and listen to what I have to say. Give me five minutes and then you can get out if you want to and I'll leave you alone. I promise you.'

'You *promise* me?' Sally stopped. She was walking up a terraced street. It was quiet, at the top end of town, as far away from Peto Court as she could get and still find places to go for drugs. 'A fucking copper?'

'You should give us coppers a bit more of a chance, Sally. Some of us just want to help you.'

'And why would you want to help me?'

'Because I don't want to see you hurt. You or Lizzy.'

'I can look after myself.' Sally started walking again.

'Of course you can. That's why you're heading off to score. I know who the dealers are round here. They'll be the same ones Lee Chivers knows. Come on now, Sally, you're a clever girl under all that dirt. You know that Lee Chivers has already sent a message out to his network. They'll be speaking to him at the back of the house while someone stalls you at the front. And Lee Chivers *really* wants to talk to you.'

'You don't know anything about me. I can disappear, you know.'

'You think? How about I drop you up at Saltwood after?'

Sally walked over to the car.

'That's right, Sally, I know where you're going. How long do you think it will be until other people get to know too? There's no such thing as disappearing, not when you gotta keep popping your head back out to get yourself a bag of brown. It makes you careless.'

'I got no choice.'

'Get in the car and I might be able to change that.'

Sally looked around her. The road was empty. 'Why would I trust a copper?'

'Sally, at the very least I'm not going kill you. Which puts me ahead of a lot of people in this town right now. Get in the car. I'll take you to a new setup I know. They're in competition with your man Chivers so there's no chance of them tipping him off.'

'You're going to take me somewhere to score?'

'No. I'm going to take you somewhere and leave you in the car, and then I'm going to go score for you.'

'Why the fuck would you do that?'

'Because you're known. You're Lee Chivers' girl. You turn up at another crew asking for product, they're going to see you as a threat and they might do something stupid. I'm here to keep you safe, not put you straight back in harm's way.'

'I'm not his girl.'

The driver shrugged. 'Way of speaking.'

'I can't say I've ever heard of a copper scoring for someone before. There's gotta be some sort of a twist to this. Gotta be!'

The driver leaned over and pushed the passenger door open, then she sat back, her hand extended. 'I'm Emily Ryker,' she said, 'And I'm not like other coppers.'

Dover Road was a long road that ran right through the centre of Langthorne. Parts of it were quite deprived, the terraced houses containing bedsits opened up at points to allow for purpose-built blocks of flats. The largest example was called Rowan Mews. Built in the 1970s, it boasted all the penny-pinching features of that era, including landings that ran around the outside of the building, open to the elements and protected by a wire mesh. The ground-floor flats opened straight out onto a grey expanse of concrete, where kids had drawn hopscotch boards and abusive graffiti in among the empty communal clothes lines.

Tracey Wickham lived in one of these ground-floor flats. Emily knew her by reputation only and had never met her. Like many addicts, Tracey had been made vulnerable by her inability to fund her addiction. A London-based gang who had been branching out into towns easily accessible by train had bullied her into allowing her home to be used as a "cuckoo" address. The gangs considered Langthorne, and Lennokshire as a whole, to be a soft target and would send their youngest, newest recruits out to gain a foothold.

Tracey Wickham answered the door on the fourth knock. Emily had seen the window curtain twitching and had stood, looking at the ground, where they could get a good look at her. People like Tracey could spot a copper a mile away.

'Who are you?' Tracey opened the door a crack, and looked Emily up and down, and then beyond, in case there was anyone waiting in the background.

'Emily.'

'What do you want?'

'What everyone wants that comes here.' Emily made a show of checking around her. 'Are you online here or what? 'Cause that's what I got told.'

Tracey didn't move. Emily had seen pictures of her, some from recent surveillance, and she was going downhill fast. She looked fragile and ill, older than her forty-something years. Her condition had probably worsened since the arrival of her new guests, who would be supplying her with a regular intake of her favourite class A drug, keeping her sweet in return for a roof over their heads. Tracey was taking risks. There was the constant danger of getting raided and evicted from her home, of being hauled into the nick, or of a violent break-in by a rival gang.

'I don't know what you're talking about,' said Tracey. She looked Emily up and down for a second time and made to push the door shut. Emily tried again.

'Look, I'm new to the town. I ain't here for me and I've got a couple of places to try so I don't really give a shit whether I get it here or not, but you could save me a lot of time.' Emily held up two crisp twenty pound notes that Sally had given her.

Tracey hesitated, her eyes on the cash. 'You think I'm stupid? I got people turning up here once before what I didn't know. I gave them the time of day and then two months later I'm down the nick, ain't I? They was coppers.'

Emily knew that Tracey had been caught dealing drugs to anyone who came to her door. She tried to think on her feet. 'Tell you what. What about I give you this forty quid and then I fuck off. Then in a few minutes I'm going to walk back past your flat and there might just be two white, two dark, and anything extra that gets chucked in for the inconvenience left on top of that bin there. Then it's got nothing to do with you, right?' Emily waved the money at Tracey, who seemed to be thinking hard. Finally she made a decision, snatched the money from Emily's hand and closed the door.

Emily walked round the corner of the block of flats and checked her watch. It was nearly 3.30 p.m. The day was flashing past and there was much still to be done. She gave it two minutes, most of it spent fidgeting with her hands and wishing she had bought a pack of cigarettes. She walked back to the flat, checking for any uniform cops who might be around. A tissue had appeared on top of the bin. She grabbed it, feeling something firm inside. She made her way quickly back to the car.

'Fucking hell, I was just about to come looking for you. You took ages.'

Emily threw the package onto Sally's lap and started the engine. 'Yeah. Seems people are wary of the police round here.'

Sally tore hungrily at the tissue. Five wraps spilled onto her lap, three contained a murky brown substance and two were lighter in colour and firmer. They were tightly wrapped in bits of torn up blue-and-white carrier bag.

'Five for forty?'

Emily shot a glance at Sally's lap. 'They obviously want you back.'

Sally looked like a starving person staring at a big plate of food. After the events of the past day, her pangs were back with a vengeance. 'Anywhere in Hythe will do,' she said, scooping the wraps back up and pushing them into her pocket.

'I told you I'd take you to Saltwood. I can drop you round the corner if you like.'

'Round the corner from where?'

'From where you're going.'

'So you know everything, do you?'

'Yeah. It's kind of my job to know everything. Although days like today, I wish I didn't.'

'What was going on earlier? Something happened on the Leas that had you lot all running towards it. How come you're not there?'

'We all have our jobs to do. I did a good few years of running towards stuff. Now I'm supposed to be one step ahead.'

'You didn't see that coming, though.'

'No. No one did. It sounded pretty serious.'

They drove to Saltwood in silence. It was one of the more affluent districts.

Sally broke the silence. 'I lied earlier.' Emily didn't reply. 'I have had a copper score for me before.'

'Your dad?' Emily said.

'You really do know everything! Did he tell you? I didn't think he would ever tell anyone about that.'

'No. You kind of both told me. You're quite alike, you know.'

'We're definitely not.'

'I mean you're both pretty see-through.'

'My mum always says I'm impossible to read. But then it takes an effort to get to know someone.'

'I expect it would take an effort to get to know you.'

Sally produced a tight smile. 'I guess I can be difficult. Most people will never understand what I need and why. I've given up trying.'

'That's true, and when they love you more than anything in the world, it makes it ten times more difficult.'

'My mum detests me. I'm everything she didn't want her little girl to become.'

'I wasn't talking about your mum. And I doubt that's true. You respected her enough to use her maiden name, after all.'

Sally shrugged. 'I needed a name so I wouldn't embarrass my dad. No one wants some loser crackhead as their little girl.'

'Your dad doesn't see you like that. He still sees his little girl.'

Sally shook her head and turned her face away, staring out of the window as the car joined the motorway and picked up speed. 'I knew that, early on when it was all starting to take hold. They were both in massive denial about the whole thing, but, fuck, I needed their help. I couldn't speak to Mum. I've never really been able to speak to her, she just flies off the handle, you know, doesn't listen. But I spoke to Dad. I told him I had a problem and I couldn't sort it out on my own.' Sally sniffed, and took a few moments to regain her composure. 'He did everything he could to help me. We tried everything. We talked about it, rowed about it, once he locked me in for ten days. They sent me to this rehab place out in the arse end of nowhere — did the lot. Nothing worked for long.'

'I've worked around the drug scene for as long as I care to think, Sally, and the one thing I always hear is just how it grabs you and it don't let go.'

'My dad had this idea. I guess we'd tried everything else. He insisted I go back and live with him and Mum and he would let me shoot up there, but only if he got it for me. He said if I was going to do it anyway then he might as well do what he could to make it as safe as possible. Fuck, he hated it and I mean hated it, but he went out and scored for me, used his own money. There was one rule.' Sally gazed towards the window. 'He said that I had to take it in front of him. I never wanted to, but when you get the hunger, you know . . . He never said a word, but I could see it in his face, the *hurt*. He might as well have stood there to watch me burn.'

'It didn't work then?'

'It just made me move out. It was the first time I ever saw my dad look at me like that — *real* disappointment. Not even that. He was disgusted with me and I couldn't cope with that. I've been in some states. It happens a lot and you very quickly lose all your self-respect, but he was the one person I just couldn't stand being that *weak* in front of. Since then I've barely been back. I can't even look him in the eye and when I do, I just feel like what we had, the father-daughter thing, I just feel that at that moment it kinda changed forever. Like there's no way back.'

Emily took a moment to compose an answer. 'I don't know everything, Sally. Don't tell anyone I said that, I have this reputation to protect.' Emily giggled and Sally managed a smile. 'But I do know that your dad loves you. I know that for absolute certain, and he misses you like crazy.'

'I miss him too.'

'And you need his help more than ever now, don't you?' Emily decided to steer the conversation towards what she really wanted to talk about.

'Just what do you think I need help with?'

'I talked to Lizzy.'

'When?'

'Since you last saw her.'

'You know Lizzy?'

'Enough for her to call me first when she realised the trouble she was in. She told me what happened, what you girls heard when she was under the bed and you were under the bath. You must have been terrified in there, Sally. Jesus.'

'I didn't hear anything.' Sally's hand went to the door handle and she sat forward a little.

'I can understand why you'd say that, Sally, but I know those flats well and you must have heard what he was saying. You have to think about what he did. I mean, it's massive, Sally, and we need to do something about it.'

'Why aren't you doing something about it, then?' Sally snapped. 'If you know what happened, if you know who was responsible, why the fuck are you here buying me drugs and running me home?'

'It's not as easy as that, Sally.'

'Yeah, it is. Someone does a crime, you know who it is, you go pick them up and throw away the key. Isn't that how it works?'

'What crime, Sally? I've got no victim until one of you tells me where he is. I've got no suspect until one of you names him formally. Without you, I've got nothing. If you help me then I can get him off the street and you won't have to be scared of him anymore, you won't have to be scared of anyone. I nick him now without your help — nothing will stick and he's back out in a few hours with the raging hump and a damned good idea who got him locked up.'

'I won't have to be scared of anyone? If I talk to you on record? You don't know everything after all.' Sally turned back to the window as they pulled off the motorway at the top of Hythe. 'You can drop me anywhere here. I'll walk.'

'Talk to me, Sally. Tell me what you know and I promise I will keep you safe.'

'Who are you to be making promises like that? You can't promise me anything. Please stop the car.'

Emily indicated and cars overtook her, blasting their horns as the Fiesta crawled along the side of the road. Emily was delaying Sally for as long as she could.

'You have to start looking after yourself, Sally. It starts here. This can be a turning point for you. I'll get you away from the area completely. Your dad will be on-board with it, you know he will.'

'Lizzy said no, didn't she? That's why you came after me. I can't help you either.' The Fiesta had now come to a halt and Sally pushed open the door.

'No, actually,' Emily said, and immediately wished she hadn't. 'Lizzy's on-board. She's going to talk to me formally once she's got a few bits sorted, and when she does I won't be the only person coming after you, Sally.'

Sally stared at Emily, who held her gaze. 'You were doing well, weren't you? Helping me out. The lift home, the talk about me. You'd almost built up a little trust with me there, but if Lizzy had talked to you, you'd be with her now and the threat to me would already be behind bars. You came to me to try and play me off against her. Well, I'm not that stupid.' Sally got out and stood by the door.

'I just want to keep you safe!' Emily shouted. She sounded desperate.

'Then leave me alone and don't mention this to my dad. If he finds out, I'll be gone, back into town, and you will have destroyed the one safe house I have. And besides, I'm not sure how he would feel about you buying me drugs.'

Sally pushed the door firmly shut.

Emily watched her walk away. The indicator ticked in the sudden silence. She swore. Her last chance had just walked away.

CHAPTER 29

Helen Webb had her phone in her hand when it erupted into life. The number on the screen had a Maidstone area code. She wasn't used to being cut off from events and she hadn't enjoyed the last couple of hours, wondering whether her career was over.

'Helen, it's Deputy Chief Constable Darren Lewis here.'

Helen raised her eyebrows. She hadn't expected the second most senior officer in the entire force to call her personal mobile phone.

'Sir!'

'Have you been kept in the loop today? I know you've gone home. Your office said you are feeling unwell?'

'Er, yes, sir, that's right. I came over a little unwell. Maybe I've been working too hard.'

The DCC ignored the comment. 'The chief was on your patch today, Helen, as you are aware. You were due to attend the same event, I believe?'

'That's right, sir, I was.'

'Helen, this may come as a bit of a shock to you, but there was an incident at that event. Someone approached and opened fire, and the chief has been injured. We think he was the target.'

'Jesus!' Helen was truly shocked. Of course she had known of the threat, but suddenly the seriousness hit home. She hadn't believed that the chief would actually get hurt. She'd imagined some bungled attempt, the offender shot by police. Not this.

'I know. It's a shock to us all.'

'How is he?'

'He's very ill, Helen. He was shot in the chest. It's touch and go. He's been airlifted to Kings, and we'll know a lot more once they can get him assessed in the right environment.'

'Jesus,' Helen said again. She bit her lip and looked round her empty kitchen.

'Look, I know it's a shock, I know you're not feeling well and this is a bit of a bolt from the blue, but would you be fit enough to return to work? We need someone to run this thing from Langthorne House. I am facing a barrage from the press up here at HQ and I can't really get away. I know you have the experience . . . and it wouldn't be forgotten.'

'Of course I can.' Helen had gathered her thoughts a little. Yes, it was a shock, in large part because she had been the one to put the chief in harm's way. She struggled to feel any sympathy for the chief. Twice, he had put her on the chopping board. He'd played her very well, covering his own ineffectiveness during this force's darkest hour, and was setting her up to take the fall for it. She was merely returning the favour. Having the DCC begging her to come back and save the day was a better result than she had dared hope for.

'That's great, Helen. Like I said, I won't forget your help. I will send a firearms team to pick you up.'

'A team? They didn't get the shooter in, then?'

'No. There's still a very real threat. The offender made off on a motorbike. We lost him somewhere on the towpaths by the Hythe canal, and we have the area locked down as we speak. I have Inspector Lance running that on the ground. You'll need to make contact with him. He can give you a full update.'

'Understood. Don't worry about releasing a firearms team to come and get me, I can drive myself in. Sounds like we can't really spare the resources until this man's in custody.'

'We can't be sure that he's working alone, Helen. This could all be part of a bigger plot. I can't guarantee your safety.'

'Don't worry. I'll make my own way in. I can probably slip under the radar better in my own car than in those blacked-out four-by-fours they drive.'

'Fine. Look, I have to go. Keep in touch, Helen. Your office has my direct number and obviously I have yours.'

'Understood.' Helen smiled.

CHAPTER 30

'That's it! It's gotta be.' PC Steve Goddes brought the car to an abrupt stop. A black bike was lying on its side, the front wheel skewed at an angle. It was lying half-hidden in some shrubs at the edge of the thick woodland that lined parts of the canal. There were fresh drag marks along the gravel towpath leading to it. 'We should call it in,' he said.

Cavan Kendall nodded. 'We should. They're going to be pissed that we're still out looking, though.'

Back at the nick, whoever was in charge had taken a breath and realised they had a lot of beat cops out in brightly marked cars looking for a man who had just shot two officers. The area was now flooded with firearms officers and everyone else had been told to leave, and to assist with road closures and cordons. Neither Steve nor Cavan were very keen on standing at a barrier for hours on end, so they had kept searching, keeping outside the area the firearms team were now looking to get sterile.

Cavan shrugged, radio in his hand. 'Zulu Echo Three, Three control.'

'Echo Three, Three go ahead.'

'Control, we are at the towpath, east of Hythe in line with the golf course. We have an abandoned black motorcycle with fresh drag marks half concealed in woodland, close to the canal bank, no signs of any other persons or vehicles at this time, but we haven't investigated too closely.'

'*Received that, Zulu Yankee One Zero, did you receive the last?*' Zulu Yankee One Zero was the call sign for Inspector Barry Lance, who had been designated Bronze Commander.

'*Yankee One Zero, confirm we have a sighting of the bike?*'

'*Zulu Echo Three, Three are reporting an abandoned bike matching the description with fresh drag marks. It's on the towpath, but further along, just within the search area, sir.*'

'*Received, control, I didn't think we had anyone searching that area?*'

Cavan and Steve exchanged a glance. 'Here comes the bollocking.'

'*Have them remain in their vehicle. I want them to withdraw to the entrance to that road or the obvious access point and effectively manage a cordon from that point. They are to pull away with any sign of movement around that bike, or any aggression towards them. I'm sending a firearms team over on flash.*'

'*Zulu Yankee Three, three did you receive the last?*'

'Yes, yes.'

'Well, that's put the cat among the pigeons. You reckon he's in here somewhere?' Steve scanned the woodland area from the car window. The area was dense in places but too small to hide in for long. Their man would look to move away from the canal altogether. He would either use one of the numerous places to cross, over the golf course and towards the sea, or back towards the road where the two officers had been instructed to stand. Cross this road and you could get lost in the tight streets and homes of Hythe town.

'Who knows? You can get anywhere you like from there, it's a big old area to search,' Cavan said.

'True, but he won't get far on foot, not quickly at least.'

'Right on cue!' Cavan smiled and leaned out of his window, peering up at a low-flying helicopter that hung overhead. Steve suddenly realised that the Bronze Commander would no doubt be looking at a live feed from the helicopter's camera, mounted underneath and able to turn 360 degrees with high-definition clarity. They hadn't driven away as they had been instructed.

'We should get out of here, before we get in any more trouble.'

* * *

Back at headquarters in Maidstone, DCC Darren Lewis was also watching the feed from his office. His PA stood next to him with her arms crossed. He had four minutes until he was due to give another update to the press, and right now there was nothing much new to give them.

'Excuse me, sir.' The door to Darren's office was usually open — he hated working any other way. He saw Detective Chief Inspector Steve Jones standing on the threshold.

'Steve! Come in. Did you get greyer, man?'

Steve's hand automatically went to his head. 'We're all getting greyer, sir!'

Darren turned his attention back to the monitor. On screen, the camera had zoomed out to show two plain vehicles. A third vehicle, carrying the more traditional "Battenberg" markings ejected a police search dog and its handler. They immediately started a sweep along the path, starting from the bike and walking outwards, the dog leading the way, a firearms team with raised assault rifles backing him up. The helicopter was keeping the search team dead centre, occasionally zooming in and holding when they entered the thicker parts of the wood.

'Anything good on?' Steve joked. He had a strong Welsh accent.

'Not really. Daytime telly is always a bit shit. How you doing, Steve?'

'I'm okay. We're getting regular updates on the boss. He's a tough, cantankerous old shit, sir, with respect. He'll be just fine, I reckon.'

'And if he isn't, maybe you could write his obituary.' Darren smiled again, his attention still on his screen.

'You know, I think he'd like that.'

'It might need a little work, but there's no one better placed.' Darren was referring to the fact that the current chief of Lennokshire Police had spent some time in Wales, working as part of their serious and organised crime group, and then he had headed up child exploitation for the whole of South Wales police. He had needed to rely on having good people around him, and one of those had been Steve Jones. Steve had been promoted twice with John Stone's blessing while working on the investigative side of child exploitation. Steve owed him. They weren't friends — John Stone neither needed nor wanted friendship — but they respected each other, and Steve had been offered an opportunity not to be refused when he followed his old boss down to Lennokshire.

'This is going to take a while, isn't it?' Steve said, knowing the answer.

'Yeah, these firearms boys can't be taking risks. It's a big area too.'

'I don't see him ditching his bike and then staying too close to it anyway, do you?'

'No, but we have to be sure.'

'Of course.'

'We're doing some checks on the bike's chassis number, but it's probably nicked. Helen Webb should shortly be established as Silver, so we can expect stuff to start happening then. She doesn't mess around, that woman.'

'I heard she was on her way down there. Sir, I need to talk to you, if I may, just a few moments of your time.'

Darren turned his attention away from the monitor and met his colleague's stern gaze.

'This must be serious indeed,' he said, still continuing to smile. 'No problem. Anne, would you mind giving us a second?'

The PA nodded and stepped out.

'What's so urgent? I need to be out speaking to the press right now, Steve.' He checked his watch as he spoke.

'It's about Helen Webb.'

'Helen Webb?'

'Yes.'

'You still look serious. You have a problem with the area commander?'

'Not really, not personally anyway. I don't really know her, to be honest. I just know that the boss had an issue with her. Part of his day down there was going to be spent speaking to Helen.'

'Speaking to her?'

'He was telling her to step down. He was going to let her walk away, but he had enough to get rid of her if she refused. He was proper pissed. I know he can be quite abrupt, but he was even worse than usual.'

'He told you this?'

'Yes.'

'That's not like him, to speak out about that sort of thing, not before she even knew.' Darren tilted his head a little, clearly unconvinced.

'I agree, and I think it shows just how rattled he was.'

'Okay . . . ?'

'I spoke to Helen's PA. He met with her before he left for the ceremony. After the meeting, Helen went out. She called her PA to tell her she wasn't coming back in, that she was feeling unwell. At some point before she went home, she made a call to your Bronze Commander. She said she'd reassessed the security needs for the ceremony and stood the armed personal protection team down. Barry Lance's team were searching some missing person's house when the shooting started. The bloke with the gun was tackled by a beat copper in his dress uniform, who took a bullet for his troubles.'

'And you don't think this is circumstantial?'

'The boss has been doing some work on Helen. I don't know the full ins and outs of it, he'd said far too much to me as it was, but if you were to speak to someone at PSD they might know a bit more about it.'

'PSD?'

'Yeah, someone senior I would guess. I'm pretty sure the boss had them doing some work on Helen. He never said it directly but he more than hinted, if you know what I mean. It has to be relevant — us detectives don't really do circumstantial.'

Darren rubbed at his chin. 'That sounds like good advice. So, what? We think she was somehow involved in the shooting of the chief constable?'

'That is quite a leap. But she had a meeting in which she fell out rather badly with him and faced losing her job. Maybe she was aware of the threat to the boss, and did what she could to move away our resources.'

'That's not such a leap.'

There was a soft tap, and Darren's PA stood in the doorway. 'Sir, the press are waiting. You know what these people are like. I'm so sorry to interrupt.'

'Don't be, it's not a problem. I'll follow you out.'

His PA left the door open.

'Thanks, Steve. I just need to deal with these cretins from the press and then I can get more of a handle on this.'

'You have Helen down there leading this thing from Langthorne House?'

'I do, yeah. There's not too much I can do about that right now, to be honest. I think we're going to have to let this play out, but at least I'm a lot more aware of the background now. If she steps out of line, I will be on it. I don't have the resources to deal with her while all this other stuff is going on. It'll have to be something that's done slow time.'

'Understood,' Steve said.

'For now, could you stay by the monitor? I won't be long but if anything significant happens you have my absolute permission to come and pull me out of there. That okay?'

'No problem.'

The DCC left and Steve Jones turned back to the monitor, still showing a close-up image of the search teams of six armed officers. They remained in tight formation, shouting instructions at bemused dog walkers who could be seen being hastily patted down then moved to another part of the open area by a second team of armed officers. One thing Steve felt sure of, as he watched the team disappear into a dense clump of trees and the helicopter's camera panned back out: this was not going to be resolved peacefully.

CHAPTER 31

Kane Forley grinned, even though the door had opened to reveal a snub-nosed pistol held at head height.

'This how you greet all your guests?' Kane said.

'You need to turn round and fuck off, right now.' Ed Kavski's voice was shaking with rage.

'Can't do that. This town is crawling with cops.'

'That's why you need to fuck off. What the fuck do you think you are doing coming here?'

'Where else would I go?' Kane thrust his hands behind his back and leant forward as if to inspect the weapon more closely. 'If you had agreed to speak to me I would have told you that this was always part of the grand plan. You might even have been able to talk me out of it. Instead, we now have to have this rather tiresome exchange on the doorstep of your exclusive residence. The last thing you want to be doing on a day like this is to be stood at your own front door, in public view,' Kane stepped back a little, 'With a gun in your hand.'

Ed hesitated, but not for long. He kept the gun raised and moved backwards into the hallway. Kane shrugged, and then stepped in after him, grimacing briefly as he stood on his left leg.

'Nice place. I don't suppose the kettle's on?'

'What plan?' Ed growled. 'Just start talking.'

'Pardon?'

'This *grand* plan. What do me and this place have to do with it?'

'Ah. Well, you will know some of it at least. I have no doubt that Tommy was on the phone to you by the time I got back to my bike.'

Ed sneered. 'You turned up off your face on coke, talking shit about taking out the chief constable of Lennokshire Police and wanting a shooter off him. Sensibly, he told you to fuck off.'

Kane sniffed. He seemed bigger than Ed remembered him, in every sense. He was a more imposing figure somehow. Ed had met him earlier in the year when he'd become aware that they had a common enemy in George Elms, and that Kane wanted him dead. Ed had helped Kane. He had put him in touch with the man who could supply the tools, and with a couple of blokes at Langthorne House who owed him favours. When Kane had come to him, he had been a sinewy mass of barely contained anger, and Ed wasn't sure if he wanted to get involved with him. Tommy Cotter had always said that Kane would cause them problems, but since Kane was taking all the risks, Ed hadn't been too bothered.

Kane was different now. He was even more unpredictable, still sniffing the Class A drug that fuelled his anger and wrecked his judgment, but more solid, less stringy. Kane wore black leathers. He'd unzipped the top half and it hung round his waist, loosely tied at the arms. A plain white T-shirt was stuck to his chest with sweat, revealing a muscled torso. A large black rucksack was on his back.

Ed stood facing him. 'You must have known that if you came here I would shoot you in the face rather than let you in. I had you down as cleverer than that.'

'You didn't though, did you? Shoot me in the face, I mean, and I'm in, aren't I? You're not that stupid. This town is jammed full of very nervous, very excitable coppers. You wouldn't want a gunshot and a body in your house today, would you? Or worse, have to get rid of it by getting out of the town? That ain't gonna happen, is it? I imagine the roads out are blocked. They'll be searching anyone that tries to leave Hythe.'

'So why run here? Why not run as far away as you fucking can? Give them a bigger area to search, less chance of finding you?'

'Because they're so predictable. They have systems — standard operating procedures they call them — for just about every type of incident. Today, for example. I left them my bike to find. Soon as they do, they stick a pin in a map and start working away from it. Slowly. Fucking hands and knees to start with, sticking their noses through just about everyone's house and garden. They'll have this town terrified, because they're fucking terrified themselves.' Kane's face lit up, and his eyes were wide and excited. 'If I can get to their chief, if I can shoot him in broad daylight when he's stood mourning the last six coppers I took out, they have to know I can get to any one of them, at any time.'

'But they have George Elms for that. That's what you wanted, you stitched him up good. Why would you make them think it might not be him?'

'Because they weren't scared anymore. I had them all terrified, one bastard shot and dying in the car park on the way home, one bleeding out under his fucking motorbike. I had them dying while sitting in their cars or turning up to 999 calls. They had never felt fear like it. *That* was what I wanted. It weren't just about George Elms. And when Elms went away, they stopped looking over their shoulders. They went back to normal. Well, it ain't normal. I'm still here and I can still get to them whenever I fucking want to.' Spittle gathered at the corners of his mouth.

'Tommy was right about you. You're a fucking liability, and you're going to put us all under the spotlight.'

'Not you. Not him either, just me. Tommy did me a favour, Ed. He wouldn't give me a clean one, so he forced me to use the same cannon that shot them officers, the one they never got back. They're gonna work that out. Can you imagine the questions that will come up when they do? And when they find my crash hat in the bushes at the end of your road, they'll get the DNA off that and it will match those six executions. Can you imagine the fear!' Kane's face was twisted, he was breathing heavily. 'It'll be worse than when they thought Elms was on the rampage. Then, they had an idea who was doing it. They had someone to chase. I'll have them again, Ed. I'll have every one of them back under my spell, terrified.'

'You're losing it, mate.'

'Am I?' Kane stepped closer to Ed, who still had the gun raised. He pushed his forehead into the barrel. 'They don't know me, Ed. There's no record of me anywhere on their system, no DNA to compare, no fingerprints. You told me yourself that as far as they were concerned, I didn't exist. That's how I know I can do what I want, because they're not looking for *me*. As long as I stay off their system, I'm just a ghost.'

'George Elms knows who you are.'

Kane laughed. 'Fucking right he does. It'll be eating him up inside. If he so much as whispers my name to his pet rat inside that stinking prison, I'll wipe out his family and I'll make sure he gets to see the highlights.'

'They'll release him. Because of you.'

Kane took a step back. Ed lowered the gun slightly.

'I'm banking on it. That way I get to destroy him all over again.'

'But you need to get out of this mess first. You reckon you can wait it out here? Like they'll just give up and go home when they're done?'

200

'Not at all. We've got three hours max until they're here. The bike and the crash hat are a reasonable distance apart. When they find those, they'll drop and do fingertip searches round them. It'll slow them up a little but you and I need to be a long way from here by then.'

'You and I? What you talking about? I'm not going anywhere.'

'Jesus, Ed, are you really that stupid? With your background, I thought you'd be way ahead of me here. They'll be going house to house, taking details. This place is on the books at Lennokshire Police, right?'

'How do you know that?'

'Same way I know where you live, Ed. You got sloppy. Everyone out there knows who you are, where you are, and who you've got in your corner. So, we give them some shadows to chase and *then* I disappear. This way they know that I was right under their fucking noses. And that means I can be again.'

'I know how these people work. You're playing with fire, Kane. They'll throw a match at you and watch you burn.'

'Of course you know. This is your bag ain't it? You're still one of them when it comes down to it. You're so certain that all you have to do is throw people, forensics, search teams — the lot — at a problem and it gets solved. Fuck, I'm not even being careful. I made sure I put some good prints in that crash hat to go with the masses of DNA. They've got everything they need. But they're still dying, ain't they? And it wasn't the rank and file this time, was it? It was the top dog with his own personal protection team of armed men. When they don't catch me, when they know they were wrong about Elms, when they see that no one is safe, that's when I'll have them on their knees, all of them. Get someone scared enough, you cripple them completely.'

'This still has nothing to do with me. I don't need to go anywhere.'

'You really believe that? What will it take though, Ed, for it all to come crashing down? How long till they stick the press release out asking if anyone's seen someone make off from a crashed motorbike in Hythe? I know I got seen limping up your road, probably even up your drive, Ed, it seems like that sort of neighbourhood. Do you really think you can stand up to the scrutiny of your house getting turned over? I don't reckon that's the only piece you've got here, is it?' Kane gestured at the pistol that now hung by Ed's side.

Ed rolled it on his palm, looked down at it, contemplating Kane's words. 'So this is your big idea? Turn up on my doorstep, make it my problem, and just hope I can get you out of Hythe?'

'Yup. We all know about your links with the coppers, senior ones too. You make a call, they make a call, and we're away from here.'

'Fuck.'

Ed and Kane still stood in the hallway. It had a small step up into the living area. Ed sat on it, using the end of the pistol to rub his head, and considered his options. He would like nothing more than to put a bullet through this piece of shit, but Kane was right. His house *was* going to be searched. If he refused, the best he could hope for was that they'd sit outside while someone went and got a warrant, if Helen hadn't already stitched him up.

'This is where it all falls down,' Ed managed, shaking his head. 'This big idea that you have. This is where it becomes impossible.'

'Nothing's impossible. A year ago, I swore I wouldn't rest until this police force paid for what they did to me and my family. Look at me now.'

'But don't you see where you are? You've become this fucking parody of yourself, hell-bent on killing every copper you come across, using the chief as a trophy kill. And now you want one of the most senior coppers to help you out, to come pick you up. She's not stupid, Kane. She won't fall for that.'

'I never said it was going to be easy for you, Ed, but you're a clever chap. Maybe you don't tell her the details, maybe you just say that you and an associate need to be out of here and she needs to do what she can to facilitate that. She knows you might reveal your little arrangement.'

'She still might not help.'

Kane slid his rucksack off his back. 'Mind if I go and change?'

Ed flicked the pistol to signify that he could leave. He watched Kane go. The only option open to him was to shoot that fucker himself. But not here.

CHAPTER 32

Helen Webb's phone burst into life. It was the cheap Nokia she used for Ed Kavski, and she couldn't run it through the car's system. She pulled over and fished round in her bag. She had considered ignoring it. But he might know something about the shooter, maybe even where he had gone or, more importantly, if he had managed to get away clean.

'Mr Kavski, it seems I'm being called back into work. There's been a nasty incident, I'm told.'

'We have a problem.'

'I know that, Ed. Do you have any update on your source? Did he get away clean?'

'No.'

'What do you mean? You haven't had any update or if he's been caught?'

'He hasn't been caught. He's here.'

Helen reeled. 'He's at your house?'

'Yeah, and look — we've lost control of him. He's going to bring this whole thing down unless you do what you can.'

'Wait. *We've* lost control of him?' Helen was angry. 'This morning I didn't know this fucker existed, and now you call me and tell me *we've* lost control of him. If he's at your place, I suggest you deal with him. Don't you have the perfect opportunity to make sure he can't speak to anyone *ever* again?'

'It's not as simple as that—'

Helen cut in. 'Seems very simple to me.' Ed's apparent weakness made her feel that she was back in charge.

'He's clever,' Ed said, almost apologetically. 'He knows his position and he knows ours. The gun that shot the chief is the same one that killed the officers in Langthorne. He's left his DNA in a helmet close to his bike. He wants your lot to know that he's the man who did those jobs, not George Elms.'

'Why would he do that?'

'Look, it's complicated. *He's* fucking complicated, but that don't matter right now. Right now you need to get me and him out of here. I don't need you to get us far, just far enough that I can clean this up without one of your search teams knocking on my door.'

Helen sighed again. 'Jesus. I don't know what you think I can do. I can't just have someone come pick you up, can I?'

'No. You'll have to come here yourself and take us away. No one's going to ask questions of you driving in and out of a sterile area, are they? You can go where you want, when you want.'

'I have to have a fucking reason, Ed,' Helen hissed. 'I have to be able to tell them why!'

'Then think of one. We don't have long, he's made sure of that, he's forced our hand. But once you get me away from here, I can take back control. For the both of us.'

'Jesus fuck, Ed, I need to think. I'll call you back.'

Ed started to say something but Helen switched the phone off and threw it onto the passenger seat as if it had suddenly become toxic. She tried to think.

This time the ringtone came through the car's speakers. It was her office calling.

'Helen Webb.' Her voice was tired, almost resigned.

'Ma'am?' Sure enough it was her excitable PA.

'Hey, Jean.'

'Ma'am, I understand you are on your way back in.'

'That's right, but I think I might go straight to the scene. Is there a rendezvous point assigned?'

'Yes, I'll find it, but I wanted to give you an update that's just come through to me here.' Jean's tone was ominous, her voice breathy. Helen knew her PA very well indeed and Jean was definitely building up to something that wasn't going to please her.

'What's the matter, Jean?'

'I'm sorry, ma'am, but it's become a murder case. The chief passed away a few minutes ago.'

Helen grabbed the steering wheel for support. This had all got out of hand, but now she had a chance to put it right. Or at least to cover her tracks.

'Did anyone speak to him? Before he died, I mean. Did they get a chance . . . ?' Helen's voice petered out.

'Well, I don't see how anyone could. I don't think he ever came round, ma'am.'

Helen concentrated on softening her tone. 'Jesus, I'm sorry to hear that, Jean. We need to focus on finding the man responsible, and then maybe we can all get our heads round what's happened.'

'Yes, ma'am. Quite.' Jean's voice shook with emotion. 'There's just been so much tragedy recently, so much.'

'There has. It will get better, Jean. We need to keep it together and see this one out. It will get better.'

'I hope you're right.' Jean sniffed.

'What's the latest on the ground, Jean? I'm playing catch-up here a little.'

'They've found a bike in Hythe. They're pretty certain it belongs to the man we want. They've started searching the area. Hythe's pretty much closed off, so we're getting a lot of questions from the media and a lot of upset residents who aren't being allowed home.'

'I bet. Is there anything out to the news people yet?'

'Social media only, but the main media are quoting them. We've just said there's an ongoing incident in Hythe and asked for patience — the standard stuff. There was talk here about putting out an appeal for information but we don't want to panic people, so there's some discussion about the wording.'

'Don't do that, Jean. Nothing goes out without my sign-off — I'll get something together. I need to speak to Barry Lance on the ground and I'll be better placed to get something done from there. I'm on this number any time you need me.'

'Thank you, ma'am. Understood.'

* * *

Kane Forley had changed into a fitted, crisp white shirt and a pair of grey dress trousers, plus black formal shoes. He'd washed his face and slicked back his hair.

Ed Kavski stood in the kitchen with his back to him. Kane noted that his weapon was on the kitchen counter, as though he'd forgotten about it. 'I feel a lot fresher,' he said cheerfully.

Ed looked out over his garden to the distant sea beyond. 'I'm going to miss this place.'

'I heard you speaking to our police friend,' Kane said.

'Yes. She's coming for us.'

'No, she isn't.' Kane was still smiling.

Ed turned to face him. 'What do you mean "no she isn't"?'

'She isn't coming, Ed. At least, if she's true to form she won't.'

'What are you talking about?'

'Predictable, Ed. What was I saying? They're completely predictable. Why would she come here? It's all over for her, and you, whether she comes here or not.

There's going to be a lot of attention on this house, it'll all come out in the wash and she knows it. She'll be using this little bit of time to give herself a head start, my friend. You said it yourself, if she comes here, she just gives me another high-profile target and if there's one thing I can't resist—'

'So what's the plan now?' Ed cut in.

'Now that you've made the call I needed? I just need to leave your door blowing in the wind, my bike leathers where they are, lying on your bed, and leave your body bleeding out on this expensive-looking floor.'

Kane's right hand was in the bag. Ed's eyes went to where his pistol lay on the work surface, but Kane had already brought his weapon from his bag and levelled it.

The weapon spat two bullets in quick succession. Both slugs ripped through Ed's body, shredding internal organs before emerging to make two neat holes in the floor-to-ceiling glass windows. Ed Kavski still looked puzzled as his heart stopped and his lungs emptied for the last time.

Kane Forley dropped his weapon back into his bag and pulled out a polished metal badge with neat black lettering. He attached it to his right breast pocket. It read, "Kane Mitchell, Front of House, Hythe Imperial Hotel."

CHAPTER 33

'Oh! You scared me,' Sally's mother, Denise, said.

'Sorry, I didn't mean to.' Sally hadn't meant to be seen at all. She had seen her mother arrive home, and had concealed herself beside the porch. Her mother must have seen her from the drive and must therefore have seen Sally scrambling on her hands and knees, trying to hide.

There was an awkward pause. Denise was carrying a small cardboard box with a piece of cake in it. She fumbled with her keys, dropped them and turned to Sally. 'Are you coming in then?'

'If you don't mind,' said Sally.

'Of course I don't,' Denise snapped. 'You know you're always welcome here,' she added, sounding more friendly. She pushed open the door and Sally followed her inside.

'What time is Dad home?'

Denise sighed as she checked her watch. 'Well, your father should be home by now, but there's been some incident and he's staying on for a bit. I have no idea how long.'

'Okay.'

'There's something going on in Hythe. I was working down at the shop and they even stopped me and searched my car, I don't know what they were looking for but they carried on even when I mentioned your father.'

Sally knew that her mother was a volunteer at one of the charity shops in Hythe's high street. She had been there for years. Sally had spent some time working there as part of one of her many rehabilitations. She'd hated it, as well as the group of bitter old women who spent the day complaining about each other and eating cake. Judging by the box her mother carried, nothing much had changed.

'Don't worry. You can hide upstairs until he's home if you like.' Denise smiled.

'Deal,' said Sally. 'But I think I'll make a cup of tea first, you know, to take upstairs with me.'

'Good idea. I'll go and get changed now then, so I don't have to go up there again. Mine's black, no sugar.'

Sally walked through to the kitchen. It was as immaculate as ever, everything in its place. Sally was wary of moving anything. She wasn't a tidy person. Maybe she had been once, she couldn't remember.

She wiped her face with a piece of kitchen towel. Her back was sweaty. Her body was aching for drugs. She hadn't been this long away from it since a court appearance eighteen months ago when she had been held in a cell. She had gone cold turkey a few times and knew what to expect. It would get better, but it would get a whole lot worse before then. Sally didn't know what to do. She could think about nothing but the heroin and crack cocaine in her pocket. Tiny little wraps that would make her feel better, if only for a short time. But she was here, at home, and she had promised herself that she would never use here again. Maybe she could weather it out? She knew her dad was going to be pleased to see her — sickeningly pleased — and she could try and spend some time with him. She would wait until her parents went to bed before she had some of her medication. But not until then. She would just have to put up with the aches, the sweats.

The kettle boiled. She knew it was important to keep busy. She'd drunk a lot of strong coffee the last time she'd gone cold turkey. The act of making it took her mind off her pain, for a few minutes at least. It forced her to stand up, to concentrate on something other than the craving.

The phone ringing made her jump so hard she dropped a mug, and it smashed on the tiled floor. 'Shit!'

'Sally?' her mum called down from upstairs. 'You okay?'

'Yeah, sorry. Damn phone made me jump.'

'Can you get it? It'll just be your dad. He'll make an effort to get back if he knows you're here.' The shower was running and Sally heard her mother step into the bathroom.

Sally answered the phone.

'Hello?'

'Sally? Thank fuck!'

'Lizzy?' Sally began to whisper, but there was no need. Her mother couldn't hear.

'Yeah, it's Lizzy. Sally, I need to talk to you.'

'You're okay?'

'Yeah, no probs. You okay?'

'Fine. How did you get this number?'

'What you mean? I thought you knew. I called it the other night when you needed picking up. It was on your jail gear when they kicked you out. It had "Dad" next to it so I assumed it was someone who might help. I know you said your dad's dead, but, whatever.'

Sally vaguely remembered that Lizzy had told her she'd called someone to come pick her up. They had been smoking strong weed, so the conversation was pretty hazy.

'My stepdad,' Sally lied.

Lizzy said, 'Whatever,' again. Then, 'Sally, we need to meet up. I've spoken to Lee, everything's cool, he ain't even mad at us.'

'You've spoken to Lee?' Sally had raised her voice, and she looked around her.

'Yeah, like I say, he ain't even pissed. He wants a sit down to get some stuff sorted, talk about what happened. He knows that we was in the flat earlier and that, and he thinks we might have misunderstood, is all.'

'A misunderstanding? He said this was just a misunderstanding?'

'Yeah, thassit.'

'Come on, Lizzy! You're not stupid. We know Lee, don't we? He doesn't work like that. Nothing's ever just a misunderstanding.'

'Sal, I've been with him today, he's cool now that we've had a bit of a chat. He was pissed at first 'cause I lied to him, said I weren't there, but he knew. That fat twat down the road had dobbed us in. But if you come back we can have a talk. I reckon Lee will chuck a bag or two in for us, you know? We can have a good smoke and a relax. Have you got any? You must be feeling shit.'

Despite all that Sally knew about Lee, she considered going back to the flat for a smoke. 'I feel okay, Lizzy. I'm fine here. I'm going to stay here for a bit, just to work some stuff out. I'll come and see you soon, though. I know where you are.'

Lizzy didn't reply.

Sally caught sight of herself in the hallway mirror and turned away, disgusted.

* * *

Lizzy shrugged. Lee rubbed his index finger and thumb together, and Lizzy nodded.

'Listen, Sal, he's going to need that cash back. You know Lee and money. We fucking panicked, yeah? I know that, you know that, and we snatched some. I told him that, but he wants it back.'

Sally bit at her bottom lip. 'I don't have it, Lizzy. I had to get here and I had to get some shoes and that. I don't have it any more.'

'You spent it all?'

Lee had been looking at the floor, and his head jerked up.

'No, I got like sixty left or something, I think.' Sally actually wasn't sure but she knew she had more than three twenty pound notes.

'That's perfect. I said to him you took sixty. He don't know what's in there, does he? Not without going all the way back through what he thinks he's owed, and he ain't gonna do that. You turn up with the sixty and it's job done, we're all sorted.'

'I can't come back, Lizzy, not now. I gotta get my head down, have a think about what's going on and then I'll let you know. I can't come down now, it's been a long fucking day.'

'Jesus, Sal. Listen to me, you gotta get that money back. He's being good to me, he's apologetic, a bit humble like, but that money — you know what he's like. It will be a real sticking point, and he's only got me here to blame. Alright, Sal, I get what you're saying. Have a few days to get your head straight. Can we meet up though? Me and you? I can get away from here, tell him some shit to keep him sweet. I think he's out on his chores for a while anyway.'

'I can't. Look I'm all fucked up, I can't get out tonight, okay? Maybe in a couple of days.'

Lizzy shook her head at Lee. He was grinding his teeth. 'Listen, Sally, just you and me meet up, okay? I need that money back. I don't want to take the brunt, Sally — that's not fair, is it? You got to help me out.'

Sally exhaled. 'Yeah, I can meet you,' Sally came back. 'I can give you the money back and you can give it to Lee. Then I can come and see you both in a couple of days or something.'

There was another silence, and Lizzy and Lee signalled to each other. Finally Lee nodded. 'That'll be okay,' said Lizzy. 'Where are you?'

'I can meet you somewhere.'

'Can't I just come to where you are? Rather than out on the street?'

'Nah, this isn't my place, it's not fair to be bringing people here for my shit. I can meet you at junction 11, the motorway services there, do you know it?'

There was another pause. 'Yeah, I think so. Stop 24 or something?'

'Yeah, that's it. There's a coffee shop in there, first place you come to on the left when you go through the doors. I can get there in an hour or so.'

'An hour?'

'Yeah, so around five.'

'See you there at five.'

Lizzy ended the call and looked at Lee. 'That okay? You okay to drop me up there? We'll get your cash and then she can come back with us if she wants.'

'You think this is about the money?' Lee's eyes were cold, and his whole demeanour changed. Lizzy was sitting on the bed and she slid away from him. He got to his feet and stood looking down at her.

'You said you wanted the money back at least.'

'I don't give a *fuck* about the money.' Lee punched her. Lizzy fell backwards. She grunted, shocked. Lee picked up one side of the duvet and pulled it over her, wrapping it around her, exposing the white tarpaulin sheet underneath. She tried to say something and he punched her again. He rolled her in the tarpaulin. Lizzy realised immediately what was about to happen. Her eyes opened wide and she tried to scream. It emerged as a husky moan. Lee produced a knife. It was an ugly thing, eighteen inches long and tapering to a fine point. He rolled Lizzy over so he could see her face, and look into her eyes.

Lee brought the knife down fast. He raised it and brought it down a second time. Beside himself with rage and frenzy, he stabbed again and again until Lizzy was still and the duvet was red with her blood.

* * *

Sally was back in the kitchen. Her mum appeared, dressed in a crisp white robe and dabbing her head with a towel.

'Was that your dad?'

'No, actually.'

'No?'

'It was a friend of mine. I gave her this number in case she needed to get hold of me. I've got some of my things at her place. I'm just going to pop out and pick them up.'

'Oh, okay.' Denise didn't believe her daughter, but knew better than to ask questions. 'Do you want me to take you?'

'No. No thanks, Mum. It's not far, I can get a taxi.'

'Oh, alright then. Well, as long as you'll be okay.'

Sally smiled. 'I'll be fine.'

CHAPTER 34

'Barry Lance.' Barry sounded rattled. Helen knew he wasn't a man who got rattled easily.

'Barry, it's Helen Webb. The DCC has asked me to head this thing up. I know you're on the ground. What's your update?'

'You're running this? I was reporting directly to Darren Lewis.'

'I just got off the phone with him. You'll be reporting directly to me from now on. Is there a problem?'

'There is a problem, ma'am, yes. We have an armed man somewhere in Hythe who has already shot two officers. If my team had been in place we wouldn't be in this situation now.'

Helen Webb took her foot off the accelerator. Her nose twitched in annoyance. 'Well, for now, we just need to get hold of the bastard. We can conduct a full review of our actions after it's done. I need your support, Barry, and I need it instantly, or my first job will be to find someone who will give it.' There was a silence. 'This is what you're trained for, Barry, but if you insist on making a point, I'll find another team.'

Barry sighed. 'What do you need to know?'

Helen smiled. 'Good man. I need you firing on all cylinders down there, Barry. I know you're the best man for the job. I need you and your team more than ever.'

'I'll pass that on.' Barry's tone was cool.

'What's the latest? I've been getting various updates, but it's all been third-hand.'

'We have an armed offender who made off from the Leas in Langthorne in the general direction of Hythe. The area was searched and we have located a motorbike, which appears to have been abandoned. We've cleared a hundred metres round the bike in every direction and cordoned it off for forensics. I've been down there and the bike has crash damage, which fits with what happened on the Leas. The offender got as far as he could on it before it broke down completely.'

'So maybe he has nowhere to go?'

'That's the thinking. He's been forced to ditch it on the canal path. He's made a half-hearted attempt at hiding it and then he's carried on, on foot.'

'The towpath? I know it reasonably well. Parts of it are wooded, aren't they?'

'Yeah, there are thick brambles, bushes, and woodland round where he ditched it, and of course there's the canal itself. We've got the dogs out. The handlers are confident that the dogs would have found someone if they'd been holed up, and the helicopter's done a run with the heat camera.'

'So are we extending the open-area search or looking at houses or buildings?'

'Both. The helicopter was high enough initially that you wouldn't be able to hear it, but it had to come down to help with the search round the bike. That might have prompted our man to force entry to a property, if he hadn't already. At the moment we're going street by street outwards from where the bike was found, with the helicopter constantly monitoring for movement. We're searching houses voluntarily if there are people in, and checking for signs of forced entry for those that aren't. I have a log here of houses we haven't been able to get into.'

'Sounds like you have it all under control.'

'It's labour intensive, slow-going. The team need to be on alert all the time. I've put out a request for more armed resources down here so I can swap them out.'

'Okay, I'll see where we are with that.'

'Appreciated.'

'I'm going into Langthorne House and then I'll make my way down.'

Barry was silent for a few moments. 'You're coming down here?'

'Well, yes. I won't stick my oar in, Barry, don't worry. I can make myself useful, deflect some of the stuff away from you so you can just continue running this thing.'

'I see.' Barry didn't sound convinced, but Helen didn't need him to be.

'I'll see you shortly.'

Helen ended the call as the BMW rumbled up to the speed-gates at Langthorne House. Eight feet high and thick steel, they formed part of the expensive new defences, erected in response to the cold-blooded murder of one of Langthorne's own in this car park. It created the illusion of safety and control.

CHAPTER 35

Stop 24 was a large site, a flashy new motorway service station near Hythe, with a glassy expanse of shopping units.

The customers hadn't arrived. The location was all wrong. It was too close to the Channel Tunnel station and the Port of Dover. Anyone needing refreshment would just stay on the motorway for another few minutes.

Sally peered out of the taxi's window. She couldn't see Lizzy.

'Do you mind waiting?' Sally leant said to the overweight driver.

'I can wait for a little while, darling, how long do you need?'

'Ten minutes?' In truth, she couldn't be sure. Lizzy wasn't the most reliable person at the best of times and she had clearly been under the influence of something when they had spoken earlier. Still, ten minutes should be enough time for Lizzy to get there and for Sally to convince her to come and stay with her in Saltwood. That was kind of as far as she had got with her plan. She knew it was risky, which was why she had wanted to meet away from the house. Lee Chivers had a way of getting into your head, of making you forget what he was really like. When both of them were safe, she could take some time to think.

'Ten minutes, darling. Call it eight quid to here.'

Eight quid. That was steep, but Sally needed him sweet and handed over a tenner. 'The change is for the wait, see you in ten.' She smiled reassuringly and pushed the door open. Her new trainers found the tarmac and the driver was already focused on his phone.

Stop 24 reminded her of an aircraft hangar. It was brightly lit and hushed. She looked up at four large flat-screen TVs fixed in a square in the middle of the central walkway. The screen facing her ran the BBC News channel with subtitles clumsily trying to keep up with a politician's bullshit.

The coffee shop was the first unit on the left. It wasn't the usual Costa Coffee or Starbucks, but some Italian-themed place that she hadn't heard of. Sally had once been into good coffee. A long-haired, handsome man greeted her with an expectant smile as she made her way into the almost-empty café.

'Hey,' she managed.

'Hey! What can I get you today?' The lad was about her age, a bit of a stoner she reckoned — she could tell them a mile off — but heathy-looking and with a cheerful smile. His name tag introduced him as Jake.

'Coffee, please. White.'

'Just the one?'

'Yeah, for now. I'm waiting for someone.'

'No problem. You want me to bring it over?'

'No thanks, I'll take it.'

Sally looked around for a table. She saw a lorry driver, tucked away round the side of the counter. A middle-aged couple with matching fleece jackets over shorts and wearing similar glasses, who Sally reckoned were foreign, and a younger couple close to the toilet door. Their toddler was standing on one of the chairs, pushing brown liquid around the table with a straw. Sally enjoyed people watching. When she had previously gone cold turkey, when the hardest part of that first week was over, she would sit on a bench in the middle of the town or on the Leas, or down the front, and just watch people. She liked to work them out, tell herself stories about them. It would take her mind off the rest of it, her hunger, the void that was left when the class A drugs were gone. She would sit and watch *normal* people going about their business. If she did it long enough she could begin to feel normal too.

She reckoned on a table close to the couple with the toddler. She knew they would soon be gone, and she wanted to be able to see out, and watch for Lizzy coming in.

Jake turned to place the coffee on the counter. 'There you go . . .' He tailed off, looking round his coffee shop.

But the girl with the greasy hair and pretty eyes had gone.

* * *

'Say a fucking word and I'll cut you,' Lee hissed. Sally had known it was Lee Chivers before she had even looked at the figure that had appeared at her side. She had just *known*. He'd said nothing, merely raised a hand with a knife concealed in the palm. A pretty knife. Sally remembered seeing it in the flat. She also remembered Lee demonstrating just how sharp it was.

Sally felt helpless. She thought about making a run for it, shouting for help, but she knew Lee. He would talk his way out. And Sally needed to find out where Lizzy was.

'What happened to Lizzy?' Sally asked as Lee took her hand and hurried them towards the exit.

'She's back at the flat.'

'Why didn't she come up here?'

'What makes you think you get to ask questions, Sal? You and me got a lot to talk about, ain't we? Seems you think you can use my flat when you want, hide in there and steal my money.'

'You better not have hurt her.'

Lee's grip on Sally's hand tightened until it hurt. She tried to pull it away and Lee pressed harder, until the pain became excruciating. 'This is just a chat, Sally, like what happened with Lizzy. We had a chat and she told me the truth, and it was all fucking sorted out. I need to know who you've spoken to today. She's back at the flat. She'd had a bag or two and she needed a bit of a rest up. We're going back there to do the same, just as soon as you talk to me about what you did today.' Lee released her hand.

'I got out, I scored, I went to a mate's house. That's it.'

'Who's your mate?'

'No one you know and they don't know you.'

'Where'd you score from?'

'A new setup, nothing to do with you.'

Lee took hold of Sally's hand again as they walked out through the double doors. A hundred metres away, the taxi driver saw them walk out of sight and muttered, 'Fucking skagheads,' and the taxi moved off in search of another fare.

The lorry cab closest to Sally had a noisy generator that kicked out hot diesel fumes. Behind the trailer was Lee's Mitsubishi pickup. He'd made damned sure she wouldn't see it when she arrived.

'Get in.'

'Where are you taking me?'

'I told you. We need to talk, all of us.'

'So I'm going back to the flat? Can't we meet her somewhere else?' Sally did her best to sound casual. 'We only ever seem to argue there. I don't want to argue with you any more, Lee. Maybe a neutral place would be better for us all.'

'Get in the fucking car,' Lee snapped. Sally was standing by the passenger door, with Lee immediately behind her. The knife was back out of his jacket, Sally could see it glinting. Her hand rested on the door handle.

She knew this was the point of no return. Once she was inside the car he would have complete control over her. She thought of Lizzy, and what he would do to her if she managed to get away. The generator in the lorry clattered away. The occupant would be settling in for the night. The last thing he would want was some girl banging on his door, screaming for help, a bloke with a knife behind her. He probably wouldn't even unlock the cab.

Sally pulled at the door. Lee walked round the car and dropped the knife into his door bin. As the engine turned over, he faced Sally with a dangerous smile.

'Put your seatbelt on, Sal. We don't want you getting hurt, do we?'

CHAPTER 36

Helen Webb used the public entrance to enter Langthorne House. A couple of punters stared at her as she clicked past. One of the counter staff had been sitting down and he hurriedly got to his feet. He needn't have bothered. Helen didn't acknowledge anyone, or even turn her head. She pushed her leather badge-holder at the sensor on the door. It didn't work at first, and she slapped it impatiently, cursing under her breath. The red light changed to green and she tugged the door open so roughly it collided with the wall.

The lift doors parted and Helen bustled into the confined space, jabbing at the button for the fourth floor, and ignoring the uniform officers nodding greetings. The doors clunked shut and she was on her own. She was relieved to find that the fourth floor was ghostly quiet. Her office door was closed, as she had left it, but the desk outside, which Jean normally occupied every second of the day, was empty. Even the lamp twisted over her keyboard that she used all day, was extinguished. It was all a little odd but it suited Helen. She wanted to get in and out again fast and the last thing she wanted was a conversation with anyone. Helen pushed her door. The first thing she saw was her monitor, lit up and unlocked, showing a page she didn't immediately recognise.

'Ma'am,' he said. His tone was confident and angry, certainly not that of someone who had just been caught out. Helen looked at the man facing her computer screen.

It took a few seconds to put a name to the face. 'Paul Bearn. What the hell are you doing in my office?'

'I needed your computer.' Paul replied calmly.

Using a senior officer's personal computer? He should be shitting bricks right now.

'You *needed* my computer? Do you realise the implications of coming in here and using my computer?'

'I do. Only too well.'

'I will be taking this up formally, PC Bearn. You will face action for this—'

'The implications,' Paul cut in, 'are a man released from jail. And, who knows, maybe you replacing him there.'

Helen's anger admitted a flicker of self-doubt, not quite panic — yet. Her eyes flicked back to her screen. She recognised what was there. 'You don't know what you're talking about.'

'Your PA helped me unlock your computer. She knew your password. I didn't even know you had children.'

'Why would you? Now I suggest you get out of here, PC Bearn, right now. Every second you delay will make things worse for you.'

'DC.'

'What?'

'DC,' Paul repeated. 'I'm a detective constable.'

'I don't really think that is the issue right now, is it?'

'I disagree. It's the detective part of me that has kept me going all this time. Despite you trying to keep me away from any sort of detective work, any work at all, actually, I carried on investigating, ma'am. I carried on investigating what happened that night when my mate got shot. You remember Sam, right?'

Helen sniffed. 'Of course I do.'

'Well, she was killed by someone, but it wasn't George Elms. I know that and, from looking at your computer, you knew it too.' Paul gestured at the monitor. 'This is the CSI database, where they upload all their findings from crime scenes. They then share with us what they need to share and your rank affects what you see, for the major stuff at least. Accessing it on your PC, for example, means that I can see anything I want to.'

'And what did you see that has filled you with this misguided view?' Helen sneered.

Paul bit his bottom lip. 'There's DNA evidence. From three of the crime scenes at least. The skipper who died holding on to his bike, the young lad dead in the alley, and from Sam's.'

'So?'

'It doesn't have a match, ma'am. You don't have to be a detective to know that this means George Elms is either taking the rap for someone else, or he was there but he wasn't working alone.'

'We found George's DNA at your friend Sam's scene, too, and he was holding the weapon that shot her when he was nicked. What do your detecting skills say about that? You cannot deny his involvement.'

'Why wasn't the fact that the DNA of another offender was found at all the scenes included in the investigation?'

'Who says it wasn't?'

'Your report to the Crown Prosecution Service is on your PC. Relatively well hidden, granted, but I found it in your outbox. The report was an attachment — you should clear them out more often, they're very good evidence — and it shows you didn't mention it at all.'

Helen sighed, she even smiled a little. 'Not on the email copy, I don't, no. We didn't have all the DNA work back by then and I got told off about sending it on email at all. Seems I should have sent it by more secure means. The complete case file is a hard copy which was driven over directly by two uniform coppers. It was literally under guard.'

'Who took it? And where's your copy? You must have kept one.'

Helen sniffed again.

'Of course.' She went over to the cabinet next to where Paul was standing. 'Do you mind?' she said.

There were no files in the drawer. It was a junk drawer, full of stuff that the chief superintendent had thrown in there during her time in the office, stuff she didn't need any more. Including her police issue steel baton.

Paul didn't see it coming. Even if he had, his left arm was limp and useless. But he wasn't even looking in her direction when the steel bar smashed into the left side of his skull. He fell back against the wall and slid to the floor.

Helen watched him make an untidy pile in the corner of her office. Her eyes were wide with the shock of what she had done. Blood trickled down the side of Paul's bald head. His breathing was erratic and laboured, his eyelids twitched, and his legs spasmed. Helen dropped the baton. The sound seemed to snap her out of her trance. She needed to leave. Now.

Helen started at her office windows. She turned the blinds in, making sure there were no gaps. Then she went over to a low cupboard with a table on top, positioned under her window. The door to the cupboard slid open. Behind it was a solid floor safe that was anchored to the steel skeleton of Langthorne House. She steadied her hands on the black metal dial and turned through the code. She reached inside. Paul uttered a moan and she checked over her shoulder. He was beginning to come round.

Helen grabbed hold of a blue document folder, pulled the flap open and ran her fingers through the first few documents. She tipped it up and a pen drive slid into her hand. She had found what she was looking for. She

227

slammed the safe door shut, spun the dial and closed the cupboard. She dropped to her knees and pulled out the plug that powered her computer. She considered taking it with her, but changed her mind. It was too late now.

Helen opened her office door and stepped out. The corridor lights were ablaze. Someone else was there.

'Ma'am?' Jean was at her desk. She spun to greet her boss, the cup of tea in her hand still steaming.

'Jean!' Helen took a second to steady her voice. 'I didn't think anyone else was around.'

'It's a little quiet up here today. All the bosses have had a bit of kick about being out and about with the troops while this incident plays out down in Hythe. It feels a bit like déjà vu, you know? All the normal bobbies are grounded and milling around waiting for firearms to bring the bloke in.'

'I guess so Jean, yeah. It'll all be over soon.'

'You okay, ma'am?' Jean looked at her over the rim of her cup.

'Yes, yes, Jean. I'm still a little under the weather is all.'

'Yes, of course. Can I make you a coffee?'

'No, no thanks, Jean. I've got to get out and about. Like you said, it's all hands to the pump today and I need to be down in Hythe.'

'Yes, I was made aware that you were heading down there. Mr Lance wanted to know when you were on your way. Did you want me to let him know?'

Helen rubbed her face and looked back at her closed office door. Jean was acting very cool, considering that she had been involved in sharing Helen's personal information. She must think that Paul had finished in there. Helen wanted to drag her over the coals for it, but she knew it would be a wrong move right now. She didn't have much time.

'Yes, please. Let him know I'm just leaving.'

* * *

228

Helen waited until she was twenty minutes away from Langthorne House and the BMW barely grumbling at seventy miles per hour. She brought her phone up on the centre screen. It rang through the speakers.

'Hello?'

'Mum, it's me.'

'Helen! Everything okay?'

'Yeah, of course.'

'You sound stressed, love. Are you sure you're okay?'

'I said three words, Mother.' Her mum had always been astute.

'Did you want to speak to the girls?'

Helen hesitated. This was why she'd called, but now she found that she didn't want to speak to them at all. 'No, Mum, I'm going to drop in. I'll speak to them then.'

It was her mother's turn to hesitate. 'Oh, right, okay. Do you mean now?'

'Is that okay?'

'Yes, of course, they're in from school and their homework should be done. I'll tell them straight away, they'll be thrilled!'

Helen broke into a genuine smile for the first time in quite a while. 'I hoped they would. I'm on the motorway, about ten minutes away. It will only be a flyer, Mum.' She hesitated again. For a second she thought she might break, tell her mum that she needed her help, that she didn't know where to turn or what to do. 'A quick cup of tea, maybe.'

'Of course. You can stay as long as you like.' The phone call ended and Helen knew she could expect more questions when she got there. After all, when did she ever drop in on her little girls out of the blue?

Helen sighed again. Her phone's display was still up on the screen and she punched in the numbers from memory. The speakers rang again and she allowed the car to slow down. This shouldn't be a long call, and she wanted to still be on the motorway when it ended. It was the best place for someone looking to discard a mobile phone where it would never be found.

CHAPTER 37

'Sir.'

Barry Lance had been bent over a monitor set up in the rear of a large marked police van which had the words, "Incident Control Unit" branded along the side.

In the back was a computer with a keyboard and printer, a second radio, a table, and an urn that plugged into the van's power source, providing hot water. Bronze Command hadn't yet found the time or the will to make a cup of tea, although his throat was dry with tension. He was watching his team on the screen. The area search up the canal bank had been completed as best and as far as they could manage, and the dogs and the helicopter had come back with no sign of the target. Both crews had said that, had their man been in there, they would have found him. Barry was equally confident that he hadn't gone very far. Witnesses to the motorbike spill had described a hard fall. The rider was probably injured and he would be aware of the scale of the manhunt. He would have heard the helicopter and, if he had any sense, he would be looking for somewhere to lay up, under cover. He was in Hythe somewhere and Barry knew that finding him was just the start.

'What is it?'

'We've had a call come in, sir. It's anonymous, but it gives a specific address and says our man is in there.'

'Right.' Barry's eyes remained fixed on the monitor in front of him, where the helicopter was supplying a feed. 'Put it with the twelve other crackpots that have called in. And that's before we've even got the press release out. Once everyone else knows about it, we'll get all sorts of *help*'

'This one seems a bit different, sir.'

Barry dragged his eyes from the monitor stream showing his team emerging from a large detached house and moving towards the next. 'How?'

'I'll read it as the call taker has typed it in, sir. It says a female has called in, claiming to be a senior officer named Helen Webb. She states that the suspect is at 14 Cliff Road, Hythe, where a male lives who is a former police officer. It goes on to say that this man is called Ed Kavski, known as "the Russian." Apparently he is well established in the local drug scene.'

'Ed Kavski?' Barry snatched the paper from the officer. 'Helen Webb?'

'Yeah, it goes on to say that Helen Webb is the chief superintendent—'

'I know who fucking Helen Webb is! Jesus.' Barry scanned the printout. 'It says here that she received a phone call from this Ed asking her to pick them both up and convey them away. 'Has this been verified?'

'Checks have been done on the phone number. It's the area commander's phone.'

'Jesus. How the fuck has she got herself caught up in this?'

The officer shrugged, waiting to be excused. Barry turned back to the monitor, made a decision, and picked up his radio. The messenger took his opportunity and stepped from the van.

'Foxtrot One to all units. I need teams two to six back to me at the RVP immediately. Teams seven to eleven to continue with the cordon. Please confirm you have received this transmission.'

Once he'd heard from everyone, Barry transmitted again.

'I will be running an armed entry based on new intelligence. We need to move on this as soon as possible. Straight away please, teams.'

His teams confirmed. He expected them to be able to muster in the supermarket car park in minutes. From there they would be raring to go.

* * *

Back in Langthorne House, Martin Young had been monitoring the same radio station and he certainly wasn't aware of any new information regarding where the offender might be. This wasn't a great surprise. With Barry Lance leading the operation from the ground, Martin's role was to try and make sure the residents of Langthorne and the surrounding areas who had other issues were getting serviced. People were still having domestics, stealing from shops or houses and crashing their cars. The late turn inspector had come in and Martin was angling to try and get away, but everyone was expected to stay on duty until the Bronze Commander updated.

Martin yawned as he held his private phone to his ear. 'Hello?'

'Denise, hey.' Martin always hated calling his wife when he was working late, especially when he had no real idea when he might get away.

'Oh, Martin. I thought it might be our Sally.'

Martin sat up in his chair. 'Sally? Why would it be Sally ringing?'

'She was here, Martin. Sat on the step when I got home, said she needed somewhere to stay for a while.'

'Well, of course she can! You didn't turn her away, did you?'

'Of course not! She's my daughter too. I said it wasn't a problem. She was making us both tea and I was in the shower when the phone went. Well, I thought it was you so she picked it up, turns out it was one of her friends. Then all of a sudden she had to go out — said she was picking some of her stuff up from this friend of hers.'

'What friend?'

'She didn't say, Martin. You know what she's like. But she was different today, you know. She seemed kind of . . . sad.'

'Sad?'

'Well, maybe not sad, just like she really did want to stay with us. She was nice to me for a start, and that's not normal, is it? Anyway she went out, she wouldn't let me drive her. That was what, an hour and a half ago. I don't know why I'm so worried about her. I wouldn't be normally, but she seemed so different today. You know how nothing ever bothers her — drives me mad, it does. Well, today I just thought that maybe something really *was* bothering her.'

'Did she say where she was going? Did she say anything else?' Martin felt panic rising. He didn't know why himself, yet, but if it didn't feel right to his wife, who was normally so unconcerned about their daughter, then he knew he should be worried too.

'She didn't say anything more than what I've told you, Martin. Then I went out to my car and Mrs Wakelin from over the road said she saw our Sally talking to someone in a small yellow car earlier today, half a mile from the house. She must have got dropped a bit up the road so we wouldn't see the car, but you know what Mrs Wakelin is like, she's everywhere that woman, and she drove past them on her way home. She said it looked like our Sally was upset with whoever she was talking to. I don't know what that's got to do with anything. Do you think she's okay? Should I go out and look for her?'

Martin had got to his feet. Two calls graded immediate were coming in at the same time. 'No, Denise, you stay there in case she comes back. I'll do the looking. I can escalate it far easier from here if I need to.'

'You think she's okay?'

'Don't worry, love. You know Sally. How many times has she had us worried out of our minds for no reason?' Martin hoped he sounded more convincing than he felt. 'Did Mrs Wakelin say anything more about this car?'

'A young girl was driving, short dark hair. I guess that's her friend.'

'Yes, probably.' Martin's thoughts were already elsewhere.

'Do you think she's in trouble?'

'No. I'll let you know as soon as I have an update here. Hopefully I'll be home soon.'

CHAPTER 38

As the truck rumbled to a stop in front of Peto Court, Sally Morgan faced Lee Chivers. He was gripping the steering wheel, as he had done all the way back. Sally wondered if he was contemplating his next move. She was certainly considering hers. They were back in his territory but they weren't inside yet, and maybe she still had a chance. She had tried asking him questions but Lee hadn't said a word. He'd seemed almost to be in a trance, staring, unblinking, at the early evening traffic. By now, Peto Court was a black outline with squares of dull orange marking out the windows lit from within.

'Can Lizzy come out so we can talk? I know you don't want me back in there, and that suits me to be honest. I told you I wasn't coming back—'

'You did come back though, Sally. Didn't you?'

'Did you hurt Lizzy?'

Lee let go of the steering wheel. His right hand went to the knife. He held it up in front of him, as if he were admiring it. 'You will do exactly what I tell you, Sal. So far all you've done is fuck me about. Now we're going to go back into the flat, we're going to meet with Lizzy, and we're going to talk this whole fucking misunderstanding out. You understand?'

'I don't want to go in there, Lee.' Sally tried to keep her voice steady. She sat turned slightly away from him.

Lee's left hand shot out and grabbed a handful of her hair. He yanked it downwards so she was looking up at the roof of the car. He rested the knife-blade against her neck.

'You don't get to tell me what you want to do.' Lee's lips lifted in a snarl which showed his teeth. 'If you try to run, I will catch you and you will not last this night. Do you understand me?'

Sally's eyes squeezed tight as Lee increased the pressure on her neck.

'Do you understand?' Lee repeated.

Sally couldn't open her mouth. She managed to jerk her head, away from the blade.

'Good.' Lee shoved his door open and got out of the car, his left hand still holding Sally by the hair. He dragged her over the centre console into the driver's seat, then pulled her out of the car by her arm.

The communal door was solid and heavy. Lee used Sally's body to jam it open as it swung back. She took the blow in her right shoulder, but she was careful not to cry out.

There was a sudden commotion on the stairs. A group of men had dropped a drinks can, or found one on the stairs, and were kicking it down, laughing and swearing.

Lee let Sally go. 'Walk up to the flat, don't talk to no one, don't say nothing,' he hissed. Sally stopped at the bottom of the steps, with Lee behind her. She knew that if she walked up those steps she would never come back down. The group of men came into sight, down the last flight of steps, and came to a halt in front of Lee and Sally. Three of them, all drunk. They recognised Lee and made comments, offered handshakes and fist bumps. Lee ignored them and tried to push past.

'Fuck him, then,' slurred one.

'All right, Geeeeee?'

They were a few steps up from the bottom. The man at the front was holding a packet of cigarettes. He pulled at one to offer it to Lee and a handful came out and scattered across the floor. One of them fell at Sally's feet.

'Ah, fuck.' The man bent down to retrieve it and at the same time, Sally bent too. The man lurched forward towards Sally.

'Help me! Please,' she hissed. She handed the cigarette back to him and they both straightened up. The man looked at her in confusion. Suddenly he caught on, and his face cracked with a smile.

'Here, boys!' he shouted. 'She wants my help!'

The other two men cheered loudly and offered some lewd comments. Lee glared at her.

No one was going to help her. Not here.

* * *

Emily Ryker had been pacing her office. She had left a message on her boss's mobile, requesting a call back. She wanted to tell him what had happened, everything she knew. She needed to tell someone. It had been six minutes now. She was wondering how long she should wait before ringing again when Martin strode into the office, making her jump.

'Sir!'

'Sally Morgan. She has disappeared.' Martin stopped in the middle of the office. He stood stiffly before her, fidgeting with his hands, his mouth slightly open.

Emily's hand went to her nose, she was nervous too. 'Okay . . .'

'Do you know where she is?'

'Well no, sir. I wasn't aware she was missing.'

Martin stared at her. 'I assume you still use the custody nurse's Fiesta for trips out? You should know better than to use a mustard yellow car if you're looking to blend in. You know a lot more than you're letting on,

Emily. This isn't about source confidentiality now, it's far more important than that.'

Emily was a little caught out. 'Look, I drove her home — to your home, and I left her there. If she's not there now, then I only know what I told you yesterday, where she hangs out and where she's been staying — but I don't think she'll be there.'

'Peto Court,' Martin stated. He lowered his gaze. 'With that Lee Chivers animal. Why wouldn't she be there?' he demanded, watching her intently.

'They've had a falling out.'

'Did that piece of shit hurt her again?'

Emily shrugged.

'What is his door number?'

'Sir, if you want to go down there to speak to him you'll want a whole team. I can see if there's anyone spare to do the door knock, but—'

'His flat number.' Martin raised his voice, then repeated more quietly, 'Which flat, Emily. That's all I'm asking from you.'

Emily hesitated. 'Forty-nine,' she said, almost in a whisper.

Martin turned on his heels and walked out of the door.

* * *

The last door. Then Sally would be on the landing that led to Lee's flat, and there would be no turning back. She wanted to see Lizzy, she'd believed Lee when he said she was in the flat. She knew Lizzy had gone back to him and was stupid enough, or had been made scared enough, to stay in the flat and wait for him to return while he went out to pick her up. Sally could picture Lee giving Lizzy a bag of heroin. After the day she'd had, a long day without, it would have switched her off completely for the time Lee was out. She would be starting to function again about now, and they would walk in to find her lethargic and chilled, like a drunk on a sunny park bench.

Maybe they would talk about what they'd heard. Maybe Lee would be able to explain it away. Maybe it *was* all just a misunderstanding. Sally hesitated at the communal door, with the palm of her hand against it.

Lee waved his card at the sensor and she shook her head, dismissing her thoughts. It was no misunderstanding. Lee Chivers had beaten someone to death earlier that day, and now the only two people who could point the finger at him would be back in his flat and under his control. Suddenly Sally realised the seriousness of her situation. Maybe Lizzy was dead already. She was now certain that in a very short time she would be dead too.

Sally spun round to face Lee. She had seen him fiddle with the knife. She was certain he had tucked it in the back of his jeans and she knew her only chance was to get hold of it. She bent her head and went for his midriff in a kind of rugby tackle, her hands grabbing for the weapon.

Lee was caught out. Sally wasn't heavy but the surprise impact of her head in his midriff made him take two steps backwards, where his foot came into contact with the raised grip strip that marked the top of the steps. Sally kept pushing, her hands fiddling with his belt.

Lee got his feet more firmly grounded, but he was still off balance. The brand new rubber of Sally's trainers squeaked on the concrete floor as she pushed forward with all her strength. She could see the steps drop away just behind Lee, but he started to push back. Sally felt her feet losing traction. She had one more big push in her. She stepped back to give herself momentum and dove forward.

But she didn't get the chance. As she rocked back, Lee brought down both his fists into the small of her back and she folded in half. Lee fell on top of her. He used the fall to bring his knee down hard into the back of Sally's head, pushing her face into the concrete. She cried out.

'Bitch!' Lee brought his knee down again, against the back of Sally's head.

She groaned in pain, but managed to twist her head enough to avoid taking the impact on her nose again. Lee raised his knee and brought it down again, and again, his face twisted into a snarl.

'Fucking bitch! This what you fucking want?' Lee smashed his knee into her one more time.

Lee looked up. Frank from number 59 stood in the doorway, taking in the scene. Lee stood up.

'What the fuck you want?' Lee panted.

'She okay?' Frank was trying to peer round Lee.

'What the fuck's it got to do with you?'

Frank met his gaze without flinching. 'I don't like blokes that hit women.'

Lee smiled — a flicker, and then it was gone. 'I don't just hit women.'

The two men stared at each other. Frank broke first and took a step back.

'Now fuck off.'

Frank slunk back into his flat.

Lee stood over Sally. He rolled her on to her back. Her eyes were half open. Her breathing was shallow, but she *was* still breathing. Lee smiled. She was going to come round very soon, and then she would be all his.

He took hold of Sally's feet and dragged her down the corridor and into the flat.

* * *

On any other day, Martin might have enjoyed the drive. He had taken a marked Ford Focus from the rear yard. It had been the only one whose keys still hung on the board. He activated the siren and the rush hour traffic struggled to part for him.

Peto Court was only a few minutes from the police station but Martin swore at every car that blocked his route, every red light that snarled the traffic further, every headphone-wearing pedestrian that walked across a zebra crossing. A mini-roundabout at the end of the High Street marked the top of the hill leading to Peto Court. The traffic there was at a complete standstill. The blue flashes from the Ford bounced off shop windows and the polished metal of railings, shop complexes and other vehicles, until it seemed that the air itself was pulsing blue. The siren reverberated from wall to wall like an injured animal, trapped among the tall buildings. All this did nothing but close the gaps.

'Fuck,' Martin said. He beat the steering wheel. The red mist was descending.

* * *

Sally rolled on to her side and retched. Lee emerged from his bathroom with water dripping from his head. He had changed into a tight-fitting white vest. Sally spat onto the sheet and gave a convulsive jerk. Her hands and feet were bound with thick tape.

'You can wriggle all you like, Sal, it won't do no good.'

'Let me out of here, Lee! What the fuck are you doing?' Sally screamed.

'You won't get out of that shit, Sal, and you won't get out of here.' Lee looked down at Sally. She lay in the middle of a plastic sheet. 'This is how I know you're fucked!' Lee swung the baseball bat like a pendulum above Sally's head.

Sally saw dents and dried blood on the bat's metal surface. 'Fuck, Lee. You don't need to do this. I won't be talking to no one about nothing, you don't need to do it.'

'We were coming here to talk, Sal, weren't we? Then you hit me, Sal. You tried to run away, and that made me wonder why, and who you was going to go running to. I can't have you just running to anyone, Sal.'

Sally's voice was quiet, almost resigned. 'I just wanted to go home.'

'You don't have no fucking home. You're a fucking street rat, that's all you'll ever be.'

'I have a home. Please, Lee, let me just go home and you'll never see me again, I promise.'

Lee shook his head. 'Can't do that, Sal. Can't do it.' Lee pointed the bat over to his right.

Sally saw a roll of plastic splattered with blood, and more had pooled on the floor. Brown hair was sticking out one end. Lizzy's brown hair.

'Oh, fuck, Lee, what did you do?'

Lee was excited. His left hand shot out and he grabbed Sally, holding her cheeks and squashing her mouth together. The bat was in his other hand. He moved it slowly across her lips, laughing as she squealed.

'Can you taste the blood, Sal? Can you *fucking* taste it?' Lee pushed her face away. He felt behind his back and brought out the knife. 'You get an option though, Sal. I'm being fair to you, 'cause you and me, we got history, right? So I'm giving you an option.' Lee dropped the bat. He took the knife in his right hand and with the other he took hold of Sally's face, pushing at her mouth again. Lee held the knife to her lips, with the flat side of the blade pushing down. He wiped it along her mouth, slowly, his eyes staring into hers.

'Now you can taste it, can't you, Sal? Lizzy chose the knife, but don't let that influence you. You gotta be your own person, right?'

Lee lifted the knife from Sally's face. She squeezed her eyes shut, and felt the cold metal rest on her cheek, barely touching her skin, as though he was stroking her with it.

'Now the slugger,' Lee continued, 'That makes a fucking mess, you know. And it can take a good while. But the knife, that's quicker and cleaner, and they say that bleeding out, it can be quite a peaceful experience if you get it right. I'll do my best for you, Sal, I don't need you to suffer.' Sally felt the knife move down, over her chin and onto her neck. It stopped with the tip on her windpipe and the blade resting on her sternum.

'Just relax, Sal, and this will all be over.' The knife moved up under her chin, digging into her neck, the point was at her main artery. Lee put his left hand on Sally's face. His eyes were level with hers. She wanted to shut them, to look away, but she was mesmerised by his gaze.

'Look at me, Sal. I want to watch you go.'

Tears ran down the side of Sally's face. She looked up at the ceiling and thought of home.

* * *

Frank hadn't expected Lee's door to be ajar. He gave it a tentative push and it swung open a little, enough for him to peer inside. He saw Lee kneeling over the girl, whose ankles were bound with silver gaffer tape. Lee had his back to Frank.

'Lee! What the fuck?'

Lee spun round. 'Fuck me, Frank. You don't know when to fuck off, do you?'

Frank took a step into the flat, and Lee was up in a flash. He reached out, grabbed at Frank's jumper, and pulled him further inside. He pushed him into the kitchen area and kicked shut the front door.

'You shoulda stayed away, Frank. 'Now you gotta be with the girls.'

Lee moved forward. Frank lashed out with his right fist. It was a lucky shot, and the fist connected with the side of Lee's face, knocking his head to the side and throwing him off balance. Frank knew his only chance was to go on the offensive, and he swung his fist again. Lee fell to one knee and Frank pushed him hard to the ground. The big man used his weight advantage, he collapsed on top of Lee, trapping his upper body and the arm that held the knife. Lee was neutralised, temporarily at least, but Frank was exhausted and had no idea what to do next.

* * *

Martin Young finally got there. He skidded to a stop in the car park of Peto Court. He got out, strode to the rear of the car, and grabbed a stack of traffic cones that he threw out across the car park. Underneath the cones was a red metal enforcer — a twenty kilo steel door ram. Martin struggled to lift it over the boot lip. He took the enforcer in both hands, and walked towards the communal door.

The enforcer would have no effect on the solid metal-framed security door but luck was on Martin's side. The caretaker of the building was in his flat on the top floor. He had been watching the comings and goings on his CCTV. He had seen Lee arrive earlier and pull a girl out of his car by her hair. He had seen the distress on her face as Lee had dragged her through the door and up the stairs. He had seen the police officer arrive, and, as the officer approached the communal door he pushed an override button that unlocked all the communal doors. Martin heard the metallic 'clack' as he walked up to it and saw the door shiver slightly in the artificial light. He put the enforcer down and pulled the cold metal handle. The door came open.

He was in.

* * *

Frank was losing strength. He was using his weight to keep Lee immobilised, but he knew he couldn't keep him pinned down forever. Lee was starting to wriggle. He was beginning to free himself. Frank needed to get hold of the knife. He brought his foot down hard on Lee's forearm to make him drop it. But he'd shifted too much weight off Lee's legs, and Lee was too much of a street fighter to let him get away with that. It was a fatal error.

Lee brought his knees up as hard as he could, connecting with the small of Frank's back. Frank instinctively straightened up and put his hands behind him.

Lee freed his arms to land two blows in quick succession and Frank moved off him to get out of their reach.

Frank shook dizzily and felt for some support. He dragged himself back to the kitchen cupboard and pulled himself to a sitting position, gasping for breath.

Lee stood up and waited for Frank to settle. Frank's arms dropped to the floor, exposing his torso. He squinted up at Lee, who didn't hesitate. He stepped forward and plunged the knife into Frank's stomach. Frank's eyes opened wide. He put his hands to the wound.

Lee moved his head closer to Frank's. Lee watched the colour drain from Frank's face, the light in his eyes fade. He pushed the knife in harder. Frank grunted. The agonising pain in his body cleared his vision.

There was a noise at the door and both men looked up.

* * *

The twenty kilo weight of the metal ram was draining Martin's reserves of strength and he considered abandoning it altogether. He felt his strength returning as he walked along the filthy corridor towards flat 49, amid the hopeless stench of damp and urine. The door to the flat was wooden, opening inward with a single visible lock. Martin was rigid with rage. The man behind this door was responsible for everything that had gone wrong with his daughter's life. He drew the enforcer back and brought it forward, grunting with the exertion.

The wood splintered and the door gave way. Martin Young looked at the scene revealed to him. He saw his daughter, bound and lying on the floor, her face, filthy with tracks from her tears and spatters of blood, turning towards the sudden sound. He wanted to drop the enforcer and run to Sally, but as he stepped through the door, a movement caught his eye. Two men were in the kitchen area. The man closest to him was Lee Chivers. Martin recognised him from the pictures he had seen on the police system. Lee stared at him. He was holding a knife which was buried deep in the other man's stomach. Martin's grip tightened on the enforcer.

* * *

Through the haze and his confusion, Frank saw a police officer. He had been pawing uselessly at Lee's hands. But the sight of the policeman galvanised him. His big hands fastened on Lee's wrists. The agonising pain fuelled his determination, he used it, he held on.

Lee pulled back, trying to free his hands and peering over at the cop. He turned to Frank, and this time Frank stared right back, gripping hard.

'You're staying with me.'

Lee's hands jerked and twisted, and Frank's pain became excruciating. He gritted his teeth and made himself think of happier times. Of his wife. He smiled. He opened his eyes and pulled Lee's hands in closer, causing the knife to penetrate deeper into his gut. He was overcome by the unfairness of it all, that his life was to be ended by this piece of vermin.

* * *

Martin froze. Then rage consumed him. All he saw was Lee Chivers. Lee started to say something. Martin swung the enforcer back. Lee saw it coming. The solid, flat head of the steel ram struck him full in the face. The force was so great that Lee's head came away from his neck and flipped back on his spine. The momentum of the enforcer carried it through the wooden kitchen unit behind, taking pieces of Lee Chivers' skull along with it.

Martin let the enforcer drop onto what remained of Lee Chivers. He turned his attention to the other man, who was bleeding heavily. The handle protruded from his T-shirt. Blood spread out from beneath him in a widening puddle. The man was looking up at him, his face ashen, his expression beaten and sad.

'Am I going to be okay?' he said, every word an effort.

'You'll be fine. I'll call someone,' Martin said, his voice shaky. He went to his daughter and rested his hand softly against her cheek. Their eyes met and he knew that she was going to be okay.

'He saved my life,' she said, and she looked over to where Frank was bleeding out.

'Are you okay?' Martin said. 'Did he hurt you?'

Sally shook her head. 'He would have. Frank saved me.'

Martin looked around him, and then his gaze returned to Frank. 'There's not much we can do,' he said. He walked over to Frank. His hands rested on either side of the jutting knife. Martin placed his hands gently over Frank's. He moved them together and pushed down on them so they put pressure on the wound. Frank was starting to drift away. His eyes were unfocused and he hardly reacted to Martin's pressure.

'I used to be an army medic.' A man spoke from behind Martin, making him jump. The Peto Court caretaker stood over him. 'If you can just keep pressure on it for a minute, I'll get my kit.'

Martin nodded. He pushed his hands as firmly as he could into Frank's gut, either side of the knife handle. Martin turned to speak to the caretaker but he had already gone.

He called out to Sally. 'I'll get you out of here, it won't be long.'

She was lying on the floor, her arms and legs trussed together, but her breathing was even.

'He killed my friend, Dad. She must have been so scared.'

'Who did? What friend?'

'Lizzy. She's lying over there, behind the bed.' Sally rolled back towards her dad. She had fresh tear tracks marking her face. 'I just want to go home,' she said.

The caretaker returned with a green bag that contained a full professional kit. Martin watched him pull at something and draw out a row of what looked like tea bags stitched together.

'What's that?'

'It's a clotting agent. You pack the wound with it and it should stop the bleeding. I've called an ambulance, they're on their way.'

Martin nodded. He stood and backed away to allow the caretaker to do his work. Frank was looking whiter and Martin wondered if there was any blood left to retain. He went over to his daughter.

'We need to go,' he said. He rinsed his hands in the sink and found a kitchen knife and cut the tape around his daughter's ankles and wrists. Sally struggled to raise herself and Martin hooked an arm under her legs, wrapped the other behind her neck, and lifted her off the floor. He knew that the caretaker's call for an ambulance, reporting a knife injury, would also alert the police. They didn't have long to get clear.

'Look after him,' Martin called out. The caretaker made no reply. He began to carry his daughter towards the door.

'Dad, the money. It's all under the bath.'

Martin suddenly remembered Emily Ryker telling him that Chivers kept large sums of money in the flat.

'Can you stand?' Sally nodded into his chest. Gently he placed her on her feet. He saw that the panel under the bath was loose, and it swung open easily. Martin tugged out a large black holdall. He pulled the zip back and he saw wads of twenty-pound notes. He whistled, pulled it shut, and grunted as he lifted it over his shoulder. It was heavy, heavier that he had expected, and he had to pause to steady himself.

'I can walk,' said Sally. 'Let's just go.'

It was a slow walk back to the police car, whose blue lights still pulsed. Sally grunted in pain as she tried to find a comfortable position in the car.

'I knew he was hurting you. I knew you were in there.'

'And you saved me, Dad. Let's get away from here. Please.'

Martin killed the blue light and gunned the engine. He drove carefully out of the car park and into the one-way system. He pulled over just a few hundred yards up the road on Tontine Street. The engine fell silent.

'What's up?'

'I need to do something quick.'

Sally's dad opened the back door and grabbed the black holdall.

'I'll be one minute.'

CHAPTER 39

The office of Langthorne Taxis was quiet. The five plastic chairs lined up under the window were all empty when Martin entered. A bored-looking middle-aged woman looked through the serving hatch over a stained mug. She clocked the police uniform immediately.

'Can I help you, boss?' she said. Her accent was local.

'I need a cab, for a delivery.'

'You people not using cars anymore? Them cuts are worse than we thought, eh?' She grinned.

'It's a personal job.' Martin smiled back, nervously.

'Sure, we can do that,' the woman said. 'When do you need it for?'

'Now,' Martin said. He dropped the bag across two of the plastic chairs.

The woman did her best to peer through the window. 'I'll get someone out. There's a couple of drivers upstairs.'

Within a minute, a smiling thirty-something Polish-looking man walked through a door next to the serving window. Martin shook his hand.

'I need this delivered to 12 Wartam Gardens. You'll need to personally hand it to a woman at the address. She's called Lorraine Robson.'

The driver smiled. 'No problem!'

Martin held out two twenty pound notes, far more than would be required for a jaunt to the top of the town. The man shook his hands and his head. 'No need for you, boss.'

'Take it,' Martin said. 'It's very important.' Martin pulled a pen and an old receipt from his pocket and started writing. 'Tell her that this is her husband's stuff, and that he meant for her to have it. This is my mobile number. Call me if she's not there or there's any problem, any problem at all.'

Martin Young fell back behind the wheel of the Ford Focus. His daughter looked even more exhausted than before. The bruising on her nose and face looked worse, and she was clearly struggling to keep her eyes open.

'I assume that's a clever front for what is actually your bank? Or you're trusting them to deliver two hundred and fifty thousand pounds to our house without having a quick look and making a sudden stop?'

'It's going elsewhere.' Martin grinned. He looked happy.

'Elsewhere?'

'Yeah. You and I, we're both making a new start.'

To Martin's delight, his daughter smiled back. It was exhausted, pained, but it was a smile. 'What you got at home, Dad? Drink-wise? 'Cause I'll toast to that.'

Martin was still smiling as the police car pulled away from the taxi rank and started up Tontine Street. A balled-up piece of tissue flew from the passenger window. It landed on the chipped tarmac, where a gentle breeze blew it into the gutter.

* * *

Thirty miles away, on a motorway washed in artificial orange light, a BMW M3 slowed for the junction leading to Helen Webb's mother, and her twin girls. Helen Webb wiped away a single tear and planted her foot on the accelerator.

She'd talk to them. Go and see them even. But not now. Not until this mess was all cleaned up.

At the same time, a squad of thirty armed officers swarmed through 14 Cliff Road, Hythe, hunting for the man behind the latest atrocities on Helen Webb's patch. That man had long since fled, leaving behind a scene laid out like a CSI training exercise. It would take them two weeks to process it completely, but the search for the culprit had begun.

CHAPTER 40

Lorraine Robson was in her living room, and the urgent knock made her jump. Daniel was engrossed in his Xbox, which Lorraine had allowed him to play with as much as he liked since his father's disappearance. It stopped the questions coming.

Maybe this was him! Maybe Tony had come back. She saw the taxi pulled untidily across the drive and her hope increased. Maybe he'd just needed some space. Maybe he had just been trying to make sense of the news about their son, and now he was back. He'd got a taxi, and he was knocking at their door. She ran to the front door. A full-length mirror hung on the porch wall — her reflection showed a tired, tense figure. She'd kill him! Then she'd hug him as hard as she could.

'Robson?' Standing at the door was a smiling man with an oversized canvas bag gripped in both hands. He sounded Eastern European. 'Lorraine Robson?'

Lorraine nodded, crushed by disappointment.

The man shook the bag a little. 'The police boss, he said to bring it here for Lorraine Robson.'

She didn't move.

The man looked confused. 'Your husband? He said it was your husband's, but he wanted it to be yours.'

Lorraine looked at him, her brain whirling. They must have found some of his stuff and if they'd found that, they would be closer to finding him, or at least a clue as to what had happened to him.

'Right, thank you.' The taxi driver's smile returned and he stepped into the porch and put the bag down on the floor. Lorraine eyed it, puzzled. The taxi driver thanked her and started to walk back towards his car.

'I don't owe you a fare, then?' Lorraine called out after him.

'No. The boss, he paid me good.'

Lorraine pushed the door shut and looked down at the bag. Daniel had appeared at the door to the living room. 'Was it about Dad?' he said.

'No,' she said. 'Just someone dropping something off for Mummy.'

'Okay.' Daniel's shoulders slumped and he turned away, back to his game. Lorraine dropped to one knee and pulled at the bag. It was heavier than she'd expected, and she didn't recognise it as belonging to Tony. She leaned forward and pulled at the zip.

Daniel paused the game. He went back to the hall, where his mother was kneeling by the bag, in floods of tears.

'Mum!' Daniel bent down to his mother and wrapped his arms around her. 'Don't be sad, Mum.'

'I'm not sad.' Lorraine took her son by the shoulders and looked into his eyes, smiling through her tears. 'I'm not crying because I'm sad, Daniel. It's going to be okay! You and me, we're going to be okay. Your dad, wherever he is Daniel, he did it!'

She pulled him towards her.

CHAPTER 41

'Long time, no see. What have you been up to?' Emily Ryker had the broadest smile.

It was a sunny autumn day. A gentle breeze stirred the first golden leaves on the ground. George Elms thought he'd never beheld a more beautiful scene.

'I know, I know! Holiday's over. I suppose it's back to work now.' George grinned.

'Not straight away though, eh?'

'Not straight away.' George pulled on the passenger door to Emily's two-year-old Volkswagen Beetle. It didn't open.

'Patience, man! Anyone would think you were in a rush to get away!'

'Open the door, Ryker.' Both were still smiling as they settled into their seats and Emily turned the key. The radio blared out Take That's latest album. George stared at Emily.

'I was having a singalong, wasn't I? Don't you fucking judge me, either. Bon Jovi! I still remember karaoke.'

'That song goes higher than you'd think,' he said.

George went quiet. He gazed at the damp lawn leading away from the stone walls of the prison. His footprints were still visible. He had wanted to walk on grass again.

'Let's get out of here, shall we?' Emily said.

'Definitely.'

'Where to, though?'

George turned back to Emily. 'Well, the world is my oyster!'

'You sure you don't want me to run you back to your family? I know you said—'

'No, Ryker. I asked you to come because you'd understand. Because you wouldn't insist that it was the best thing to do. You don't know what's for the best, and they don't either. No one does, and that's why I left them in protection.'

Emily took her hands from the steering wheel. 'Mate, I'm here, aren't I? I get what you're saying. It's just . . . there's no issue if you've had a change of heart.'

'I haven't.'

'I shall not ask again.'

'Good.' George smiled.

'When are they coming here to pick you up? Your wife and daughter?' Emily said. George frowned.

'Sorry. They're going to be torn up when they get here, that's all. I had to say it. Now I've said it, I won't say it again.'

'It was the only way I could stop them coming. They'll find out that I already got out and there'll be no need to come here. No need to put themselves at risk.'

'Your release date has been publicised as three days' time. No one knows. They could have picked you up and you'd all have been able to ride off into the sunset . . .'

'Ryker.'

'Okay.' Emily stared out of the windscreen and gripped the steering wheel again. 'So, I assume it's vengeance then, is it? You know, some sort of terrible vengeance shall befall those that have wronged you? That sort of shit.'

George's expression softened. 'Well, I was hoping for some breakfast first. You can't go out avenging on an empty stomach, can you?'

'I suppose not.'

'So the nearest greasy café, please, driver.'

'Serious?'

'Emily, when am I not serious about food?'

'Fair enough. Greasy spoon it is, for a dirty great breakfast.'

George peered back out of his window as the car pulled away, taking a last look at the building that had taken away a chunk of his life, one he would never get back, no matter how long he lived.

'And a cup of tea,' he said, still looking out of the window.

Emily nodded. 'Gotta have a cup of tea to start the day.'

'True,' George said. 'And I reckon this might be the nicest cup of tea I've ever tasted.'

THE END

Thank you for reading this book. If you enjoyed it please leave feedback on Amazon, and if there is anything we missed or you have a question about then please get in touch. The author and publishing team appreciate your feedback and time reading this book.

Our email is office@joffebooks.com

www.joffebooks.com

50625844R00159

Made in the USA
Columbia, SC
09 February 2019